save me

New York Times and USA Today Best Selling Author

HEIDI MCLAUGHLIN

COVER DESIGN: Sarah Hansen at Okay Creations
COVER MODEL: BT Urruela
COVER IMAGE: Eric Batterhsell
EDITING: There for You Editing
INTERIOR DESIGN:

E.M.
TIPPETTS
BOOK DESIGNS

www.emtippettsbookdesigns.com

~ Dan and Amy ~

Thank you for everything!

preface

Six years ago some of America's finest and most elite warriors were called into action. Four decorated Navy SEALs left their families behind to rescue a young girl who had been sent to Cuba in a sex trafficking ring being run by Tacito Rento and funded by US Senator, Ted Lawson.

The girl in question is Abigail Chesley, the granddaughter of Brigadier General, Harold Chesley, who called in a favor to Admiral Jonah Ingram. Unbeknownst to Chesley, Ingram is the father of Ted Lawson, the man responsible for kidnapping his granddaughter.

Captain Gerald O'Keefe sent his highly skilled SEALs into Cuba with what he promised to be a snatch and grab mission, only the rules changed once the SEALs touched ground.

The mission was a success, until the SEALs' orders changed. Someone at the top didn't want the warriors to come home and went as far as to declare them dead, except Captain O'Keefe finally had had enough.

When the SEALs returned, their homecoming wasn't as welcoming as it should've been. To their families, they were dead. To their families, they no longer existed. Loved ones moved on, parents accepted their son's death, wives left town, and some even sought love with others.

The biggest question arose—who had been sending the

care packages while they were deployed? And why these four SEALs?

But the damage had been done.

Evan Archer expected to come home to his fiancée waiting for him with their son; instead, he came home to her being engaged to his twin brother, Nate.

Team leader, Raymond "River" Riveria thought his homecoming was perfect, until he found out his wife, Frannie, was the one sending his team care packages.

Justin "Rask" Raskin lost his mother and father who are unwilling to accept that their son hadn't died and was alive. Despite his attempts, they ignore him.

Tucker McCoy went home, expecting to hug his wife and daughter, only he found a stranger living in his house with the whereabouts of his family unknown.

Unwilling to accept what has happened, Evan Archer sought the help of his fiancées mother, Commander Carole Clarke, JAG lawyer, along with the help of his brother and Nate's former girlfriend, FBI Agent Cara Hughes, to find out what happened and why they, the four SEALs were targeted. Questions were asked, and the truth was slowly uncovered as the lies began unraveling.

What started off as a mission to rescue a scared little girl, quickly turned into a nightmare of epic proportions, one that still continues.

This is Tucker's story.

prologue

EVERY ONCE IN A WHILE something will come on the television or radio that gives one pause. It'll make one stop and think. Sometimes that *something* is life altering. For someone like Amy, that *something* is the last thing she needs, even if she wants it.

Amy's husband Ray is grading his eighth grade history mid-terms with the television on in the background. He stops in time to watch a brief news clip on CNN about four Navy SEALs who had been reported dead, but have returned home alive in an apparent cover up. Yet, no one is commenting on the how's or why's.

Both reporters for CNN scoff at such a thing and the segment quickly ends. Ray Barnes returns to grading his papers with the thought that *this* would be a good history lesson.

"Did you see the news?" Ray Barnes asks Amy, as they

sit down for breakfast. She looks at him and smiles before shaking her head in between bites of her breakfast.

"No, I fell asleep reading my book last night." She absentmindedly rubs at a spot on her forehead and laughs. "I think my tablet smacked me in the face."

"Oh, it did. I can see some bruising there. You may want to cover that up before you go out today. I don't want anyone thinking I hit you." He laughs, as he lightly grazes the colored spot on her forehead. Amy knows the last thing he would do is hurt his wife, but living in a small town, simple things like bruises cause people to talk and neither of them want to be topic of conversation at the lunch counter. People know them, and people like to talk, even if Ray is a respected history teacher. Amy has been working at the general store for four years, her second job since moving to Pittsfield. She keeps a low profile and intends to keep it status quo.

Laughing, Amy bats his hand away. "What was on the news that caught your attention?" She stands and carries her empty plate to the sink, turning the faucet on to let the water push the crumbs left over from her toast down the drain.

"Hold on, I'm trying to find it." Amy walks over to stand behind her husband, resting her hand on his shoulder. Ray opens a web browser on this tablet and types in N-A-V-Y in the search bar before Amy has to move away. Setting her hand over the top of her pink sweater, she tries to calm the discomfort in her stomach. Amy doesn't want to know what her husband watched last night on the news, but the mention of Navy anything is enough to give her heartburn. She walks back to the sink, holding the edge of their marble counter, taking deep breaths to calm herself down.

"Hmm … I can't find it. I thought for sure it would be on here," he states much to Amy's relief. There was a time in her life when the Navy was everything, but then— No, she can't think about that right now. That was another life, another time.

"Maybe it'll be in the paper today. You can show me then." Her words are choppy. *It's just small conversation*, she reminds herself, but her gut is telling her something else.

"It seems there's a massive conspiracy going on."

Her tongue feels like it is three inches thicker than it should be. "Hmm," is all she manages to say.

Amy closes her eyes at her husband's assumptions, praying he'll leave it alone, hoping that by the time he returns he'll have forgotten. But knowing Ray, he'll bring it up down at the store and someone will have seen something and they'll start talking. It'll be all anyone talks about until the next conspiracy comes along. Living in a small town in Vermont, people have too much time on their hands and nothing much to talk about.

"I'm sure it's nothing," Amy says dismissively as she starts filling the sink up with hot water and soap to wash the morning dishes. Dipping her hands in, she picks up Chloe's cereal bowl and starts washing while listening to her husband argue with his tablet.

"Well it's definitely something to think about with our military, and something I'd like to teach in class. Anyway, it was about a Navy SEAL who was reported dead, but they found him alive. Damn, I really wish I could find it."

The moment Ray mentions the words SEAL, dead and alive, the bowl slips from her hand, smashing against the side of the sink and shattering into pieces.

"Shit," she mumbles, reaching for a towel.

"Are you okay?" Ray asks, immediately at her side and helping her pick up the pieces.

"Um … yeah," she says, catching her breath. "The bowl slipped. Don't worry about the mess. Go on, get to work." Amy pats the back of her husband's back, encouraging him to leave. "You're both going to be late." She didn't know if her suspicions were right, but wanted Ray and Chloe out of the house as soon as possible.

"We'll see you later." Ray kisses his wife briefly on the lips before reaching for his school bag and car keys. "Chloe, let's go," he hollers.

Their nine year old comes thumping down their stairs, kissing her mom before following her dad out the door. Amy moves to the window, watching the car, which carries her reason for being, drive down the gravel and dirt driveway. Once they're out of sight, she lets the tears flow as the panic she had learned to control lets loose.

Picking up her tablet, Amy rushes up the stairs to her bedroom and right into her bathroom, locking the door behind her. She turns on the shower, even though she has no intentions of getting in there right now. The moment her tablet comes to life, she clicks on her web application and types in F-O-U-R-N-A-V-Y-S-E-A-L-S-D-I-E-I-N-C-U-B-A. Her finger hovers over the search button as tears stream down her cheeks. It's been years since she's searched this article. Her thumb grazes the button ever so slightly as her eyes close. She's not sure what she's going to do if there's a new link. She opens one eye then the other to read the first line.

Four of Coronado's Finest Perish in Cuba

Amy lets out a labored breath. If Ray had heard the story right her search should've brought up an alternate link in the news category, but there is nothing. She closes her screen and sets her tablet on the counter before disrobing and climbing into the shower. It's there, under the loudness of water where her voice can be muffled, that she lets out a body-shaking scream and vows to make Ray forget about what he heard.

chapter 1
Tucker

THE WHIZ OF CARS ACCELERATING as they merge onto the interstate can be heard through the paper-thin walls. When I first arrived at the run down building I thought for sure I had the address wrong. There is no way someone as distinguished as Carole Clarke, the future mother-in-law to my best friend, Evan Archer, would know or visit a place in the run down part of Seattle. Yet, Carole has raved about her friend, Marley Johnson, being the best private investigator in the business, which is why I'm here. I need the best. I never thought about hiring a woman until Carole made a comment that women think alike and insinuated that a woman looking for a woman might be better. At this point, I have nothing to lose.

Marley's office is different from the others. Hers is cheery with brightly painted walls, flowers, and has a homey feel. The other offices I've been to felt more like a bad *Colombo* movie, and at any moment I expected the overhanging lights to start moving back and forth, but not here. Here it feels like Marley is going to give a shit about my plight and help me find my family.

I find myself sitting up straighter when the door opens and Marley walks in. She's of average height and slightly slender, reminding me of Penny. I do that often; pick out features of woman I'm staring at who pass me on the street, in parks, and the grocery store, looking for any hint that they might be my wife. Each time I see a woman with brown eyes it makes me wonder if she's Penny with a wig, or had plastic surgery. Deep down I know Penny would try Botox or color her hair, but not her eyes. She'd never change those. They're the only part of our daughter, Claire, that she shares with her. The most important part as far as I'm concerned.

Marley sits down and smiles at me. It's not one of those, "I feel sorry for you", but a genuine "I'm happy you're here" type smiles. I try to return the gesture, but its been so long since I've smiled that the muscles in my face are permanently frowning. My life, for the past six years, has been spent in the confines of hell, hunting men who I've always vowed to protect my daughter from. When I came home all I wanted to do was crawl into my king size bed and have the loves of my life hold me and never let go.

Instead, I came home to a house that was no longer mine. When I opened the door and walked in, like I did all those times before, I stood there wondering why Penny hadn't told me that she bought new furniture. After I set my bag down on the coffee table, I went to the wall to look at the pictures Penny had hung up, only to find that I didn't remember any of the people in the photos. The familiar sound of a gun being cocked caught my attention. I slowly turned around with my hands up in the air to stare down the barrel of a shotgun. It was that moment when everything changed for me. The six years I had been gone didn't matter anymore.

"Hello, Tucker," Marley says in a sweet and calm voice. I find it comforting, much like when Ryley, Evan's fiancée, promises that everything is going to be okay and reminds me that I have to have faith.

"Ma'am," I say, clearing my voice. For the past six months, I have been living where I can. Being dead for six years and suddenly coming back to life—or returning from your unclassified mission—makes it hard to acclimatize yourself back into the community. With no driver's license, birth certificate, or any proof of who I am, it's hard to find a place to live. One would think that the United States Navy would provide me with a place to stay on base, but that hasn't been the case. In fact, as far as they're concerned, I don't exist. Unfortunately for the USN, I refuse to accept the fact that I'm not a SEAL. I've worked too hard to obtain that title and I'm not about to let it go because Admiral Jonah Ingram is a corrupt bastard.

"A little about me," Marley starts. "My specialty is finding the parents who have kidnapped their child."

"Penny didn't kidnap Claire," I interject.

Marley holds her hand up, asking to continue. I nod, and slink back in the chair as if my teacher has reprimanded me for talking out of turn.

"According to your file, you came home from a mission to find your wife and daughter missing. What makes you think this isn't a parental kidnapping?"

I adjust awkwardly in my chair and try to rein in my temper. Ever since my return the littlest things set me off and I often find myself blowing up. I know, deep down, these are questions that have to be asked, but I hate them nonetheless. I also know my story is unbelievable, especially considering the lack of media attention surrounding it. It was only after Senator Lawson and Admiral Ingram were arrested, that the team became primetime news, but the story never went national. As far as the team was concerned, it was too late to make up for the lack of coverage when we all came home. What made it all worse was the one man who tried to bring attention to our return was found dead. Someone has been making sure this story stays buried.

"I'm a SEAL, stationed out of Coronado. My Team was deployed, and when I came home, she was gone. Not just gone, someone else was living in our house." I keep the amount of years I've been away to myself, knowing that as soon as I tell her it's been six years there will be skepticism in Marley's features and I'm so tired of seeing it.

"It's common for wives of servicemen to leave once their husbands deploy. I've seen it before."

I shake my head. "Ma'am, have you heard about the four SEALs that returned after a six-year mission?"

Marley shakes her head, but leans forward, acting interested in my story. "Of course you haven't." I sigh and clear my throat. "My team …" Even though I've told this story two other times, it doesn't get any easier. No one believes me and the burden of proof falls on me. "Six years ago we were deployed and four months in, our families were told we were killed in action. Six months ago, we returned home."

Marley's mouth drops open, hanging there for a moment. She sits back in her chair, with her pen between her fingers, tapping it on her pad of paper.

"Let me get this straight," she says, leaning forward in her chair. "Four Navy SEALs went on a mission, something I'm sure you do more often than I know, and your families were told you were dead only for you to come home six years later?"

I blanch at her words, but nod. The way she says it makes me think she's pitching the next Tom Clancy movie.

"What were you doing for six years?"

"Hunting," I reply, getting right to the point. I'm not willing to elaborate, either. Regardless of how I feel, I'm a SEAL through and through, and no one is going to get classified information out of me.

"Hunting. Right …" Trailing off, Marley looks as if she's pondering whether I'm telling the truth. "So you came home and your wife was gone?"

"Yes, ma'am."

"And that's it?"

I shrug. It's my new automatic response to the repeated same question. "Everything I've been told, which has all been the same, is she left right after we were buried, yet I don't know if I can trust the source. But she did so without saying good-bye to everyone." I leave out any information about Frannie Riveria being my source and her involvement because that's for me, and right now I'm not convinced Frannie has anything do with Penny and Claire disappearing. If she does … well, that just makes the bullet I plan to put between her eyes even sweeter. I don't care if River was our team's leader; his wife is a traitor and is responsible for everything that has happened to them. She'll pay.

"Have you checked in her hometown?"

My blood starts to boil and I want to ask if Marley is stupid, but I bite my tongue. "Her father died when she was younger and I never met her mother. Penny and I met in a bar. She was in San Diego on vacation. To say we hit it off would be an understatement. When she left I thought I wouldn't see her again, but she proved me wrong immediately. As soon as she made it to her first layover, she turned right around and came back to California. I knew I wanted to spend the rest of my life with her, but had no idea she felt the same way until she came back. We married quickly because there wasn't a reason to wait. Penny told me she was pregnant a few months into our marriage and our daughter, Claire, was born. She's nine-years old."

"This may be a sensitive question, but is Claire yours?"

I smile at the thought of my daughter and reach into my back pocket to pull out my wallet. I take out the last picture I received from Penny, well Frannie, and its Claire's second grade photo. Marley isn't the first person to ask if Claire is mine, but all it takes is for the person asking to take a look at Claire and see she looks just like me. Placing the photo on Marley's desk, I slide it toward her.

"Well that answers my question," Marley says, nodding.

Taking the photo back I look at Claire and silently tell her that I'm coming for her.

"If you 'died' four months into your mission and you say that your daughter is nine, how'd you get that picture?" Marley asks.

"Well, this is where shit gets complicated, ma'am. Our team leader's wife knew we were alive and kept sending us care packages so we wouldn't know something was up."

"That's fucked up." The statement must shock Marley as she quickly covers her mouth. Thing is, her response was so quiet that I almost didn't hear her, but I like knowing she's not afraid to drop the f-bomb when it's warranted.

"Yes, ma'am, it is."

"I feel really sorry for you, Tucker."

I want to tell her thank you, but I don't need pity. I want answers. I want my family back. "Please, just help me find my wife and daughter."

Marley nods and wipes an errant tear that's fallen down her cheek. I direct my gaze down at my lap because I don't want her to know how she's affecting me. I don't want to see her heart break for me because I'm not worth it. The ache she's feeling in her heart needs to be focused on finding Penny and Claire.

"Claire's in second grade?"

I sit up, rubbing my hand up and down my leg. "Third, now." The only reason I know this is because of the care packages and the reports cards I was receiving. "She's just like me with having a birthday that is later than your classmates."

"Okay. I'll need that picture and one of Penny."

I quickly hand the picture back to Marley and pull out the last one I received of Penny. If I had to guess it was probably seven or eight years old. Even when I deployed after Claire was born, Penny would only send pictures of our daughter. Rarely would she be in them. It didn't matter because I always kept my favorite picture of Penny in my helmet. I take a long look at my wife, with her blonde hair in a messy bun and her sunglasses resting on the top of her head. We had just come back from the beach and she was outside hosing off Claire's toys when I called her name and snapped the photo. Reluctantly, I hand the photo to Marley, who puts each one into her scanner. A few clicks later and they're both back in my hand and tucked inside my wallet for safe keeping. That is until I pull them out later when I'm lying in bed, wondering if they're safe.

"What's your wife's name?"

"Penelope Ann McCoy," I say with a sigh. I finally feel like Marley has listened to my plight and she's willing to help me.

While typing on her computer, Marley rattles off her next question without glancing at me. "Maiden name?"

"Kolowski."

"And Claire's name?"

"Claire Ann McCoy."

Marley continues to ask pertinent questions with me giving her everything she needs to know and then some. With each click of the keyboard, I grow more anxious. Could Marley be the one to find my wife and daughter? I don't want to get my hopes up, but maybe Carole is right and a woman private investigator will have a better chance than a man—especially one who focuses on searching for kidnapped children.

That thought makes me pause. I refuse to believe Penny kidnapped Claire. I can easily admit that Penny and I hadn't known each other long when we married, but I was in love and in the middle of a war. War makes you lonely and Penny filled that void. When Claire came along, she filled a hole in my heart that I didn't know I had.

When I left on the snatch and grab mission, everything was fine … or so I thought. No, I believed everything was fine and that my wife would be waiting for me to come home. I told her, just as I did with all my missions, that I'd be coming home to her. I have never lied to her and I never will.

"Okay, I've run Claire's name through a system I use to check every student and registered homeschool student, and have come back with nothing."

"I know. That's the answer I've been given over and over again. Claire's not registered in school, or she's not registered under that name."

"Why do you think she'd be under a different name?"

"It's a hunch. I don't know, it's hard to explain. Penny didn't take my pension, which to me means she didn't leave me. She also left in the middle of the night. Penny hated being out after dark, especially with Claire. The story I've been told doesn't add up with the person I know Penny to be."

Marley fingers moves along her keyboard, I assume adding notes to my file. When she's done, she sighs and looks at me. "Mr. McCoy I think I have enough information to start, but I'm going to be honest. Penny has been gone for a long time and usually the longer they're gone, the harder they are to find. Most people who leave their world behind are running from something, and the fact that none of your friends filed a missing persons report concerns me."

I feel as if a ton of bricks are being pressed into my chest, while a light bulb explodes right in front of me. I never asked Ryley if a missing persons report was filed, nor did I look for one, or file one myself.

"I understand, ma'am," I say, even though I refuse to believe they can't be found. People don't disappear unless they're dead, and I know they're not—I can feel it in my bones. "Please call me if you need anything, or have an update."

"I will, Mr. McCoy."

We shake hands, and I hold hers for a beat longer, hoping I can convey how important my quest is before I exit her office.

chapter 2
Tucker

"I can't believe you bought a house across from the shipyard," I say as I peer through the high-powered binoculars that Evan Archer keeps on his upper deck. Everything on the other side of the Puget Sound looks crystal clear, as if the sailors he's watching are standing right in front of him. The only thing lacking from the Puget Sound Naval Shipyard are SEALs, and I don't mean the kind you find loitering the shores.

Archer sets a beer down next to me and leans over the balcony, letting his own dangle from between his fingers. We've been friends for a long time, meeting for the first time when we were assigned to the same SEAL team. Penny and Ryley hit it off immediately and were often too chatty during the team's gatherings, making Evan and I wonder what the women were up to. We never felt like we had to worry about our wives when we were deployed, which makes me question why a missing persons report for Penny and Claire was never filed.

"I bought for the view," Archer replies, laughing. The

view from his deck is spectacular, even if it does look directly upon a shipyard. I could spend hours out here, watching the boats as they coast up and down the Sound. The water is always calling my name, so the Navy was the only choice I had for a career. It's what I wanted to do; becoming a SEAL was the icing on the cake for me.

"What goes on over there?" I ask. Ever since Evan's been back he has been watching everything. He's always searching for hidden meanings in the actions of people around him.

"Oh you know, a little bit of this and that."

I don't know if Archer is being coy on purpose or not. Either way, I don't appreciate it. I don't have time for games. Pulling the binoculars away from my eyes, I glare at him, and he picks up his beer, taking a long pull before returning his attention to the shipyard. There had to be a reason for him to buy here.

"Care to elaborate?"

Archer sighs and looks around. "Chesley's over there. About six weeks ago he arrived in the middle of the night by helo. I had noticed a lot of activity at the yard earlier in the day. They moved a sub and a carrier, and you know how slow shipyards move. That night I was watching with my night vision goggles and caught sight of the bird. Sure enough, hopping off that helo and running into building C was none other than the Brigadier General."

I don't think it's a coincidence that Chesley would show up here, especially since Archer is across the Sound.

"So why did you buy here?"

Archer shrugs. "I wasn't ready to let go, and being across from the yard gives me peace of mind. Now I'm on constant alert and have installed a state of the art alarm system with hidden cameras because I don't trust them." He points across the water at the same people who were once considered family. "We're the only ones that can bring Chesley down with Ingram and he knows it. I have no doubt that the reason he's hanging out in a Navy shipyard is because my house is in his line of sight. He's watching me. I'm watching them. What sucks for him is that I have access to the best equipment—night vision, guns, you name it I have it. He probably thinks I'm siting here sipping coffee and enjoying retirement."

"Aren't you?"

"Nah. I mean I do my thing and have my jobs, but I watch them, recording the shit they do. They want us dead and I'm not going down without a fight."

I nod in agreement before picking up the binoculars again. I watch movements—doors opening and closing, and the people who come and go—taking mental notes of what's going on. As far as I'm concerned, I'm still an active SEAL whether the Navy wants to recognize me or not and I'm always thinking like one.

The three members of SEAL Team 3 were offered early retirement once the arrests were made. The Navy was quick to dismiss any wrong doing on their part, and mostly they were right. Between the missing documents, paper shuffling, and hidden flight manifests, most people didn't have a clue what was going on. It also helped the Navy's case when Captain O'Keefe went missing, only to turn up dead later. But not before letters detailing the entire mission were found in his house. Those letters now are supposedly safe in Washington, DC. From what I've been told those will be used as evidence in the Lawson / Ingram trials.

It was Justin Rask and I who refused retirement, but for different reasons. For Rask, he wants to feel like he still has a family and the Navy provides that. The Navy is willing to keep Rask active because he's not missing his family. They choose to ignore him. Apparently he's not a lawsuit threat. But for me, my reason is simple: I want them to pay.

Evan Archer took the retirement payout, but that didn't prevent his fiancée from filing a lawsuit on their son's behalf for emotional stress, fraud, and a slew of other reasons. Ryley wants to make sure their son is well provided for as a result of the suffering they've both had to endure. Who knows if that will ever see it's day in court, but I hope to be there when it does, and pray that my family will be filing the same lawsuit once I find them. Archer is enjoying retirement as a workingman, running a security firm that works closely with the CIA on political details. His twin brother, Nate, will be running their field office in Washington, DC.

Raymond "River" Riveria was by all accounts a damn fine team leader. If he knew what was going on, he hid it well. I want to believe River was in the dark just like the rest of us, and was as surprised as we were when he came home only to find out the team had all been dead and buried for years. The whereabouts of River are unknown at this time. The day that Evan and Nate confronted River about his wife Frannie's involvement, his house blew up seconds after the Archer brothers left. No body fragments were found in the rubble.

"How'd your meeting go today?" Archer asks, switching topics. It's a habit with us; first we'll discuss our theories, but only briefly because we don't know who's listening, and then we'll talk about daily life with hopes to bore whoever may be lurking down the road.

"I'm trying not to get my hopes up, but I can't lie, they are. She specializes in finding kids who have been kidnapped by parents. I told her Penny didn't kidnap Claire, but it looks that way to an outsider."

"No one believes us," Archer says, much to my agreement. "They think we're either lying or went rogue and are blaming the military for a cover up that doesn't exist."

"Cara has the letters from O'Keefe. What's she doing with them?" Captain O'Keefe had a heavy part in our deployment and subsequent life in Cuba for six years. He was the only one to come and go, always promising that the next rendezvous point would be the last. Except each time the team would unearth another child sex ringleader and, as parents themselves, wanted to end the people involved, O'Keefe came back with more orders.

Cara Hughes is the FBI agent who has been helping us. She's also Nate's girlfriend, who I had the pleasure of meeting a few times before we deployed. Since returning, she's been by our sides trying to figure out how everything became so fucked up.

"They went missing." The anger is Archer's voice is absent. He should be pissed off. "It's okay though because we made so many copies before she turned them over. Ingram, Lawson, and Chesley, they're going down. It's only a matter of time. Cara says they have enough to prosecute Lawson on child pornography, rape of a minor, and some other shit that went in one ear and out the other. Ingram is out on bail."

"Too bad we don't know the guard," I add, knowing that if I did, I'd ask for five minutes alone with the admiral. Or I could find out what cell he's in, set up in the trees near the jail, and aim my rifle at this head. Thing is, I need answers and he has them. He's no good to me if he's dead.

We both turn when we hear the sliding glass door open. Ryley pokes her head out, smiling at us. Seeing her and EJ every day is difficult. Between the longing for Penny and Claire and the anger because I can't find them, spending time with Archer and his family is hard. But this is where I'll call home, until I can prove to the US Government that I'm alive. All I need is my birth certificate or a DNA test to do so, making the need to find Penny and Claire even greater. The other option is to exhume my mother, and the last thing I want to do is disturb her resting place.

"Hey, guys, are you ready for dinner?" Ryley steps into Archer's side and wraps her arms around him. They're a couple who have been through a lot and are persevering. Aside from Archer being gone, when the team came home, Ryley was engaged to his twin brother, Nate. I haven't been privy to all that happened between them, but I do know an attempt was made on Ryley and her mom, Carole's, life. The car accident left Ryley with a broken arm and Carole temporarily wheelchair bound. From that point forward, Archer has been glued to Ryley's hip, only leaving her side to go to work. It was Ryley who ended up asking Archer to marry her. Their wedding is set for next summer once her mom can walk down the aisle holding Nate's arm.

"I'm starving," Archer says, kissing Ryley on the forehead. The sight makes me jealous, but I'm happy for my friend. I want to believe that I'll have this again, soon but I know the clock is working against me. Even though I was declared dead six years ago, the seven-year mark of being absent is approaching. The last thing I want to find out is that Penny has remarried and moved on with her life, even though I'm suspecting that's the case.

"Tucker, are you hungry?" I nod and finish my beer. Ryley has been so cordial and accommodating to me, even though her and Archer should be alone, getting to know each other again and bonding as a family. She's opened her door, home, and heart to me, making sure I've felt welcomed since they moved back to Washington.

As soon as I step into the house, I'm attacked by EJ—the walking, talking, spitting image of Archer, but with Ryley's red hair. I pick him up, even though he's getting too big for this type of stuff, and give him a hug. I take little consolation in knowing that EJ has never met Claire so he's not missing her or asking me where she is. I'm not sure if I'd be able to handle those types of questions.

"Do you want to play hide-n-seek after dinner, Tucker?" How can I say no?

"You bet, but you have to promise to eat all your vegetables."

"Deal," EJ replies, giving me a high-five. After setting him down, I follow him downstairs where the main part of the house is. The view from the living room is still as spectacular from the porch, but the vantage point upstairs is what makes this house worth it.

"EJ and I are going to play a game of hide and go seek after dinner," I say, causing Ryley to groan. She's mentioned a few times that I don't need to entertain EJ, but I don't mind. Sometimes I need the distraction.

"EJ, make sure you don't hide in your special place. That's only for me, okay?"

"Okay, Evan."

I can't help but frown at Archer who shakes his head. Two things have caught me off-guard just now: The fact that EJ has his own hiding spot, and that he's still not calling Archer 'Dad'.

It's the hiding spot, which truly gives me pause and makes me wonder what the hell Archer is preparing for.

chapter 3
Tucker

AFTER A HIGH STAKE GAME of hide-n-seek and tag with EJ, the little guy is finally ready for bed. It's been a long time since I've played with someone so young. There were times, when I was chasing him around the yard, that I had flashbacks of doing similar things with Claire. Only when we'd play hide-n-seek she'd cheat and watch where I was hiding. Of course, Penny was helping her. I didn't mind though. Hearing Claire squeal when she found me was worth it.

Now if and when I see her again she won't even know who I am. I doubt she has a single memory of me as her father. Pictures, if Penny even took any with her, won't make up for the time we've missed and continue to miss each day we're not together. To my daughter, I'm nothing more than a stranger and maybe someone her mother talks about on special occasions.

Each day that passes is another day lost, and one more day closer to my absolute end. I have less than five months to find Penny or my marriage, as I know it, is over. Right now the law is somewhat on my side according to the first private investigator I hired. I don't know how much smoke he's blowing up my ass, but if he's telling the truth, the law puts a deadline on what the spouse could call abandonment, especially since the Navy isn't acknowledging their error, even with the offer of retirement. If Penny has remarried it will be null and void because I'm alive and well. The downside to that is something I think about every day—what if she left me? What if I'm chasing her when I should really be focusing solely on Claire?

But where is she? How come she's not in school? And if she is, why did Penny change her name? Are they running or hiding? I can't declare her missing because technically I'm still dead. That thought reminds me I need to speak to Ryley about a missing persons report and why one wasn't filed. As much as I don't want to bother her and Evan, I have to know.

Climbing the stairs, I try to make as much noise as possible so I don't interrupt them. I know from experience what it can be like to have people walk in on you when you're trying to love up on your wife. The last thing I want to do is to make things awkward between us.

Much to my surprise, Ryley is curled up in the corner of the couch and Evan is watching television. Of course, his hand is resting on her leg. He's never far from touching her if he can help it. We both know that we'll never be able to make up for the time we've been away. I'll be struggling with Claire, just as he is with EJ. His son knows Evan is his father, but hasn't called him the name he so desperately wishes for … 'Dad.'

For years, I filled Evan in on what it feels like to hear your child say dada for the first time, promising him it's going to be one of the best moments of his life. Little did I know that our lives were being ripped apart while we fought a despicable animal, which some sick fuck senator was funding, and instead of coming clean about his desire to play with children he destroyed our lives. There isn't a shred of doubt in my mind that he has a hit out on us and is waiting patiently to strike. It's just a matter of time before someone makes a move. I hope for our sakes, it's us. I refuse to be a victim to Lawson or Ingram ever again.

"Hi, Tucker. Can I get you some coffee?" Ryley asks as she closes her book and starts to stand before I hold up my hand. Evan turns his head slightly to acknowledge me before returning his focus to whatever he's watching on TV.

"I'm fine, and please don't think you have to wait on me, Ryley."

"Okay, but please know that our house is yours, so you can help yourself to whatever," she says sweetly as she settles back into the couch.

"Except my sniper rifle," Evan laughs, knowing full well that once Ryley is in bed, I'll be on the deck siting the scope to my perfection. As much as I hate saying this, I miss shooting.

"Evan, you can share your toys," Ryley chastises him with a smile. Penny used to say the same thing when Evan would come over to check out a new gun or knife I had picked up. That's one thing I like about being a SEAL—the plethora of weapons that arms dealers had lying around, waiting for us to test them. There was never a shortage of toys.

Sitting in the recliner, which happens to be closer to Ryley, I know this is the time to talk to her about the questions that have been plaguing me. It pains me to bring up the past knowing she's working so hard on her future with Evan and EJ, but this is where I'm stuck.

"Ryley, can I ask you some questions about the day Penny left?"

My question must spark Evan's curiosity because he mutes the show he's watching and sits up, moving closer to Ryley. The three of us look at each for a moment before Ryley sits up straight and reaches for Evan's hand. I can't imagine what the wives and families went through when they were told we died, but I like thinking Penny was there for Ryley since she was pregnant and helping her cope, at least for a brief amount of time.

"I'll tell you anything," she starts before taking a deep breath. "It's been a while, but my memory of that time in my life is fairly clear. What do you want to know?"

Everything, anything, and nothing at all, is what I want to say. I don't want to know that my wife left me for another man and decided to take my child away from me. I think if that were the case, Ryley would've told me by now.

"Did you or anyone else file a missing person's report?" I cut right to chase, knowing her answer could either deter or help me.

"I tried, but no one would take me seriously. The story was the same, 'husband died, wife left'. Anyone on base I would try and talk to brushed me off, and the local police didn't think it was anything since you had died," Ryley states, slightly agitated, probably because I'm asking. She glances at Evan before reaching under their coffee table for the box of tissues.

"As soon you guys deployed, Penny and I had taken Claire to the park. It was something we did on any normal day so it was nothing was out of the ordinary. Our lives didn't change because you guys were gone. The next day we were at the commissary buying you supplies and putting boxes together just in case you weren't back by the end of the week.

"As the weeks started turning into months we started our deployed wives' habits: eating at each other's houses, sending packages, always trying to do stuff together to keep our spirits up. We kept saying you guys would be home any day and we didn't want to you to see how much we worried. The few letters we received kept our hopes up, but we yearned for a phone call.

"One day, we're walking to the beach and Deefur starts growling. It wasn't the kind of growl he does when he's playing, but the hair-raising growl and he wasn't even a year old yet, I don't think. A man was coming toward us and apparently Deefur didn't like that so we followed his intuition and crossed the street. That's when Penny noticed we were being followed. She had seen the same car a few blocks over and thought it was weird and that this hadn't been the first time. She said the car really didn't fit in on the base, but couldn't pinpoint why. We chose to go home instead of the beach, which was probably for the best because Claire wasn't feeling that well. We walked back to your house and I made sure her and Claire were inside before I drove off. I kept watching in my rearview mirror for the car, but never saw it." Ryley looks at Evan and smiles, while he brings their hands up so he can place a kiss on hers.

"That night I called Penny to see if she wanted to go to mall the next day to buy some baby stuff, but she didn't answer. Thinking back, I should've gone over there because it was late, like after nine, and she never had Claire out that late. But I thought maybe you had called her and I didn't want to interrupt her knowing how much those calls meant to us." Pausing, Ryley wipes away a tear, which has fallen down her cheek. I hate that I'm asking her to relive this time in her life, but I'm hoping she has a clue as to what happened to my wife.

"It was the next day that everything went to hell. Between the Chaplin coming to my door and my parents, I never called Penny and she never phoned me either. I ... I didn't think anything of it because we were grieving and I knew we'd grieve together, eventually. I never questioned that she wouldn't be there for me. Frannie was the one who told me she had left. It was only a day or so after we got the news, I think. She said she had gone over to check on her and Claire, being that River was the team leader and all she felt it was her duty as his wife to make sure we were all okay. Now that I think about it, it should've been Penny or I checking on her since her and River had just gotten married, but I was wreck.

25

I couldn't eat or sleep and being pregnant didn't help. Plus, my parents weren't letting me out of their sight.

"Before Evan's funeral, I had to meet my mom on base for some paperwork, so decided to go for a walk and I ended up in front of your house. There was absolutely no life in the house whatsoever. I could see Claire's swing in the backyard just blowing in the wind like she was on it, but yet she wasn't. Your neighbor came out and said that Penny had packed up and left in the middle of the night, which I just couldn't believe. I wish I had asked her when she left exactly, but I assumed it was when she had been told that you died. I tried to call her, but her phone had been disconnected.

"The house—" She stops and shakes her head. "Oh, the house looked nothing like the home you and Penny had created. I tried the door, hoping that the neighbor was wrong, but as soon as I stepped in I knew Penny had left. I could tell a few of the pictures were gone, their frames lay haphazardly on the floor, but all your furniture was still there. It looked like a few of Claire's toys and clothes were gone, as well as some of Penny's things. I had told your neighbor that I would be back to finish cleaning it out, thinking I'd put everything in our garage until she came back, but when Nate and I went back over with boxes, the house had been emptied and a new family was about to move in. It hadn't been a day or so after the funerals. The Navy wasted no time getting your stuff out of there.

"Some weeks later I had voiced my concerns to Nate about Penny and Claire and how I found it odd that we buried you, but she wasn't there. My mom also looked into a few things and noticed that your pension and death benefit hadn't been touched, which I also found odd. I mean, why leave if you don't take the money? That's when I went down to the police station and tried to file the report, but they told me wives disappear all the time and more so when married to SEALs because the guys are never home. The officer wouldn't listen when I said Penny wouldn't do that and she loved you wholeheartedly. I brought up the guy who we saw that Deefur didn't like and the car, but he dismissed my claims saying that I'd probably been seeing things because of my mental state after losing Evan, even though I argued it had happened before."

Ryley takes a few more tissues out of the box and dabs her eyes, smearing her make-up in the process. I look to Evan for some guidance, who nods, encouraging me to continue.

"Did you ever see the car again, the one that had been following you? Do you remember what it looked like?"

Taking a deep breath, Ryley shrugs. "I don't know. Maybe I did. There were a lot of cars on my block after we got the news. At the time, I thought it was the press, but there was only one article about you guys dying. No one ever brought it up again. And thinking back now—I was probably followed more times than I know. Shit was weird. The street was busier. The phone would ring, but it'd be dead air or hang-ups. I told Nate that I thought the phone calls were you," she pauses and looks at Evan, "trying to tell me you were alive, but he said you were gone and I needed to accept that."

"Of course he did," Evan mutters, earning a stern look from Ryley. Evan knows that Nate holds a special place in Ryley's heart, and she hates when he badmouths his brother.

"Were you trying to call?" she asks sternly.

"No."

"All right then." Ryley turns her attention back to me with an apologetic smile. "I'm sorry about that. Evan needs a little reminder every now and again."

Evan pokes her in the side and kisses her on the cheek. I know things have been hard for him, especially knowing that his brother was set to marry his girl, but it's all worked out and Evan and Nate are on the path to becoming best friends again.

"I should've asked more questions, but I didn't know.

I had lost Evan, the only man I had ever loved, and was pregnant with his son. I was about to lose the house we had bought together because his checks stopped and I wasn't entitled to the death benefit, his mother made sure of that. I had his life insurance, but that was only going to last so long. I'm sorry, Tucker. I wish I had done more."

Reaching over, Ryley places her hand on top of mine. I fight back the tears, knowing that Penny felt unsafe while I was gone and feel solidly that she didn't leave me. My wife is running from someone or something. I just have to find her before whatever it is does.

"When we were on the beach after we got back, Frannie said she remembers a moving truck. Did you see a moving truck near our house?"

Ryley's eyes drift off as if she's trying to remember. It's only a matter of seconds until she's shaking her head. "I'm sorry, I don't remember a truck. Living off base kept me a bit secluded from on base activity."

"I hate saying this, but we all know some shit went down that they don't want us to know about. I bet there are cameras everywhere on base, monitoring everything. Someone knows why Penny left in such a hurry. We just need to figure who that person is and get them to start talking," Evan says, adding more theories to an already large conspiracy.

"Who?' I ask, shrugging.

"I don't know," Evan states matter-of-factly.

chapter 4
Tucker

EVERYTHING RYLEY IS TELLING ME is a lot to process. More importantly, I feel like an ass for asking her to relive this nightmare, but she's the only one who has some of the answers I need. These are questions I should've asked when we first came back; however, she wasn't in any shape to answer them. Dealing with Evan's return was enough of a blow and they had their own things to work out.

"The day we were at the beach, Frannie had a lot to say."

"Yeah, she was everywhere once we got the news. She was my rock. Frannie acted like our leader, much like River was yours. Only now that I think about it, it was so she could get information on us." It pains me to hear this about a woman we know had a hand in this conspiracy.

"You mentioned Penny wasn't at the funeral, but I recall Frannie saying Penny left shortly after. Do you think you can remember exactly?"

I feel like a fucking therapist asking a victim to remember her attacker or what was going on around her. A quick glance at Evan assures me that he's okay with my line of questioning.

If he weren't, he'd tell me to cool it for the night. He is, without a doubt, protective of Ryley and isn't afraid to assert himself where she's concerned. I feel the same way about Penny and I know I'd be acting the same as Evan, especially since there's already been an attempt on Ryley's life.

"I'll be right back," she says as she stands and walks out of the room, leaving Evan and I.

"Where's she going?"

"Dunno, bathroom maybe?" Evan says with a shrug.

There's an awkward silence between us, but it has nothing to do with a lack of conversation. The shit we've been discussing tonight is hard and weighs heavily on us. We've been through hell and back, lived to tell people who care to listen about it, but have nothing to show for it except our lives ... which in the grand scheme of things is better than nothing.

Ryley returns with a shoebox and sits down in the same spot. "There are things I remember and there are some things I think happened. Like I said, I was in a fog. My life, as I knew it, was gone. I was that young girl who had based every adult decision around Evan, only to be left pregnant and alone. So when he died ... part of me died, too, and I didn't cope very well. Long nights of watching home videos and sleeping in his clothes on the couch was what my life entailed. I had this amazing group of people surrounding me, making sure I didn't lose EJ, but that doesn't mean I wasn't missing Penny.

"After about a month or so, pictures started arriving from the funerals. I found it odd that someone was taking pictures, but they were military funerals and those are often shared everywhere, so it didn't really mean anything out of the ordinary. I looked at them until Nate put them in a box, saying they weren't helping the healing process." Ryley lifts the box that's sitting on her lap.

"Why didn't you tell me?" Evan asks her, his voice soft and caring. This is a side of Evan I rarely see. When we're together, we're always strong, never showing any type of weakness.

"I forgot about them until Tucker asked if I was sure Penny missed his funeral."

Ryley lifts the lid, and I have to fight my instincts to yank the box away from her to look at the contents myself. Ryley pulls out four stacks of photos, each one tied in navy blue ribbon. It only takes her a second to grab the stack she's looking for. Everything she's doing is painstaking slow and hidden from my view. Evan isn't watching either as his eyes are focused on the wall in front of him. It's fucking morbid to see pictures from your own funeral, and if I didn't know any better I'd think I'm having an out of body experience.

"Years ago I'd say these are the images from your funeral. I don't remember Penny or Claire being there, but I don't remember much from those first few days. She's not in the pictures here." She hands me the stack and I take them without breaking eye contact with her. I don't want to see what's on them because the heartbreak of knowing my wife wasn't at my funeral is a lot to bear. I should look because there may be a clue in one of the photos. Not that I'd know what I'm looking for.

"Who took my flag?" I ask as I thumb through each picture. I have very little family, having been raised by my grandmother. I got word while deployed that she had died and that Penny had followed her wishes for cremation. Sitting here now I don't even know if that's true or not.

"I don't know," Ryley says, shaking her head. "I don't remember. I'm sorry, Tucker." She sets her hand on my wrist and gives it a squeeze.

I nod, letting her know it's okay even though she realizes none of this is far from being all right. I'm not sure any of us will ever feel normal again, or feel like we don't have to watch our backs.

"Do you know anything about my grandmother?" I ask,

hoping that Ryley may know something.

"What do you mean?" she asks.

"While we were deployed, Penny ... *Frannie* wrote, well typed a letter saying that she had died. Knowing what we know about the lies, I guess I'm wondering if that's even true."

"I don't. Frannie really never discussed you or Justin, once we buried you guys. After a while we stopped talking about you all together. It was too hard."

Evan stands and starts pacing. His hands are pulling at the ends of his hair and he's muttering to himself. There's something on his mind, but he's not ready to tell us about it yet. I've seen this from him before.

"Evan?" Ryley says his name only for him to hold up his hand. When he finally drops it, it's a pissed off Evan Archer staring back at me.

"What?" I question, eager to know what he's thinking.

"We have to find Frannie."

"Isn't she dead?" It's more of a statement than fact. I think we're all hoping she's alive, but we don't know.

He shakes his head. "I don't believe she is and she has all the answers. She knows where Penny and Claire are."

I stand slowly as I match his posture.

"Frannie sent you pictures of Claire. Hell, she sent you report cards with teacher's comments. She's either a fucking whiz on the computer with age progression, has some really deep ties, or knows where your wife is and is able to get pictures of Claire. I give Frannie a lot of credit, but she assumed the lives of so many people, writing out comments about Claire and not repeating herself would be almost impossible."

As much as I hate to admit it, he's right. Frannie is the key, which ties everything together. But if the Feds haven't found her, how will I? My resources are that of a gnat.

"Babe, did Frannie ever take vacations while we were gone?" Evan asks Ryley, who is now standing right along with us.

"Yes, although I don't know if they're vacations. But every couple of weeks she'd disappear, it was odd."

"How so?" I ask.

"Well, it was like this ... each day she'd come over for coffee or be there when I'd have a doctor's appointment. Every couple of nights we'd have dinner, go to the movie, or do game night with Nate and Cara when they were still together. And then she'd say things like she's going to visit her sister and niece, but when you went to her house there were never any pictures of anyone besides her and River. I know not everyone is like me and has pictures of their family everywhere, but I found it odd. And her sister never came to visit either, especially after River's funeral."

"That's because she was probably visiting Penny and Claire," Evan blurts out before I can get the words out of my mouth.

"I'm thinking the same thing, and if that's the case, how do we find Frannie?" I ask, ready to do whatever I have to.

"I don't think it's a question of finding her, but drawing her out. I have a feeling she's close by. The sociopath part of her wants to know what we're doing. She had control over everyone's lives for so long that she won't be able to let go." Evan seems so sure that it's hard for me to doubt him.

"What are you suggesting?"

"You keep looking for Penny and Claire with your private investigator. I'm going to get someone who resembles Penny to make appearances in town and hope Frannie slips up."

"Okay, say you're right. What if you do that and she has Penny and Claire someplace and moves them? Or worse, hurts them?"

Evan's face falls at my question and I don't know if the thought of Frannie hurting Penny and Claire crossed his mind, but it should've—she hurt Ryley and her mom.

"Okay, so my James Bond technique needs some work,

but we have to find Frannie and hand her over. And we need to find Penny and Claire, although I do believe that Frannie will lead us to Penny."

"Why?" I question.

"Because our lives are nothing but a conspiracy and if we don't think outside the box, we'll never figure it all out," Ryley says, stone-faced.

At night is when I feel the most alone. It's the quiet calm that scares me. In my dreams I'm often running through bare hallways chasing the sound of Claire's voice as she yells for help, only to find Tacito Renato with a bullet in the middle of his forehead, holding my daughter at knifepoint. Each time I try to step toward her, the floor gives way and I'm falling into a black pit of nothing.

The dream feels like its only minutes long, but it's been hours since I've closed my eyes. And when I wake, I'm tired as shit and still hearing her voice. Every nine-year-old girl I see looks like Claire, even when she doesn't. For days I sat outside her school on the off chance that Penny was still in town, ready to accept the fact that she wanted a divorce. I waited for my little girl to come down the stairs once the bell rang, hoping she'd see me and remember that I'm her daddy. Each day I was let down. And the next day I'd go to the next school and then the next, searching for my daughter.

I know Renato is dead. Archer killed him. It was the most beautiful shot I've ever seen him take. We had been searching for Abigail Chesley, and once we found her we stumbled upon Renato's camp after finding a pile of little girl clothes not five to six hundred yards away. What we saw made us sick to our stomachs and before any of us could react, Archer leveled his rifle and put a bullet between his eyes. We had never heard of this guy until Abigail said his name, and from that point forward a shit storm ensued.

River was the one to radio it in, and we were told we could go home—only the extract didn't come for us, only Abigail. We were ordered to find all the players in this sex ring we uncovered.

We weren't supposed to kill Renato, which we learned after we finally came home. I think that triggered our downfall. Maybe the powers that be were thinking we'd kill ourselves, each other, or die before they brought us home and started asking questions. All I know is we were the ones who were supposed to end up dead. That seemed to be the story our families were told so why keep us alive? The risks far outweigh the rewards. Whoever is behind all this, whether its Senator Lawson, Admiral Ingram, or General Chesley, they're keeping a dark secret that will destroy someone in power, a secret which frees the four of us—Archer, River, Rask, and myself—from this purgatory we're living in.

I want all the answers given to me on a silver-fucking platter with my name engraved in gold. I deserve that at least. I've served my country. I've fought in wars protecting its freedom. It's bullshit that the people who run the country I love so much are willing to shit on my team and me.

Going to bed angry is never my intention, and I find myself pacing the room I'm staying in. Evan and Ryley have opened their home and resources to me, helping me to find my family. Even the room I'm temporarily calling mine has pictures of Penny and Claire, giving me peace. I pray every second that they're alive and waiting for me to come and rescue them.

The one person who can shed some light on all of this is Vice President Christina Charlotte, except she's dead and no one is putting the pieces together. We were sent to retrieve her daughter, who Lawson had kidnapped, but Christina was killed before we came home. If that doesn't reek of a cover-up I don't know what does. General Chesley should be on our side. We saved his granddaughter, and brought her home to his son. Instead, he's lurking on the base across the way from Archer's house, coming in under the cover of darkness thinking no one will know. Maybe he's the key to unraveling the mystery.

Tomorrow begins a new day, a new search.

chapter 5
Tucker

"WHAT ARE YOU DOING OUT here?" Evan's voice is quiet against the night air. It's different in Seattle than it is in Coronado; the air seems thinner. Maybe it's because Washington doesn't hold life-shattering memories for me.

"Watching."

He sits down next to me, and pulls a second set of binoculars out from a bin by my chair. I don't bother looking in there to see what else he has, but I imagine he's fully equipped to spy on Canada from here.

"How far is the beach from here?" I ask, wondering why he didn't buy property with beach access.

"It's a block or so. The rocks thin out quickly once you get around the bend over there. Ryley and EJ walk there almost every day. She can show you in the morning if you're needing to get your fins wet."

I laugh at his joke even if it's not that funny. Being in the Navy we have plenty of opportunities to be in the water. The water is our friend, and when you're trained like us, it's easy to hide in.

Evan's access to the ocean from his house is negated by a massive rock formation. It's as if whoever cleaned the rocks away from the beach piled them here. The rocks are jagged and undoubtedly make climbing up to this house difficult. He's chosen the best spot to watch the Navy and protect his family at the same time.

"How's Nate?"

Evan sighs and leans back in his chair, kicking his feet out.

"Are you talking to him?"

"We talk. He and Ryley talk more, almost every day. I try not to let it bother me, but sometimes it does. I'm jealous of their relationship. Her and I have lost so much time, and it doesn't matter how much time we spend together now, things are different.

"When Nate's around, they're always laughing. They have these stupid inside jokes and I hate hearing 'remember when' because whatever it is they're talking about, it's usually something that happened while we were gone. And don't even get started on Nate and EJ." He stops talking and shakes his head. "I'm grateful my brother was there for them, but sometimes I want to ask him to disappear for a year and let us be. Each time I think I'm about to have a breakthrough with EJ, Nate shows up. I know he doesn't plan it, but there's a part of me that thinks he does."

Evan and I often complain about the shit we went though and easily forget about how our families suffered. Each of us is hurting in different ways, and while Evan was lucky enough to get his family back, Rask and I haven't been. That poor kid—his parents won't even speak to him, even though a simple DNA test will prove he's their son. They refuse to acknowledge he's alive and yet, he hasn't given up hope. He says he calls them each Sunday, just as he did before we deployed. He tells me that he leaves a message because they don't answer and is waiting for the day he's met with the operator recording stating the number has been disconnected.

"Nate's good, though. I need to accept that he did what he did out of love for Ry and me. Him being with Cara helps, though. And when he does show up here, she's with him, so I'm not always on high alert when he's around."

Since I've sat down I've been watching a set of lights off in the distance. The boat's activities are strange. From what I can gather, when it shuts its lights off it's speeding into the Sound. When the lights come on, I have a feeling it's looking to see if they've reached their destination. It's as if they want to get wherever they need to be unnoticed. If this doesn't reek of something illegal I don't know what does.

"He's still enlisted, right?" I ask, lifting the night vision binoculars to my face. Now that the boat is closer I can make out three people onboard. It's nothing but a fishing trawler without fishing poles. *Who takes a trawler out with no poles?*

"Yep." Evan lifts his binoculars. I have a feeling he's looking at the same boat as I am. The Sound is quiet right now, except for this boat. "Cara wants him to retire. He wants to as well, but not until this mess is over. He's joined the lawsuit Ryley filed against the Navy and says the bigwigs are fucking pissed, but he doesn't care. He said losing me was the hardest things he's ever gone though."

"Worse than BUD/s?"

Evan chuckles. "Yeah, man, worse than BUD/s."

"Shit, man, that's hard."

"Don't I know it," he says, as the both of us try not to laugh.

Laughing is rare for me these days, but when it does happen I appreciate the moment.

"What do you think is going on down there?" he asks, solidifying my instincts.

"Drug deal, Navy style."

"What?" Evan scoffs.

"The lights are off now, and when they turn them back on I bet you the boat is parallel to us. They're searching for something in the water, so either it's a place to drop a body or they're waiting for one to pop up. I said drugs because *that* would be the easiest for me to take right now."

"No shit," he mumbles as we watch the boat speed closer to us. "Man, why does everything have to be so fucked up? And why us? I mean, what the fuck did we do to deserve this?"

"I don't know," I mutter just as the boat's engine shuts off. We both lean forward at the same time to watch whatever is about to happen unfold. The telltale sound of a bullet moving into the chamber has me looking at Evan.

"What the fuck?"

Evan doesn't say anything as he rests his cheek on his rifle. He flicks the button that allows a red beam to project and steadies it on one of the men on the boat. Shouting ensues and the engine starts up. Their lights come on while they scramble for cover and speed out of the Sound. I shouldn't laugh but it's funny as shit.

"Dude?"

Evan shrugs as he puts his rifle down. "Just having a little fun."

"What if they shot at us?"

He looks at me and I imagine his eyes are cold. "Then I shoot back. Pretty damn sure I'd hit them before they hit me."

He's right, but that's not the point.

"Anyway, if it's drugs, they need to find someplace else to smuggle. I don't want that shit washing up on the shores where EJ plays."

I nod, agreeing with him. "That was funny."

As soon as I say it, Evan busts out laughing. Our moment of hilarity only lasts a few seconds before a hangar light comes on across the bay.

"That's where Chesley likes to hang out."

"He has a girl with him. She's young," I state, looking through the binoculars. Part of me is waiting for Evan to train his rifle on Chesley, but I know he's not willing to do time, and I'm not willing to let him kill one of the men who can give us answers.

"Probably Abigail … the reason we're in this mess."

"I feel sorry for her," I say out of nowhere.

"Me too. She gets kidnapped, raped, sent to Cuba to be a sex slave, then gets saved by us only to have her mother die. That kid is scarred for life thanks to Lawson."

"Do you think Lawson killed her mother?" I ask.

"Yup, I do. Lawson is a sick fuck with all the answers. He started this shit and will likely die without telling a soul everything we want to know."

Chesley and Abigail get into a car and it speeds off into the darkness. The rest of the Navy shipyard is quiet, except for a few sailors hanging around doing grunt work. It's odd that no one was watching that trawler come in, in the middle of night. Unless, they were waiting for it and Evan scared it off.

When the sun peeks over the mountains, I stretch and yawn. I slept outside, finding it easier than sleeping in a bed. I don't care how long I've been back, after living in the jungle for six years it's hard to confine yourself to a box, regardless of how comfortable it is.

The bay is bustling with fishermen as they head out for their first or next catch of the day. I don't know what time it is, but aside from needing to be close to the shipyard I understand why Evan loves this house so much. The way the sun casts an orange glow makes everything seem right in the world. I've heard that the Pacific Northwest has some of the most amazing sunrises and sunsets, and now I can confirm that. I could get used to waking up like this every day.

The sliding glass opens and Ryley steps out. She's dressed in a Navy T-shirt and flannel pants with her hair braided. Behind me, EJ is knocking on the window, waving. He runs off, wearing nothing but his underwear and screaming at Evan.

"Morning." After handing me a cup of coffee, she curls up in the chair that Evan sat in not a few hours before. If she's leery of the rifle resting against the deck railing, she doesn't say anything.

"Sorry for sleeping out here," I say after taking a sip of the coffee.

"Don't be. Evan does it often. I understand."

I nod a thank you, grateful that she's not only willing to open her home to me, but she accepts me with all my odd habits.

"Marley called this morning and would like you to come to her office around nine. I have to head that way, so I was wondering if you'd like to drive in with me."

My body tenses. It's only been a day since I met with Marley and I don't know if it's a good thing or not that she wants to see me so soon. Ryley places her hand on top of mine and squeezes.

"It's going to be okay, Tucker. I know it doesn't seem like it now, but it will. We'll find Penny and Claire and bring them home."

"Where exactly is home?" I ask, hoping my voice doesn't break. The last thing I want is for Ryley, or anyone else for that matter, to see me cry.

"For right now, home is here. It doesn't have to be a place, or specific house. Home is where you hang up your coat and kick off your shoes. Home is where you sit down for a nice meal, and if you have your friends surrounding you, it's so much better. You are welcome here for as long as it takes, and so are Penny and Claire."

"Thank you, Ryley. You're a good woman."

She shakes her head. "I'm not, Tucker. I'm a woman who lost, too, and I know what it feels like to not have somewhere to come home to."

I look at her strangely wondering what she's talking about. She smiles sweetly and leans back in her chair, pulling her legs up. "When Evan died, the house we shared didn't feel like the one we had bought together. Everything about it was wrong. The paint wasn't what we chose; the furniture wasn't what we bought. I hated it. I hated everything about it, but I stayed because he had eaten off those dishes and had sat on that couch. I stayed because the bed that I slept in was the same one he did."

"That doesn't make any sense," I tell her.

"Sure it does. With Evan gone, I had to make it a new home with his memories. And that's what it came down to … memories. And the best thing about memories is that you can take them anywhere." She turns to me and winks, telling me that she's always right no matter how confusing she may sound.

"I'm going to go shower," I say, leaning over to give her a kiss on the cheek. "Archer is a lucky man."

"You'll be lucky, too, when you have Penny back in your arms."

Her words give me pause and hit me straight in the chest. I dream of the day when I can hold Penny again, when I can feel her nestled into my neck and her body pressed against mine.

The problem with my dream is that it seems to be quickly fading. The tick tock of the law is fighting against me.

chapter 6
Amy

I TAKE A DEEP BREATH after I get out of my car and tilt my head toward the morning sun before walking up the steps to the general store. This is my favorite time of the day, the time when everything is calm. When you can hear the birds chirp before traffic comes barreling down the road, and when you can still make out a four-legged friend who is grazing on the dewy grass across from the store. Everything looks fresh in the morning sunlight, which gives me hope that things are going to be okay. And I need a lot of hope these days.

Every morning, the same two men—John and Steve—sit on the porch in the white rocking chairs the store provides. They sip their coffee and carry on like two old ladies on a Sunday morning. They know everyone in town and absolutely everything that goes on. They are the unofficial mayors of Pittsfield. I say, "Hi," as I pass by, earning a whistle and a wink. Some think they're dirty old men, but I believe they're being nice. They make a lady feel good about herself whether they mean to or not.

I open the door and cringe at the creaking sound it

makes. We've tried to oil the hinges and even replaced the door, but the same thing happens each time. The guys say it's the ghost of the previous owner making sure we don't change the character of the store since it's on the historical preservation list—not that we would do anything of the sort. There's something about an old general store that takes people back to the quieter days of the world. The inside doesn't fare much better with its old floorboards; they tell a story of age each time they're stepped on. It's a sound of history and you get used to it over time.

"Good morning, Amy," Laura says, handing me a steaming cup of coffee. Holding it between my hands, I inhale deeply. I love the smell of her home roasted coffee. She sells it specifically for the store, along with an assortment of cakes, pastries, cheeses, and meats. Her little store is a tourist stop and is often too busy for just the two of us, but we make it work. According to Laura, her first year of ownership was a struggle, but after putting in the breakfast and lunch counter things picked up. And when she started featuring local products to help out the farmers and independent businesses in the area, people really started to come in. By the second year, her business had grown and it's still thriving fifteen years later. I've been working for her for four years now and know just about everything there is to know.

I tip my head back and welcome the warmth as the coffee trickles down my throat before I answer her. Yes, this makes getting up early worth it.

"Morning, Laura. How are things?" I ask, coming around the counter to place my purse in the drawer and grab my apron. I do everything here: cook, clean, stock shelves, serve the lunch crowd, and chat whenever someone needs an ear ... and believe me everyone has something to say. I'm everyone's favorite history teacher's wife, and when your husband is highly respected you do what you can to keep up appearances.

45

"Can't complain. Now that you're here, I'm going to run and do the banking. I'll be right back."

With a flurry, Laura is out the door before I can respond. It's normal for her; once she has her mind set, it's moving a million times faster than her body and she probably feels like she's already late. The nearest town is about forty minutes from here, so her "right back" means two or three hours later. I don't mind, really, since everyone who comes in are either locals or tourists.

One of the best things about my job is that I get to talk to people from all over. I get to hear their stories and pretend it's me having the grand adventure they're enjoying. Tourists love to share. They love that you care. I want them to feel welcomed, even if this isn't their final destination.

And when they leave, I move on to the next person and their adventure because deep down talking to them makes me miss where I came from, makes me long for the warm air, the ocean and sand between my toes. They make me question my existence and I often find myself wondering how things could've been different.

I set out and start the daily chores around the store. Laura has already dealt with the early morning rush, leaving me to clean up and make sure the store is presentable. Our busy times vary, but between five and six in the morning you can guarantee a trucker or two will be in here eating before hitting the highway. The state lacks the necessary highway system to help them get from point A to point B. This is where small towns like Pittsfield come in. If you create the atmosphere, they'll stop and become regulars.

One of the farmers from down the road walks in, grabs the newspaper, and takes a seat at the counter. After pouring his usual iced tea, I set it down in front of him.

"Thanks, Amy."

"No problem, Adam. Let me know when you're ready to order."

He nods and opens the paper, getting lost in the news. The paper here is nothing like I'm used to. You can read front to back in under an hour, or just ask one of the guys on the porch what's going on and they'll tell you. Not a whole lot happens around here, and for that I'm thankful. The less excitement we have the better I feel.

"Unbelievable," Adam huffs, grabbing my attention.

"What's that?"

He shakes his head and ruffles the paper to straighten it out. "Just that senator from Florida."

I'm not sure what Adam is talking about, as I haven't been keeping up with the news lately. There was a time in my life when all I did was watch the news, but lately it's depressing with all the children being murdered and the terrorist attacks. Each time I hear about one, I want to crawl into bed with Chloe and hold her. She wouldn't allow that, being almost ten. Apparently it's no longer cool to do those types of things with your mom.

"I hadn't heard. Do you want the usual?" I'm not trying to rush him, but don't want to get caught if more people come in. When he nods, I set off to make his roast beef and bacon grinder.

"This guy's a real piece of shit."

"Most politicians are. They're liars and thieves, taking the taxpayers' money for hammers and toilet seats that they put in the books for an exorbitant amount. I'm not sure I've met one who doesn't lie." Bringing his sandwich and a bag of chips over, I rest my hip against the counter.

"Nah, this guy is the scum. Says here he's being charged with all kinds of crimes against children, like prostitution and rape."

I cringe at what Adam says. Being a mother, it's our job to protect our children at all costs. I know I do. I've taken measures before to protect Chloe. These men and even woman that sexually harm children … I have no words for them. They should not be walking amongst us, I know that, but as I stand here I have to keep my opinions to myself because Ray doesn't believe in the death penalty.

"I'd like to get my hands on this guy and squeeze the life out of him," Adam states in between bites.

"What's his name?"

Adam returns his focus to the paper before replying, "Lawson. Says here he's being charged with rape and pedophilia. What a sick fuck."

Everything around me stops and my body grows cold. I'm having trouble forming a sentence, or getting my mouth to move. I want to tell Adam that he has no idea how deranged this man is, but I can't. It's my secret to keep and mine alone. It's been years—six and a half to be exact—since I've heard that name, and I could've honestly gone the rest of my life without ever hearing it again.

"Amy? *Amy*!"

Adam's yelling gets my attention and I try to compose myself as I look at him. "What?"

"You're um … well, you're holding the knife like you're about to kill someone. I've read stories about people blacking out and committing murder, and honestly I don't want to die today."

I glance at the knife in my hand, one I don't remember picking up, and set it down on the counter. Wiping my hands on my apron as if they're dirty, I step away. I need some water or something, but moving seems so unnatural right now.

Suddenly, the bell above the door chimes and a family walks in. They're loud and the kids take off in opposite directions, searching for what their hearts desire.

"Amy, are you okay?"

Glancing at Adam, I fake a smile. I nod as memories that I've long hidden come rushing back.

The doorbell chimes throughout the house, waking Claire from the nap she was taking on my chest. We've been up for who knows how long dealing with her cough and runny nose that sleep has evaded us. I drag my tired ass to the door, pleasantly surprised to see Frannie together with a man dressed in a suit standing there.

"Hey, Fran," I say, letting her come in. The man follows her, eyeing Claire the entire time.

"Penny, this is my friend from high school, Ted Lawson. He's a state senator making his rounds and thought he'd spare me some of his time today. This is Penny McCoy. Her husband is the SEAL I was telling you about."

"What about Tucker?" I ask, mid-yawn and handshake.

"Oh, just that River is his team leader and I've been making sure all the wives are doing okay since they've been gone." Her smile is sweet and on the inside I'm rolling my eyes. She doesn't know jack shit about Ryley or me and is trying to weasel her way into our lives. Frannie married River a few days before the guys deployed. That doesn't make her the queen bee around here.

"You look tired," she says, her tone laced with pity.

"I am. Claire isn't feeling well, and we haven't sleep in what feels like days. I haven't even showered."

Frannie reaches for her, and Claire goes willingly. "Why don't you go and take one now? I'll watch Claire for you."

The thought of a nice hot shower does sound like something I need. "Thank you, Frannie. I won't be long." I kiss Claire on the top of her head and make a beeline for the stairs. Before I head up, I take a look at her friend, finding it odd that she brought him here. However, I'm so tired nothing makes sense. He's sitting on the couch, reading my recent fashion magazine and seems harmless. Besides, he's a state senator; I guess I should feel lucky he's in my house.

I stay in the shower longer than I had planned, and even take the time to blow dry my hair before heading back downstairs.

"Frannie, I can't thank you enough," I say as I come down

the stairs, stopping short when I don't see Frannie, but only her friend. He's lying on the couch without his shirt on and Claire is lying on top of him, naked. It takes my mind a minute to register what I'm seeing as his hand is caressing her bottom.

"What's going on here? Where the hell is Frannie?" I pull Claire off of him and wrap her in my arms; she's lethargic and limp. "What'd you do to my daughter?" I scream at him as he moves at a snail's pace.

He puts his hands up. "I was just helping her feel better."

"By taking off her clothes? You're a sick fuck. You need to get out of my house." I move quickly around the room, searching for her clothes, but can't find them. "Where are her things?" I ask, but he doesn't answer. I can feel him behind me and I go rigid.

"Good-bye, lovely Claire. Until we meet again."

Turning, I glare at him. "What the fuck are you talking about? You will not come anywhere near my daughter. I'm calling the police."

He sets his hand on my shoulder and leans closer. "You'll do no such thing, or your worst nightmare will come true."

Before I can comprehend his words, he's out of my house and I'm standing there with a baby that is barely moving and completely naked. I run upstairs as fast as I can and get her dressed. Rushing back down the stairs, I open the door—half expecting him to still be standing there—and put her into the car. My first stop will be the hospital to have her checked out. The second stop is the police. Whoever this man is, he needs to be called in for questioning. If he hurt my baby, I'll be his worst nightmare.

Only when the bell on the front counter dings again do I snap out of the day that changed my life forever.

"My name is Amy Barnes," I mumble under my breath, forcing myself to remember who I am and reminding myself that Ted Lawson can no longer hurt us.

chapter 7
Tucker

RYLEY DROVE ME TO MEET with Marley this morning, claiming that it was no big deal because she had to go make an appointment with a wedding dress consultant. When I asked Archer why he wasn't going, I got the death glare. I know when Ryley is out of the house it gives him time with EJ, but I also know when he's not near Ryley, he starts to panic a little. He's also preparing himself for the arrival of Nate and Cara, who called last night to say they're coming to town in a few days. Evan isn't happy; Ryley is thrilled. I'm hoping Ryley is thrilled because Cara will be here and not just Nate, given the history between them.

I'm waiting. It's all I ever do these days. Marley has a client in her office, and from what I'm gathering this was a spur of the moment appointment. Without a secretary or a two-room office, she has standing room in the hall to wait and from my experience last time, Marley is punctual.

It's been just over a week since I've seen her, and even though she called last week, she had to cancel our meeting saying her lead didn't pan out. Today, I'm physically in the hallway outside her office at her request.

When her door opens, a woman comes out. Our eyes meet briefly and I can tell she's been crying. It's probably not a good thing as I can only imagine the news she was given isn't good. For all I know, I could be facing the same sort of news when I step in.

Marley greets me at the door with a soft smile. Almost hesitantly, I follow her into her office and take a seat across from her desk. I quickly glance at the file sitting there and see my name. It's gone from being thin to thick in a week's time, and I don't know if that's a good or bad thing.

"Hi, Mr. McCoy."

"Please, call me Tucker or just McCoy. None of that mister crap."

She nods and opens my file, taking out a piece of paper. "I'm going to just cut right to the chase." That'd be nice. Even though she's not only being paid by the hour—by Ryley— we're still working against the clock.

As if in slow motion she sets it down on the table and slides it over to me. I know I'm supposed to lean forward and look, but my body is frozen in place. Anxiety and fear run rapidly through my system right now. I'm torn, needing to know what's on that paper, but also afraid of what it says.

"I'm afraid to look," I tell her honestly. If she's surprised by my admission she doesn't show it.

"I understand," she replies, pulling the sheet of paper back to my file. "I think you probably feel lost, but be assured I'm here to help. With that said, I don't want to withhold any information that I find from you. In my line of work it's going to be good and bad, but nonetheless it's helpful in what I'm doing."

I take in everything she's saying, but I'm still fearful of what's on that document. *Is Penny remarried? Did she file for divorce from me? Is she dead? What about Claire?* I have these questions every day, yet there are no answers to fill the void.

"The fear I feel, I've been trained to not feel this way and yet I can't … I can't stop feeling like I've failed Penny and Claire when all I ever wanted to do was protect them."

"I understand, Tucker." She pauses, taking a deep breath. "My line of work can be rewarding and also very painful. It's never fun to tell people that their spouses, who they think are working late, are actually having affairs, or living secret lives. But sometimes, I get the happy … like reuniting long lost siblings, or people searching for their adoptive parents or those parents searching for their children. While not all of those are happy, most are. I want to believe your case is going to be happy."

My heart beats a little faster when she finishes. "Did you find something?" I ask, trying not to get my hopes up.

"I did, and while the news isn't good, it does tell me what I'm looking for."

With a furrowed brow I stare at her questioningly, waiting for her to continue. She picks up the sheet of paper I wouldn't look at and reads it out loud.

"My name is Sgt. Doyle. Penelope McCoy entered into the police station with her young daughter at approximately 1900 hours stating that a man molested her daughter. I took her complaint, noting that the child had already been to the hospital, but the report was inconclusive. The child is two years old and I did not ask her any questions due to her age. I did not notice any visible physical damage / bruising on the parts of her body that were not covered by clothing.

"Mrs. McCoy attests that her friend, Frannie Riveria, came to her house with a friend, Ted Lawson, who represented himself as a senator and she left her child in the care of Riveria while she showered, stating that the young child has been sick and her friend offered her a small break. Mrs. McCoy states that her husband is currently on deployment with the United States Navy to which I asked why this matter isn't being brought up to the police on base and she states they dismissed her claim. Mrs. McCoy goes onto state that when she came down from her shower, she found Lawson prone on her sofa without a shirt on and with her naked daughter lying on his chest. He was caressing her bottom, and when she took the child from him, the child was limp and lethargic leading Mrs. McCoy to believe he had drugged her. The report from the hospital says lab results are pending. When Mrs. McCoy informed Lawson that she was reporting this to the authorizes, he told her that if she did her worst nightmare would come true."

It takes every ounce of control not to pick up the desk in front of me and throw it across the room. That fuck touched my daughter and Frannie led him right to my baby.

"Doe—" I clear my throat and pinch the bridge of my nose. "Does it say anything else?"

"Just the date."

"When?"

"August fourteenth, two thousand and nine."

The date isn't lost on me. I know, from Ryley, it's the day before we died.

"Does that date mean anything to you?"

I nod, reluctantly. "I died on the fifteenth of August."

I sit there, trying to comprehend and make sense of the report Marley read to me. I take it from her, reading and re-reading the words over and over again. Penny filed a report with base and was brushed off, so she filed a report with the local police.

"Did they investigate?"

"Sgt. Doyle brought Lawson in for questioning, but didn't have anything to hold him on so they had to release him."

"Was Claire drugged?"

Marley nods and slides another sheet of paper over to me. "Her blood had traces of a sleep aid and cocaine."

"Cocaine? Why would he give a baby coke?"

Marley seems uncomfortable as her eyes wander from my file to her computer and to me. "I asked the same thing, so I did some research and found out that in children so young it relaxes them beyond control. Pedophiles use it—"

I hold my hand up, silently asking her to stop talking. I don't need to know that this piece of shit was going to rape my daughter.

"I'm trying to wrap my head around this. I ... uh ..."

"I know, me too. Unfortunately, Sgt. Doyle had a massive heart attack last night, only hours after he sent that report."

My eyes snap up to hers as the color drains from her face. She's smart. She must know what I'm thinking.

"I understand if you want to quit this case," I tell her, even though if she does I'll never find my family. However, I wouldn't be able to live with myself knowing something has happened to her because of me.

"I'm not quitting. Why would you think that?"

"Because people are dying, people who know the truth. This woman, Frannie, she pretended to be our friend only to make our lives hell. She's behind all of this and we don't know where she is and why she's doing this. Lawson is her brother and their father is Admiral Ingram. Lawson is in jail and hopefully not coming out anytime soon. Now you're telling me the sergeant you were speaking with is dead?"

"Sgt. Doyle was over seventy and obese. I think his heart attack is a result of age and an unhealthy lifestyle."

I let her words sink in and my only response is a joke. "Those donuts will get you every time."

She smiles for the first time since our meeting started, and oddly enough that takes away a small bit of stress.

"The hospital report, which I was able to dig up, showed no signs of trauma to Claire. It's my best guess that he didn't get as far as he planned or it took the drugs longer than he expected to work."

"I'm going to kill him."

Marley glances up at me with shock and slowly shakes her head. "He's locked up."

"I'm a sniper and a SEAL. Do you really think a prison is going to keep me from putting a bullet in his head? He touched my daughter and threatened my wife. And after she reported it, we're all dead. He's the reason we were deployed." My voice is rising, and it's only after I realize I've given out classified information that I shut my mouth. I hang my head, in shame, discontent. I've said things I shouldn't have and wish I could take them all back. All except for saying I'm going to kill Lawson because I am. He's going to die and so is Frannie.

"My wife ran," I state, and Marley nods. "She didn't leave me, she ran. If the police didn't listen and I'm dead a day later, she ran for her life and for Claire's."

"She's protecting your daughter from these people."

"And from me."

When Ryley picks me up, I'm quiet. I'm afraid to tell her what I've learned, for fear of her reaction. I know she's already upset that she can't provide more information, and telling her this about Penny and Claire will likely make her feel worse and I can't do that. Ryley doesn't deserve any more heartache.

Back at their house, I stand outside and look for any signs that this place is booby-trapped. I see none except for the basic security camera. What the potential intruder doesn't know is that it's taking a full body scan when you cross the line and Evan will know if you're armed when you come to his house. He's not taking any precautions. I don't blame him.

I step out on the deck and see that he's out here teaching

EJ how to scale the rock wall the house sits on. Knowing Evan, he's teaching him in case they need to evacuate.

Evan isn't taking any chances when it comes to his family. As I watch him instruct EJ on how to get down, I find myself wondering if I'm going to get the same chance with Claire. *Will we be living in fear for the rest of our lives? Or will this shit end?* One thing I know is that if Frannie is still around, we'll never be safe. She's fucking deadly and crazy. The shit she's been doing to us, whether she was threatened or not, isn't right. Singlehandedly destroying lives as if they don't matter.

And my daughter? Frannie led her to slaughter and didn't bat an eyelash. Why would any woman do that? Aren't women, designed by nature, built to protect children? Just thinking about her standing in my living room, holding Claire against her, cradling her because she's been sick only to hand her off to a monster who pumped her full of drugs so he could rape her, fills me with rage.

Rape her.

If I had known this when I returned, Frannie would be dead. There wouldn't be an all-points bulletin out for her right now because she'd be buried six feet under with her husband.

Lawson was going to rape my two-year-old daughter and I'm going to kill him.

Evan and EJ climb back up the rock formation and onto the deck. I think about helping EJ over the edge, but know that he needs to do it himself. Evan isn't going let anything happen to that little boy.

"Wow, EJ, I don't think even I could do that." I motion toward the rocks and earn a big beaming smile from him.

"I'm going to be a SEAL," he says, and proceeds to make a barking sound causing me to laugh.

"Just like your dad?" I point to Evan to make sure EJ knows who I'm speaking about.

"Yep, and you and Uncle Nate."

Well at least Nate is sporting the right familial title.

"EJ, why don't you run and see what kind of trouble you can get into with Mommy."

EJ high-fives Evan and takes off into the house. I say a prayer for Evan that Ryley doesn't kill him later.

Once the door is closed, I look at Evan and shake my head. "I want to kill him, Archer."

"Who?" he asks as we both sit down to face the ocean.

"Lawson. The PI informed me today that day before we "died" Penny had filed a police report against Ted Lawson because he was molesting Claire." I finish the story, recounting everything I learned today for him. I lost count at how many "mother fuckers" he let out during my recollection.

"I'm going to go see him."

"Not without me you're not."

I shake my head, not wanting him involved. "You have a family to think about. I need to do this."

Evan looks at me, stone-faced. "We're a team. I want that fucker to pay for what he's done. He's hurt each of us in different ways and needs to be dealt with. He needs to know that his sick lifestyle is going to be the end of his life. And besides, we're family and family supports one another no matter what."

"Thanks, Archer, that means a lot."

"Don't fucking thank me. You know I hate that shit."

We sit in silence, watching the ships move in and out of the Sound. The activity at the Naval yard seems normal— no nondescript cars or people moving around stealthily— although tonight might be a different story.

"I don't know where they're holding him," I break the silence, admitting that my plan to see Lawson is flawed. I'm assuming he's in DC or maybe San Diego, but I don't know.

"Cara will make sure we get in to see Lawson. She'll know where he is," Evan says, confidently. "Maybe Nate can scope out the area and find us a good vantage point."

"To kill him?"

Evan shakes his head. "No, to scare the shit out of him and bring that fucking bitch Frannie out of hiding."

I nod in agreement. I'd never hit a woman, but I'd welcome a few rounds with her. Hell, I'd love to see Ryley take her on. I'd pay good money to watch her take that bitch down.

chapter 8
Tucker

As I suspected, the arrival of Nate seems to have Evan on edge. It's either that or what I told him yesterday about Penny is really messing with his mind. He's trying to protect Ryley and EJ; all while trying to figure out who set us up and help me find my family. He's pacing more now than on a regular day.

The last I knew he and Nate were "okay" and Evan was wanting to work with his brother in the security business, but Nate stayed in the Navy to finish his enlistment … or as Ryley likes to say, he stayed to keep an eye on her mom and to be the eyes and ears that we need on the inside. Either way, Nate is pulling into the driveway and Evan looks like he's about to have a full-blown panic attack.

Ryley, on the other hand, is excited for Cara's arrival. She says with her here they can talk wedding stuff, and it's something us men wouldn't understand. She's right, especially where I'm concerned. Penny and I were married in front of a justice of the peace with no witnesses other than the people who were there to get married after us. I promised her a real wedding, but she got pregnant with Claire and we decided to delay it until our fifth anniversary, which happened while I was deployed.

Giving her the wedding of her dreams is something I still plan to do, assuming she wants to be with me. I can understand if she's moved on. I probably would've. It's just hard to think of life being like that since this situation is no fault of ours. I now know she didn't leave me, or choose someone else. I think she ran to protect our daughter. The question I have is did she know of the danger she was facing, or did she figure it out? There are so many unanswered questions that loom and pop up every day, and I'm afraid I'll never have all the answers.

The loud knock on the door sends EJ screaming down the hall until he's crashed into it. He swings it open and jumps into Nate's arms. I glance at Evan and see the torment on his face. He has to know EJ loves him, but he isn't going to forget that Nate was there when he should've been. I know he's thankful, but the pain is still fresh. I pray that I'm not in the same situation as him when I see Claire. To find out your child loves another man as their father has to be the worst heartache ever—that and losing your wife.

"Rask?" Our teammate's name falls from Ryley's lips coupled with a gasp. My eyes land on Justin Rask, standing in the doorway with his bag slung over his shoulder and Ryley's arms wrapped around him. Nate glances over his shoulder, smiling.

"I thought this guy looked a little lonely on base so I brought him with me," Nate says, making Rask smile as Ryley disengages herself from his hold.

While we've all dealt with our own personal tragedies, his has been just as difficult and completely different. Rask was a year out of BUD/s when we deployed. He joined our team six-months before we left and was immediately brought into the fold. The bar-be-cues, bonfires on the beach, and birthday parties, he was a part of them from day one. He's an only child, born later in life to his parents who were retired by the time he graduated from high school, so he chose the Navy to help pay his way through college and found the SEALs instead. All he has is us. In fact, we're all each other has because our story is so outlandish no one wants to believe it can happen. Hell, half the time I'm pinching myself to wake up from this fucking nightmare.

"Rask, it's good to see you." Stepping forward, I pull him into a hug. He stalls before wrapping his arms around me. He did most of his growing up in Cuba while we were deployed and really needs a family. I'm happy that Nate thought to bring him here.

"You too," he replies, patting me on the back. Even when we'd meet at Ryley's backyard in San Diego, he never said much, but now that he's had time to digest everything that's been going on maybe he'll open up more.

"Rask, you son of a bitch, it's about time you left Coronado," Evan says, pulling him into a quick hug.

"Yeah well this ugly mug finally told me to get my sorry ass off base and start exploring." He nods toward Nate who shrugs and is still holding EJ.

"Well I'm happy you're here," Ryley says with a wink. "I didn't really want Evan to hear the wedding talk with Cara, so with all of you here, you'll be able to keep him busy." She pushes Evan, who smiles.

"Where's Cara?" Evan asks.

"Later flight, but she'll be here. She has a lot to tell us." Nate puts EJ back on the ground.

When Evan cocks his head toward the stairs, Nate and Rask both nod.

"We'll be downstairs, babe," he says to Ryley as he kisses her on the cheek.

We follow Evan down and into the back of the house. I haven't seen this room yet, but knew there was something he was hiding. He punches the code on the door and waits for it to click. The lights come on as soon as the door opens, and when I step in I feel like I'm in the belly of a submarine.

"Ready for war?" Nate asks, as he looks around the room. There are monitors along one wall, all hooked up to surveillance cameras outside. One in particular faces the shipyard, showing us exactly what's going on. Maps line one wall while the other wall is covered in pictures and notes of the people responsible for our deployment and the aftermath.

"It's reinforced," Evan explains. "If someone shows up, Ryley knows to bring EJ down here and lock herself in. This monitor here," he points to one on the far left, "shows her who is at the door, so if someone is telling her it's clear, she can see them. If the power is cut to the house, the authorities are alerted and come out regardless of being called or not."

"Jesus, Evan, you're planning for an apocalypse or for a nuclear bomb by the looks of it." Nate seems worried, maybe even confused.

Evan nods and points to the monitor that's trained on the shipyard.

"Chesley is across the Sound. Now, you tell me why someone like him is suddenly worried about the shipyard. You and I both know from growing up around here, no one pays much attention to this base. They send ships in, get repaired, and move them back out."

Nate moves over to the monitor and takes a closer look.

"What's going on?" Rask asks, taking a seat at the small table.

Evan shuts the door, motioning for us to take a seat. "I'm not sure where to start, but I have a feeling we're being watched. Who knows you're here?" The question is aimed at Nate and Rask.

Nate speaks first, "Carole, Cara, and Master Chief York. I had to tell him, plus Poole. He drove us to the airport."

"My parents," Rask says, quietly. "I still call them and tell them stuff."

"Do you think Rask's parents are in Chesley's back pocket?" I ask Evan, who nods.

"It makes sense in my head, but right now the craziest things make sense to me." He shakes his head and looks over at Rask, who has his eyes focused on the table. Evan bumps his shoulder into Rask. "I don't mean anything bad, but shit, they don't give you the time of day. Why would they keep your secrets?"

"They wouldn't," Rask admits regretfully, making me feel even worse about his situation. "They never take my calls. Hell, I'm not even sure why I call anymore. I guess I feel like one day my mom will answer and even if she doesn't say anything I'll know she's listening."

The room grows uncomfortably quiet as Rask's words set in. I feel sorry for him, as I'm sure he feels for me, but I don't need to tell him that. We're lost right now. Hell, even Evan is and he has his family back.

"Can someone please start from the beginning?" Nate all but begs by throwing his hands up in the air.

"Within days of buying this house, I'm sitting outside minding my own business when a helo shows up and drops off Chesley. Now, I'm thinking it's not a coincidence, but I'm trying to give the Navy the benefit of the doubt. Except days are going by and Chesley's not leaving … hell, he's not even moving."

"How do you know?" Nate interjects

Evan points to the monitor. "I watch there and upstairs on my deck. Plus, the video records so I can watch when I'm bored."

"That's really creepy, Evan." Clearly Nate isn't as impressed as I am.

"Call it what you want, Nate. All I know is that Chesley isn't leaving that hangar except for the other night when McCoy and I were screwing around with a suspicious trawler.

After we scared them into leaving, Chesley and Abigail left in a black car, returning around six a.m."

"Isn't that who we saved?" Rask questions, earning nods from Evan and me.

"Yeah it is." I clear my throat and take my turn telling the guys what I learned yesterday from Marley. Between the holy shits and motherfuckers, I think I have them convinced we're in danger, even if neither Evan nor I can prove it.

"Who the hell did we piss off?" Nate asks while all of us shake our heads.

"Wrong CO in O'Keefe? I don't know, maybe it wasn't us and someone else," Rask remarks, throwing out another theory.

"I can't think of anyone I've pissed off," I add.

"It wasn't us," Evan states. "It was River. We've never had a dirty mission until he married Frannie, or whatever her real name is, and all of a sudden we're being sent out to rescue the daughter of the vice president because she was kidnapped by the senator she was having an affair with?"

"Plus, the vice president dies weeks before you guys return, and I'm sent out on a bogus training mission before you come home," Nate says, adding to the conspiracy.

"Holy shit, this is worse than one of those books my mother used to read," Rask says, with a shrug.

Evan opens a notebook and pulls out a stack of papers, handing each of us one.

"Here's what we know. When we left, River had just married Frannie, who happens to be Ingram's daughter and Lawson's sister. As far as I can tell, Lawson and Frannie have different mothers, neither of which are or were married to Ingram. River hadn't known her long from what I remember, and days after they married we're sent to Cuba on what O'Keefe called a snatch and grab. River tells us a few days, tops. We find the Chesley girl and kill Renato, setting off a chain reaction.

"At this point, O'Keefe should've brought another team in to assist, but doesn't. We stay and uncover a child sex ring funded by a US man, who we can assume is Lawson since he's currently in jail for raping Abigail Chesley. And again O'Keefe needed to bring in another team, but doesn't, telling me now that there was a reason for us to stay."

"Because Lawson was trying to rape or kidnap my daughter," I continue, as I put in my two cents. "We know he kidnapped Abigail from the emails NCIS found, and my PI was able to locate the police report. By this time, we should've been home, but my wife files a police report and now we're dead."

"His surprise visits with our mail should've been our first clue that something was wrong, but we were warriors and there were children involved," Rask adds.

He's right. None of us would've left those children behind and we couldn't really turn them over to the government in Cuba because we weren't supposed to be there.

"You're right, Rask. We also should've paid attention to our ammo, we always had supplies so O'Keefe or someone was cooking the books and not keeping an inventory. Someone had to track O'Keefe every time he took out a helo or a C-130. Everything is logged—how come no one was watching for all these trips to Cuba?"

We all shake our heads because no one knows the answer.

"O'Keefe ended up dead after we came back," I remind Evan, who takes a note.

"What else?" Nate asks.

"Let's see … the police report McCoy's PI saw says that Penny was threatened by Lawson that if she told anyone her worst nightmare would come true. I'm guessing McCoy dying is her worst nightmare?"

"It's not," I say, shaking my head. "Losing Claire or not being able to protect her would be. That's why I think she ran. She knew death was a part of my job, but if she lost me *and* Claire, she'd have nothing to live for."

"So we think Penny is on the run?" Nate asks.

"I think so, or she's living somewhere under a different name. I don't know, but it makes sense." At least it makes sense to me because I'm not willing to believe she left me.

"What else?" Nate asks again.

"The file Cara took back to DC went missing almost immediately, but she has multiple copies so they can still prosecute. Ingram is out on bail but under house arrest. And then there's Chesley. I can't figure him out yet. I don't know what he's doing over there, but we need to find out. At best he should be thanking us, but he's not and I have a feeling he's waiting for something big to happen. He's part of this cover-up somehow, and not just the Brigadier General and grandfather. He has to know what was going on there and he's protecting someone."

"But who? Every time I enter a room on base, it goes quiet. I haven't deployed with my team since you guys have been back. Honestly, I'm biding my time until reenlistment. I ask questions no one will answer, and Carole has to tread lightly so she doesn't lose her job and pension."

"Nate's right, our hands are tied there," I add.

Evan nods, but doesn't say anything.

"We need someone on the inside," Rask says.

"But who?" I question. "We can't trust anyone."

"Does anyone know you're dating that Feds chick?" Rask asks Nate, who blanches at the way Rask refers to Cara.

"Her name is Cara and no. We've kept it pretty low-key. It's another reason we don't travel together."

"Maybe she can help," Rask suggests.

"How?"

"By getting me in to see Lawson. He knows where my family is and I want answers." I lean forward on the table so Nate can see I'm serious. "Maybe if we scare him enough he'll start singing. Remind him that he's about to become

Bubba's bitch."

"Unfortunately, I think our answers are back in Coronado, and I have a feeling the person who is going to be able to help the most is Slick Rick."

"The bartender? Are you nuts, Evan?" Nate barks out, asking the question before I can.

Evan shakes his head. "Tell me who else has access to everyone that comes in and out of his bar, and the ability to talk your ear off until you're divulging all your secrets over a pint of beer. Alcohol and truth telling go hand-in-hand, especially when you have secrets."

"Remind me to never drink around you." I punch Evan in the shoulder as we all start laughing.

"As much as I hate to admit it, I think you have a point." Nate rolls his eyes at the compliment he just paid his brother. For all the unease Evan was showing upstairs toward Nate, its definitely not being shared now. It must have to do with Ryley and EJ when Nate's around, because right now you wouldn't know that there's anything wrong between these two.

chapter 9
Tucker

AFTER WE FINISH REHASHING HOW we ended up dead and returned home alive, Evan shows us the gadgets he has installed in and around his house. Nate, who thinks this room is overkill, is happily playing with everything. Even I'm impressed and I've been staying here.

"What about guns? What do you have on-site?" Nate asks, as he moves one of the cameras around.

"What do you want?" Evan shrugs and glances at something on his phone. I already know a few of the guns he has, but have a feeling there's a whole arsenal of weapons stashed somewhere around here.

Nate looks at Evan and shakes his head, but not before he cracks a huge ass smile. I'm guessing he has a pretty decent idea of what Evan is hoarding and appreciates it.

"Cara's here and Ryley says she's ready for dinner," Evan says, pocketing his phone. He opens the door and waits for us to leave before turning off the light and locking back up.

The four of us walk up the stairs so quietly you'd think we were on a mission. It's the training that never leaves; always light on your feet, ready to go when the phone rings.

Honestly, I miss the phone ringing. I miss having a job and a place in this world. Being in the Navy, being a SEAL gave me purpose and some fucker has taken that away from me when I didn't deserve it. I've always done things by the book, even exceeding the requirements because I had to prove to myself that I could. If the assignment were to run a mile, I'd try for two. When others would take shortcuts, I went the long way.

I stayed out of trouble, always doing what I was told, so why me? Why my family? And why River? He seems to be the missing link, along with why Frannie chose him. And Lawson—is my family on the lam because that prick wanted my kid and couldn't have her? Or is it because we saved the girl he raped and sent her back to her mother, a woman that left him?

As soon as I reach the top of the stairs I'm hit square in the chest by what I see. Nate is standing with his arm wrapped around Cara. Evan is with Ryley with EJ on his back. Rask is staring out the sliding glass door with his back to everyone, and I'm feeling sorry for myself, watching happiness unfold in front of my eyes. And I have to ask myself again, *Why me?*

"McCoy, wanna help with dinner?" Evan asks as he hands Nate a plate of steaks and ribs.

"Yeah, Archer." Only after I say his name do I realize having the twins in the house could be awkward when it comes to their names, but then again if I need one, they'll both come running so it could be comical.

"Tucker, do you remember Cara?" Ryley asks, always the hostess.

"I do, but I don't think we've ever been fully introduced." I extend my hand to shake hers. "I'm Tucker McCoy."

"It's nice to officially meet you, McCoy."

"You too?" Ryley exclaims, throwing her hands up in the air. She comes over and molds herself to my side before placing her hand on my chest. "Why can't you call him Tucker?"

Cara shrugs. "Because in our line of work we go by last names. To the guys I'm Hughes."

"But you're a woman. Don't you want to feel like a woman when you're in the presence of these men?" Ryley points at all of us. "I mean, look around, Cara. We have four highly trained lethal weapons who are willing to do whatever we ask. Just think of how they'd turn to mush if you said their names with a bit of honey added."

I stand, frozen in place, not knowing what to say. If I didn't know Ryley, I'd think she's trying to come on to one of us, or trying to entice Cara to. I don't know, but I'm suddenly hot under my shirt and trying to step away.

When Evan starts laughing, Ryley rolls her eyes and flips him off.

"Shut up, Archer," she says, pushing him away from us. I pull Ryley behind me, intent on protecting her from her soon-to-be husband.

"I'm sorry, babe, but come on what the hell was that?"

"I'm sorry," Ryley says as she comes out from behind me. "I'm here all day with you and Tucker, and all I hear is McCoy and Archer. And now Nate and Justin are here, so you add them to the mix. I just want Cara to be a girl. Is that too much to ask?"

"Yes," Nate says. "My girl is a bad-ass-gun-toting agent and I like when she calls me Archer."

"I agree," Evan adds.

Ryley throws her hands up in the air, much to everyone's delight, and kicks us all out of the kitchen, including Cara.

"Well I'm sorry I'm not girlie enough for her," Cara mumbles, causing Nate and Evan to laugh.

"It's okay, we've never been girlie enough for her. The only one that appeases the girlieness is Lois," Nate tells us.

"Yeah, she misses Lois," Evan says, as we all step out onto the deck. Rask is tending to the grill and Nate and Evan go over to help him, leaving Cara alone. Lois is Ryley's best friend from high school. Lois and Carter, who happens to be Nate's best friend, followed Ryley to San Diego, but chose to stay in California instead of moving back to Washington.

"I don't want to be too forward, but I'm hoping you can get me into see Lawson?" I feel like I'm asking for her to do something dirty to me by the way my heart is pounding. Of course, it probably would've been better coming from Nate or Evan since she knows them better.

"Why do you want to see him?"

It's a fair question, so I tell her what I found out at the PI's office. Her eyes widen and I see a hint of tears as I recap my story and that of Penny's when she found Lawson with Claire.

"I see," Cara says, shaking her head. She stares off, out into the distance without saying a word. Her silence speaks volumes and has my mind spinning on how I'm going to get in to see him. Shit, maybe I'll just break into Ingram's house and get him to start singing about his involvement.

"I'm not sure if I have clearance, but I'm still on his investigation. Let me work a few angles and see what kind of strings I can pull. It'd have to be without his lawyer present because if that bitch is in there, Lawson won't say anything. Not that he will anyway. The bastard is smug and just sits there saying nothing during questioning."

"I'll make him talk." I shrug when she looks at me. "Especially if no one is watching. I'll make him fucking beg for his mother, and that bitch of a lawyer, too. He knows about my wife's disappearance and I want answers."

Cara nods slowly before a mischievous smile appears. "I think I like you, McCoy. I'll see what I can do."

"Thank you."

"What's your name, cowboy?"

I look around wondering who the leggy blonde is talking to. I don't see anyone with a cowboy hat at the bar so she must be blind, which means she's right up my alley because she won't see how truly ugly I am.

"No cowboy here, ma'am." *I pick my pint back up and finish it off, signaling for Slick Rick to bring me another one.*

"Well what would you like to be called?" *She sits down next to me and places her large purse on the bar.*

"Ma'am?" *I question.*

"You want to be called ma'am? Are you into cross dressing or something?"

It's a good thing I didn't have a mouthful of beer when she said that or she'd be soaked. Although, she has what looks like a nice rack and she is wearing a white T-shirt so maybe her being wet isn't such a bad idea.

"What's your name?"

"Penny," *she says in a sweet voice. One of the things I notice about her is that she's sitting on the stool and not leaning into me, showing me the goods. Most chicks that come in here wear next to nothing for clothes so you can see everything they have to offer.*

I look at her as if I'm inspecting her, but I stay focused on her face. Her eyes are light brown and her blonde hair frames her face. Her lips are definitely kissable.

"What?" *she asks as a smile plays on her lips.*

"Nothing. I guess I always thought that if I were to meet a Penny, she'd have copper hair, but you don't, unless you're not a true blonde."

"Well there's only one way to find out!"

I look at her inquisitively and watch as her cheeks turn bright red. I can already tell she's not this forward, which I have to say I'm thankful for. I've had my fair share of women throwing themselves at me and it never lasts long.

"Wow. I … uh … yeah, I don't usually talk like that, but my friends over there didn't think I'd be able to get your number if

I just asked for it."

I hold my hand out for her to take and when she does, I bring it to my lips and press them softly against her skin. Her eyes turn dreamy and she sighs. I can't help but smile before pulling my lips away.

"Let's start over. I'm Tucker McCoy."

"I'm Penelope Kolowski."

"Penelope, what a beautiful name."

"To go with a beautiful woman?" she asks.

I shake my head, but immediately realize my mistake. No man should ever tell a woman she isn't beautiful.

"Beauty isn't only on the outside. Everyone can make themselves pretty with hair and make-up, but it's their character that counts the most."

"Wow, what do you do for work? Do you write Hallmark cards or something?"

I shake my head once again and look around the bar. It's filled with Navy personnel, but mostly SEALs and officers.

"I'm in the Navy." I leave out the part about me being a SEAL. Most women think it is a glamorous life when they truly don't understand what it means to be involved with a SEAL. We're gone at a moment's notice. It doesn't matter if it's at the beginning of family dinner while meeting her parents or about to blow your load. You get the call you go.

Her mouth forms an O and I'm wondering if she knows what that means.

"You know you're less than a mile from a Navy base and this bar is known to cater to SEALs, right?"

"No, I didn't know that. I'm in San Diego on vacation and my friends said this bar is the place to be."

Leaning to the side, I look over at her friends and wave. They giggle and whisper amongst themselves.

"They're cute, your friends. But yes, you're in a Navy bar and most women come in here to pick up a sailor."

"And a SEAL, apparently."

"Looks that way." I wink at her and watch as she blushes uncontrollably. I find it cute that she doesn't know anything about SEALs. I would've been turned off immediately if she did. "Why don't we take a ride down the coastline? It's a nice night and I'll have you back before your friends are ready to leave."

"How much have you had to drink?"

"Just one beer."

She looks over at her friends once more and back at me. Her lower lip is pulled in between her teeth, causing me to caress her lip away from the hold they have on it.

"Okay," she says almost breathlessly.

I throw a few bucks down on the bar and yell at Rick, "If I'm not back in two hours with her, tell Archer to hunt me down." I wink at Penny as I take her hand in mine and lead her out of the bar.

"Have you ever been on a motorcycle before?"

She shakes her head. After climbing on, I help her onto the seat behind me.

"Don't worry, I'll go slow." I pull her arms forward and wrap them around my waist.

"That's what I'm afraid of," she whispers against my neck.

Firing up the bike, I feel her move closer to me. Her grip becomes tighter as soon as I release the kickstand and start toward the street. She may be scared now, but in a few minutes, after the wind blows through her hair, she'll feel the exhilaration. She'll welcome the night air against her skin and the view she's about to see will be some of the most spectacular sights of her visit. I don't know what her friends have planned for her, but at least tonight I'll show her a glimpse of my life.

As soon as I hit the highway I fight the urge to show her what my bike can really do. Instead, I do as I promised and keep it slow, allowing her to take in all that she can.

Every few minutes her hands wander. They start around my waist then under my shirt, only to retreat back to the outside of my shirt.

It's not often I bring anyone out on my bike. It's mine and for my enjoyment. It'll go into storage when I deploy, being neglected until I return.

If I return.

Having Penelope on my bike now, with her hands caressing my skin, even if she's not meaning to, makes me realize that I like her there. I'm enjoying the way her legs are pressed against my hips and the way her fingers graze my skin so innocently.

Pulling off to one of the lookout points, I set both feet down and shut off my bike.

"Watch," I instruct, pointing to the sky. Without hesitation, she rests her head on my shoulder and I instinctively lean into her. I like it. I like the way I'm feeling with her right now. She's here because she wants to be, not because of who I am.

"What am I watching for?"

"Birds."

"It's dark, I can't see a bird in the dark. No one can."

Realizing my mistake, I shake my head. "Fighter jets. They'll be coming to land in a second."

"How do you know?"

Because I wanted to be one until I found the SEALs.

"When you live on base, you follow patterns." Before I can say anything else, two jets appear and align themselves for landing.

"Are you a pilot?"

"No, I'm not cool like that."

"So what do you do?"

Kill bad people.

"I'm the guy who protects you while you sleep."

chapter 10
Tucker

I STARTLE AWAKE, SITTING UP abruptly and holding my head from the impending headache that's about to come from my instant head rush. Beads of sweat pebble on my neck and forehead while my body shakes uncontrollably. My heart races as I struggle to calm my breathing. The last thing I want to do is have a full-blown panic attack, which would require Evan or Ryley to come to my aid. They don't need to see me like this. This isn't who I am.

Pushing my hands over my face and through my hair, I work to bring myself back to reality. It was just a dream, of the day that Penny and I met. But I saw through her. I recognized her embarrassment when she spoke words that she didn't intend and I knew I wouldn't let her get away.

Except, I didn't want her to stay. I didn't want her to fall in love, only to be hurt when I didn't return. Or returned as a man she didn't know. I didn't want those things for her, but she wanted me. Telling me over and over again that loving me whether it was for a day, a week, or a hundred years was worth the potential heartache she may feel down the road.

Penny was the optimist in our relationship.

After that first night, we spent the rest of her vacation together. When I'd get off work, I'd go pick her up and bring her back to base. We'd sit on the sand with our toes buried, watching the waves, the ships, and planes land. I didn't wine and dine her like I should've because I needed her to see what my life was like. When I was off work, that's what I did, besides go to Magoos to hang out with my friends. She needed to see how mundane and laid back things were for me.

I introduced her to my friends and she fit in as if she had been a part of our lives since basic training. I knew I had to do something to let her know I was interested, but didn't want her to think that she had to give up her life back home to be with me.

So I kissed her, underneath the moonlight and on my motorcycle with birds flying overhead and the crash of waves surrounding us, and I didn't stop until the sun was peaking over the horizon. I didn't want to stop, but work called and so did her return flight.

When she left San Diego to return home I didn't take her to the airport. I left that to her friends. I had already monopolized all of her nights and I didn't want to take away their good-byes as well.

I tried to occupy my time at work, waiting for her to text me and let me know she was home, but it never came. I had no doubt in my mind that once she got home she'd realize a life with a SEAL is near impossible. A lot of women, and some men, can't handle the military. It takes a special type of spouse to marry a service person. You give up a lot, for very little in return.

The night Penny left, I went to Magoos to drown my sorrows. Tomorrow would be a new day, but that night I was going to mourn what I could've had if things had been slightly different. I know that if I weren't in the Navy I would've never met her, but it was still nice to think about.

Two beers in, I felt a tap on my shoulder. I tilted my head slightly, never looking behind me, only to tell the female that I wasn't interested. Then she spoke. The way my name fell off her lips had my body zinging. I turned on the stool and took her in, with her blonde hair pulled into a ponytail and her sunglasses resting on top of her head. Penny stood in front of me with her luggage at her feet.

Hi was the only word I could muster. Penny had made it to her first stop, only to get off and buy a flight back to San Diego.

That night, dressed only by the light of the moon, I made love to her. She moved in that same night. I had a small studio apartment off base and we made it work.

A month later I asked her to marry me, and she said yes. What followed was frantic planning which was tossed aside when orders came in for deployment. Her dream wedding was no longer an option for her and we went to the justice of the peace instead.

Our wedding night consisted of lovemaking until we could no longer keep our eyes open. She knew I was saying good-bye without using words. The war had escalated and too many of us were dying. I wanted her to know and remember how much I loved her.

My first piece of mail from her was a radiology image of what looked like a bean. The card accompanying the image said 'Hi, Daddy'. I was going to be a dad and I prayed for the first time in my life that I'd be there when my child was born. And I was.

Days before Penny was due I got papers saying I was going home. To this day, I stand firmly behind the fact that I caused Penny to go into labor. I didn't tell her I was coming home and since it was only a few of us returning, the surprise was easy to pull off. I knocked on the door of our on base housing—one she had to move into all by herself—

and waited for her to answer. Her belly, plump and with my child growing inside of her, was the first thing I noticed. The squeal brought my eyes to my wife for the first time in eight months. The sheer panic that spread across her face seconds later literally brought me to my knees. Within hours of coming home, I was a dad to a beautiful baby girl.

I wipe away the trail of tears falling down my face. Muffled voices above me let me know everyone is awake, and it's only a matter of time before I hear EJ running up and down the stairs, wondering if I'm awake.

The only thing my dream and early morning recollection of Penny have done for me is remind me I need to be back in San Diego. Where she disappeared to starts from there, not here, and while I appreciate that Marley is here, I can't stop searching for my wife and daughter.

And I want my bike. Not that I know where to find it, but I'm going to look in the last place I left it.

As my bare feet touch the plush carpet I resign myself to having to tell my friends I'm leaving. Of course, I'll have to borrow money for a bus ticket, but they know I'll pay them back when I can.

The laughter upstairs is warming. When I reach the top, no one stops talking and they carry on like I've been awake with them all morning instead of sitting in bed remembering my wife.

"Breakfast is in the oven. Do you want me to make you a plate?" Ryley asks from the dining room table where everyone is sitting.

"No thanks, I can do it."

I make my plate and take a seat next to EJ who is patting the chair.

"Wanna play hide-n-seek?"

"Maybe later, buddy." EJ shrugs as if it's no big deal that I don't want to play. I do, though, because I love spending time with him. In my mind, my time with him is preparing me for when I see Claire, although boys and girls are vastly different. Plus, she's much older.

Once EJ is done with breakfast, Ryley excuses herself to go give him a bath, leaving the rest of us at the table.

Nate and Cara are talking about going to the cemetery to visit his dad's grave, and Evan is talking about heading to the gun range to shoot some of his guns. He wants to make sure they're working. Rask says he wants to go with Evan.

"I think I'm going to head back to Coronado," I blurt out, interrupting their conversations. It grows quiet and eight eyes turn toward me. I feel like I'm on the stand and just confessed to a crime that I didn't commit.

"Why?" It's Nate who asks and not Evan like I suspected him to.

"Yeah why? I thought you hired a private investigator here?" Rask inquires.

"I did, but I feel like I should be doing something to find Penny and being here isn't where I need to start."

"Where will you look that you haven't already?" This time it's Cara asking, and her question gives me a small bit of confidence in my desire to return to California.

"When I came back I looked in only the obvious places— housing, parks—and the PI's I hired there said they didn't find anything at any of the schools in the area. They also said the highway patrol cameras weren't working that night, but I don't believe them."

"Why not?" she asks, pulling out a notepad from behind her. It's like all Federal agents have a supply of notebooks in their back pocket.

"It's too convenient. Those cameras are always working, it's how the state makes their money, and for them to be suddenly down when she's leaving? I don't buy it. Not anymore after learning what I have.

"Also, the more I think about the other PIs, I realize they only asked if Claire was in school or if there was someone matching her description.

"Don't you think your PI is doing that now?" Cara questions.

"I'm sure she is, but there's one thing I need to check." I take a deep breath. "Every time I deployed, regardless of how long, Penny would have my motorcycle put into storage. She didn't want it to fall on Claire if she was to get into the garage and she didn't want it damaged. So I'd leave and she'd call a tow company to come get it and take it to storage."

"Where's your bike now?" Rask inquires.

"I don't know. Honestly, I forgot about it until this morning. It's the last thing on my mind, but I'm wondering who the storage owner sold it to because if Penny is gone, she isn't making the payment, right?"

They all nod, but don't say anything as Ryley walks in.

"Why so quiet?" She moves to stand next to Evan, placing her arms around him. "You guys look like you've seen a ghost … or three of them at least." She laughs at her own bad joke.

"I'm talking about heading back to San Diego because there are some things I need to check out. Things I didn't remember until this morning."

"Okay, so why is everyone so glum about it?"

"Because, babe, it's not safe and we can't protect McCoy when he's there."

Throwing her hands up in the air, Ryley huffs. "Archer, yes I'm looking at you, too, Nate … you guys, come on. Tucker is a big boy and if he needs to go back to his home then you let him."

"Thanks, Ryley."

She sends a wink in my direction.

"But what about meeting with your PI?" Cara is the logical one. "She's already uncovered things the others couldn't, or wouldn't. I'm sure she'll have more."

"I won't be gone long. I just need to check out a few

things that I didn't before."

"I'll go with you. You can't fly yet, but I can escort you on the plane. I'll have to make a few calls, but it can be done."

"I can take the bus," I say to Cara. "I don't want to take time from you and Nate."

Cara brushes off my statement and gets up from the table.

"I'll go, too. EJ and I haven't seen my parents in a while, and I can do some wedding stuff down there." Ryley's words cause Evan to freeze. The Archer brothers are going to kill me.

"Ry—"

"Don't, Archer. *If*, and that's a big if, Frannie is there, which I doubt she is, I'll be with Cara. EJ will be safe at my parents."

He sighs, knowing he won't win this battle with her.

"Okay, we're all set," Cara says when she comes back into the room. "Tucker McCoy, your under arrest."

"For what?" I balk.

Cara shrugs. "Don't know, but I thought it'd be funny to say that. Either way, you're in my 'custody' although that doesn't really mean anything since we just faked the documents."

"Gotta love the government." I'm trying not to laugh at the situation, but it's funny. I can't fly because the government doesn't accept that I'm alive, but yet they let a Federal agent escort me on the plane. It'd be easier if they just gave me my driver's license back.

chapter 11
Amy

THE REST OF MY DAY went on as if I never heard the name Ted Lawson. I focused on my tasks, greeted each customer, made the best sandwiches, and did it all with a smile. When Chloe's classmate came in to get a milkshake while she waited for her dad to get off, I happily made it and listened to her talk about her day and what her and Chloe did during recess. Her chatterbox mouth and sweet smile reminded me why I did what I did—to save my daughter.

When Laura returned and the nighttime crew showed up, I hesitated at the counter, staring at the newspaper. I didn't want to touch it for fear the dirtiness of Lawson would get on me and taint the life I've built, but I had thoughts of sitting in the courtroom during his trial so I could see his smug face as his verdict is read. But I won't. I'll never see him again and if I do, I'll kill him.

My drive home is quick, which doesn't allow me much time to decompress and gather my thoughts before I see Ray and Chloe. I have to keep a straight face, show that I'm solid so he doesn't ask questions. Ray needs to see that I'm his doting wife despite how I'm feeling on the inside.

When I enter the house, the warm aroma of freshly baked bread surrounds me. The benefit of being married to a teacher is that he's off before I am and can start dinner. It's how we've always done things and I'm not complaining. Dinner was never my forte anyway.

"Dinner smells good," I say as I step into the kitchen through the mudroom. One thing I had to learn when it comes to living in New England—there are extra doors and odd rooms. While most people enter through a front door, homes here have two and you use the one attached to the mudroom so you can take off your coat and shoes before you enter a home. It took me a long time to remember that.

"Hey, you." Ray comes to greet me, taking my bag and setting it on the back of the chair. He gives me a soft kiss and I try to return it, but my feelings are muted right now. If he notices he doesn't say anything.

"Dinner, which is pot roast, will be ready in about twenty minutes."

"Okay, I'm going to go upstairs and check on Chloe."

"Wait, before you go." Ray reaches out and grasps my wrist, keeping me from leaving the kitchen. "I heard from Bob today. He said that Adam came in for lunch."

Everything in me turns cold. Of course Adam is going to share with Bob, Ray's friend, that I freaked out at the store today. We live in a very small town where word spreads fast.

"Yes, Adam comes in almost every day. Why would today be any different?"

"Oh I don't know, Amy, because my wife blacked out and was unresponsive with a knife in her hand?"

I brush it off. "It wasn't anything like that. I was listening to a story Adam was reading and got lost in thought."

Ray nods, but I can tell he's not convinced. I pull my arm out of his grasp and head toward the stairs to see Chloe.

"Amy," he calls when my foot is on the first step. I can

pretend I don't hear him or I can answer him. I hesitate too long because he's now in the doorway looking at me.

I smile sweetly. "Yes, Ray?"

"What was the story?"

"I'm sorry?"

"The story that had you so consumed you blacked out—what was it?"

I shake my head. "I don't remember." The lie falls easily from my lips. It's been years since I've lied to him and I hate how I can fall back into the pattern so easily.

"You don't remember?"

I shake my head. "I blacked out, remember?" With that I continue my trek upstairs and into my daughter's room. I realize once the words are out of my mouth that I've slipped. I've admitted that I blacked out today and knowing Ray, he's not going to let it go.

I stand in her doorway, resting against the jamb. She has headphones on while she's doing her homework and her head bobs up and down. The mirror on her wall shows me her reflection. She looks up and sees me, giving me a radiant smile that reminds me of her father. Someday I'm going to sit her down and tell her about him, but not now. Ray doesn't even know, and I'd really like to keep it to myself for now.

"Hi, Mom. How was your day?"

"It was good." I step into her room and shut the door, something I rarely do. We're big on having open doors around here as long as everyone is awake and dressed. I like to sit at the bottom of the stairs and hear her moving around. I wouldn't be able to do that behind a closed door.

"How was yours?" I ask, sitting on her bed.

"It was good. I have a test in history that I'm studying for." I can't help but laugh as she rolls her eyes.

"Has he ever failed you?" I can't bring myself to ask if her dad has failed her. Ray isn't her dad, but he's all she's ever known. Her father would've never failed her, not in life or anything else. He was smitten with her from the day she was born.

"No, but Dad holds me to a higher standard than the other students."

Of course he does. But I don't say it out loud. I can't speak ill of Ray; he's a good man and saved me from myself.

"Are you okay, Mom?"

"I'm fine, sweetie. Dinner will be soon. Da—" I have to clear my throat. "Dad's making pot roast."

I get up and open her door. "And fresh bread," I add with a smile before I walk down the hall to the bathroom. Once inside, I lock the door, turn on the faucet, and pull out a towel. I found myself here months ago after Ray bought up the death of a Navy SEAL, and I find myself here again.

I hold the towel to my face and scream into it, sobbing as my body convulses. My heart aches, my lungs grasp for air, and my head spins. I've been living a quiet life and one article has changed that. I should take comfort in knowing he's behind bars and can never hurt my daughter again, but I don't because *she's* still out there and for all I know she's doing the hunting for him.

One article reminds me of the worst time in my life. A time when I made the choice to run so I could protect my daughter from a monster who informed me that my husband was dead a day after I reported him to the authorities.

The Greyhound bus made a stop and we got off in this small town, which was divided by a highway, and I found a run-down motel that rented rooms by the week. I had enough money for a week before I'd have to find a job. That job came in the form of cashier at the only gas station in town. I took the job because they'd allow me to bring my little girl to work as long as she stayed out of the way.

She did and I earned enough to continue to pay rent and feed her some healthy food. With my only bills being rent and food, I was able to save enough for us to move from a run-down motel to an apartment where my daughter and I shared a room. It wasn't until I met Ray that things started to change. I know he took pity on me, the single mom working at a gas station, but he never let on if it bothered him that I was destitute.

When he asked me, Amy Jones, to marry him I said yes because he was going to provide for my daughter. He was going to protect her when I couldn't. He was going to give us a house with land and a stable income. All things I couldn't provide for her.

But I still love the husband I could never bury, the man who gave me my daughter and made my world so bright. To this day it pains me to know that he was alone when they set him in the ground and that his wife and daughter weren't there to say good-bye. Someday, I'll go back and tell him how much I love him. I know he'd be proud of me, knowing I did what I had to do to protect our daughter.

Pulling the towel away from my face, I toss it in the hamper, and then make an effort to remove the rest of my make-up because it's the only way I can explain my red eyes. Washing my face with hot water will also give my blotchy skin an excuse.

I take a deep breath and avoid looking in the mirror. I don't care to see myself right now. The person staring back is not me. Not anymore. I can feel my world starting to crumble. Ray will never understand the lies I've told.

As I head back downstairs, Chloe and Ray are sitting at the table carrying on a funny conversation. I hate that I wasn't here to hear the story, but maybe they'll share with me.

"Have you been crying?" Ray asks. There's an undertone to his voice that I can't describe.

"You okay, Mom?"

I smile at Chloe and set my hand on hers. "I'm fine. And no I haven't been crying. I got soap in my eyes when I was taking off my make-up," I tell my husband who has grown quite sour this evening.

We eat dinner in silence and when it's done, Chloe helps clear the table while I take care of the dishes.

When Ray puts his hand on my waist, I jump. I don't mean to, but it's not like I can tell him that.

"Amy, what's going on?"

"Nothing, Ray. I'm just doing the dishes, you scared me is all."

"I called your name a few times before I touched you. I thought maybe you had earphones in."

I shake my head and offer him a sweet smile. "I'm sorry, I didn't hear you."

"Do you want to talk about it?"

I look at Ray in his pale-green button down and black slacks. His hair is always perfectly styled and his face freshly shaven. I asked him once if he thought about letting his facial hair grow, especially on the weekends, but he said he'd never do that. I miss the feel of stubble against my fingertips and along my cheek. I miss the way I used to be kissed, but I couldn't ever tell him that.

"I'm fine, Ray. I promise."

"Do you think you could be pregnant?"

I shake my head sadly and watch his face fall. He's wanted another child for years, but I've been secretly taking the birth control pill since we started dating, fearful that I'd never be able to love another child the way I love Chloe.

He nods and moves back toward the table. With my back to him I finish washing the dishes. He talks about his day and I respond at the appropriate times.

"You know our politicians leave something to be desired."

"Uh huh." *Please change the subject, Ray. I beg of you.* I close my eyes and pray he moves onto the next topic.

"Ted Lawson," he tsks as I fight back the tears. "Hopefully he's put away for life."

"Or gets the death penalty," I mutter under my breath. Shutting off the water, I excuse myself to retreat back to the bathroom where I empty the contents of my stomach.

chapter 12
Tucker

I'M A FAN OF FLYING and jumping out of airplanes. What I'm not a fan of is walking through the airport in handcuffs, but that's what Cara had to do to make this an official prisoner transport. Of course it doesn't help that EJ is asking, very loudly, why I have to be handcuffed and why he can't wear some, too. The only benefit is that people are steering clear of me and offering sympathy to Ryley because they're all assuming I'm her fugitive husband.

Being a "fugitive" means we don't have to sit and wait with everyone else. The first class lounge is very nice, and even with it being my first time in here, I find that I could get used to something like this. Being in the Navy doesn't exactly pad the pocketbook—therefore, if it takes handcuffs to get into the first class lounge, so be it. Unfortunately, when we get on the plane we'll be in coach like everyone else, except we have the luxury of getting on first. You know, dangerous criminal and all.

I have to say, Ryley isn't playing the role of doting wife to me right now; she's chasing EJ around. Cara is talking with security, and I'm sitting on a leather chair with my coat wrapped around my hands trying to figure out how to pick up the glass of water the hostess sat down on the table for me. Mind you, she should've never given a criminal a glass, but that's beside the point. I'm thirsty and the water is mocking me.

As soon as our flight is called, Cara is at my side, being dutiful. She walks me toward the gate, flashes her badge and our papers amongst the whispers, and escorts me onto the plane. Ryley and EJ are sitting across from us, with us all being in the first row of coach.

"Let me see your hands," Cara says as I lift them toward her. After this, you can bet your ass I'll be following every law mandated because being unable to use my hands is not my cup of tea. As soon as Cara unlocks the cuffs, I instinctively rub my wrist. Even though they weren't tight, the metal still rubbed against my skin causing an irritation.

"How long's the flight?"

"Under three hours," Cara replies while scrolling through her phone. "When we land, Jensen will be there waiting for Ryley and EJ. You and I will get into a black town car and meet them at the Clarke's."

I frown at the realization that we've had to go through so much trouble to get me back to San Diego. I should've just taken the bus, which is how I ended up in Seattle to begin with. The security is so much less strict, and they're not paying attention once you show them your military ID.

The plane starts to fill and I keep my hands under my coat so as to not cause a panic. The passengers need to think I'm still under Cara's control. They need to feel safe, and if that means hiding my hands, giving them the illusion I have cuffs on, so be it. The last thing people need is fear when they get on a plane. People can't help but stare, even the few eyes I've made contact with as they've come down the aisle has them questioning what I'm doing on the plane and whether

I'll be causing a ruckus.

There's some mumbling as people walk by and Cara makes sure to have her badge around her neck, so everyone can see it. I hate that I'm making them uncomfortable. I look over to Ryley, who is watching me, to see an expression of pity. I don't need it, but I know it's inevitable. She turns away and whispers something in EJ's ear. The next thing I know he's coming over and sitting down next to me and showing me his iPad. Maybe Ryley feels that if people see me with EJ, they'll soften. Thing is, Ryley doesn't know how comfortable she's just made me by having him sit next to me.

Aside from a few comments behind us, the flight goes off without a hitch. Once again, I'm escorted off first and the people in first class whisper as I walk by with my jacket covering my once again cuffed hands out in front of me. I know they're pissed they're still sitting down, and if my situation were different I wouldn't care, but these people have no idea what I'm going through and it pisses me off that they feel they can pass judgement on me. If it weren't for guys like me, these people wouldn't be so careless with their freedom.

Jensen is waiting at the baggage carousel when we finally make it down there. EJ races out of Ryley's grip and into his grandfather's arms. Watching them … hell, watching any child hugging a parent or otherwise, chokes me up.

I feel my resolve slipping, my determination wavering. I know I have to fight, but fighting thin air is tiresome. I want a reward, a nugget of information which tells me that Penny and Claire are alive. That's all I need to get me to the next stage.

Jensen gives me a hug. It's nice even though I don't know him well. We've met maybe a handful of times. Carole, I know better but the hug is welcoming nonetheless.

"Shall we get home?" he asks, focusing on Ryley and EJ. I can't imagine how he feels about everything. I know he and Evan were, and maybe still are, close. He was there for

Evan and Nate when their dad died, and once Ryley followed Evan to Coronado, Jensen and Carole did, too. But now that they're back living in Washington, I can't imagine how lonely he must feel. Even though he hasn't lost his family, I'm sure it feels like it when you can't drive over and see them on a Sunday afternoon.

Jensen piles our luggage onto a cart with the assistance of EJ, while I stand here looking like fucking scum for not helping. It'd be nice to have some semblance of an identity by the time I leave. It'd be nice to belong again.

As Cara said, there's a black town car waiting for us. It's not Federal or military issued so she must've rented it for us. It's something I'll have to pay her back for, when I can.

We both climb in the backseat and take off, driving faster than normal, but living up to the pretenses that everyone has about the Feds. It's funny and I find myself laughing at the absurdity of this whole situation.

I'm a decorated member of the United States Navy and because they won't acknowledge that they made a mistake, Rask and myself have to live like illegal aliens. Worse really for me since Rask lives on base—at least they're acknowledging his existence, even if he can't do anything. I'm just a blimp on their radar and they're just waiting to take me out.

"Do you think they'll kill me before I uncover the truth?"

"What's the truth?" Cara asks as she uncuffs me.

"I don't know." Shrugging, I direct my gaze out the window. The familiar scenery lulls me into a false sense of security. This place has the answers, but I don't want to be here, not without my family.

"The truth is out there, we just have to find it. Someone has the answers we're looking for."

"Probably Lawson," Cara says.

"He's going to die."

Cara sighs and crosses her legs. "You can't talk like that if you want me to take you to see him."

Closing my eyes, I lean my head against the window. The sun feels good as its warmth radiates through.

"The other day you told me about Penny filing a police report. I want to go interview the officer who took it."

When I look over at Cara, she's on her phone—always working.

"He's dead," I reply coldly, and meet her gaze so she knows I'm not giving her the run around.

"How?"

"Massive heart attack."

"Well shit," Cara mumbles.

"Yup, my thoughts exactly. I thought maybe he gave Penny some direction on what to do, or gave her a number to call."

When we pull into the Clarke's, Cara and I immediately get into Nate's car. Carole arranged for it to be picked up from base so Cara could drive it since technically she's off duty.

Our first stop is my old house. Cara wants to look around; I really want to stay in the car, except I can't.

"Here, you need this." She hands me a badge, which has the name Duke Riggs on it. "It'll be easier to get information."

"Makes sense." We both get out of the car and I find that I have to give myself a little pep as I walk up the steps. It may not be my name, but for right now it gives me an identity. Now I can't screw up and give her the wrong name.

"Can I help you?" the small-framed woman asks us. She doesn't look familiar and I don't believe she's the same woman who lived here six months ago.

Cara flashes her badge and the woman's eyes go wide.

"I'm SA Hughes and this is SA Riggs. We're with the FBI," she says as the woman's face pales. I guess I'd be shitting bricks if the FBI came knocking on my door, too.

"Ma'am, we have reason to believe that a crime took place in this house approximately six years ago. How long have you lived here?"

"Um …" She stalls before shrugging.

"You're not sure how long you've lived here?"

She drops her head, giving it a slight shake. When she glances at us, fear is written all over her face.

"Am I in trouble?"

"Is there a reason for you to be?" Cara returns the question.

"Shit. Look, I'm not supposed to be here, okay? I met him at bar and his wife is out of town. Fuck," she says as things start turning frantic.

"I see. Well, why don't you go on home?"

She nods. "Yeah, that sounds like a good idea." She grabs her purse and bolts down the stairs without shutting the door. We wait until she's down the street before stepping in.

"Well that was easy." Cara pulls on some gloves, then hands me a matching pair. "Put these on before you touch anything. I don't have to tell you how important it is that you put everything back in its place."

"I know this is my house, but what am I looking for?"

Cara lifts the corner of a painting off the wall. "Anything that looks familiar, and also in places where you hid shit."

I take off up the stairs, pulling my gloves on as I do. I had various hiding spots throughout the house for many things: money, guns, and passports. My job was dangerous, and the last thing I wanted was for people to show up at my front door and find anything untoward.

I pause at what would've been Claire's room and rest my hand on the doorknob, but don't enter. I'm not sure I can bring myself to go in there yet. Instead I go into the bathroom where the remnants from last night's rendezvous are still present. This guy's a fucking douche for cheating on his wife.

Getting down on my knees, I open the cabinet doors under the sink. Much to my surprise there's only towels under there, making it easy for me to pull them out.

In the back corner there's a small hole. Using the tip of a hairbrush I found on the counter, I lift up the piece of plywood and take a deep breath. When I look, I can't contain my excitement and let out a, "Yeehaw."

Sitting there nice and pretty, covered in a layer of dust is my Glock 19, along with the ammo that I need. I pick her up and use the towel that's on the floor to clean her off. She hasn't been fired in so long, I'll have to take her to the gun range and if Cara lets me keep my new identification, I'll be able to do just that.

Putting everything back the way I found it, I shake off the clump of dust and put that in the garbage. No one will check there for anything suspicious anyway.

Next, I go into what would've been mine and Penny's bedroom and head right to the closet. My side was always the left, so I look on the right, where Penny kept her shoe rack. The rack in here looks like it's the same, but it probably isn't. I move the two boxes that are in the way of where I need to be and get back down on my knees. I pull at the carpet, but it doesn't budge.

"Fuck," I say. I continue to run my hands along the edge where the wall meets the carpet, but nothing comes lose.

"Does this look familiar?" Cara says from behind me. I turn to see a red box with a red ribbon. I gave this box to Penny for our first Christmas and she used it to put things she wanted to keep in there.

"Penny had a box like that," I say as I reach for it. It's not heavy, but there's definitely stuff in there.

Taking a deep breath, I lift the lid and immediately fight back the onslaught of tears. Inside, staring back at me is a picture of Penny, Claire, and me days before I deployed. The next picture is just Claire along with most of the pile. When I get to the last one, there's a face and it's circled in red marker or crayon. When I flip it over, I almost lose the contents of my stomach at what I'm reading.

'*If you're finding this and I'm not here, this man is responsible. His name is Ted Lawson.*'

Cara must see my turmoil because she takes the picture from me. "Lawson," she says, and I nod. "Where's this taken?"

"I took it. I remember the day. We were outside playing and this car pulled up. He got out and looked around. He watched us for a few minutes until I said something. He never answered and I snapped the picture. I took it to security to find out who he was, but no one remembered seeing him. I meant to follow up—"

"But you deployed?"

"Within twenty-four hours."

"We need to find your wife."

I look at Cara, a mixture of confusion and frustration running through my mind. "Lawson has people on the outside. They're probably searching for her," she says, increasing my anxiety.

The thought tears at my insides and I pray Penny has armed herself or is out of the country.

"Anything else in the box?"

I dig through some of the mementos she kept until my fingers touch a key ring. Smiling, I hold it up.

"It's the key to my storage unit and motorcycle. I doubt it's still there, but maybe the owner forwarded mail to her or something."

"Most likely not, but let's go find out."

I put everything back in the box, including my gun, and take it with me. It's a not clear sign of her whereabouts, but at least I know why Lawson came after me ... us.

chapter 13
Tucker

CARA SPEEDS DOWN THE ROAD heading toward the storage unit where I kept my bike. It's crazy that after being gone for so long, I remember everything. Nothing seems out of place or new as we traverse the city streets.

I'm hoping Penny continued storing my bike after I left, but considering how everything happened so fast my gut is telling me she didn't have time. Now, more than ever, I want to get my hands on Frannie. I want to shake the truth out of her, torture her until she tells me everything. Where's my family and our belongings, and more importantly, why? Why the fuck did she target the four of us, or was it just me and the others were part of the casualties?

"Is Lawson really that fucked up to go after my kid because I asked around?"

Cara shakes her head. "Remember Renato?"

"Unfortunately."

"He had a list of buyers looking for specific children. Some blonde, some brunette, some with green eyes, and one of the most sought after feature was virginity."

"Excuse me?" My stomach lurches at the ugliness of this situation. Thank God Archer killed that mother fucker when we had the chance. If we had captured him, I have no reason to believe he'd be behind bars. Someone bureaucratic bullshit would've had him walking out the front doors of justice. That's what Capitol Hill money does—it makes problems go away.

Cara nods as she turns the corner. Down the street I can see the storage facility I've always used. Before we get there, she pulls over and types out a message on her phone. "I'm getting a warrant just in case they don't want to talk to us." Setting her phone back down, she turns toward me.

"I shouldn't be telling you this because it's classified and I know this is going to be hard to hear because your daughter was involved, but what your wife did, saved her life. Lawson was tasked with finding children for Renato. In exchange, Lawson got to live out his deranged fantasies. Abigail Chesley was not the first child he raped … there were many others, except we can't pin those on him because they happened in Cuba. Renato wanted American children and Lawson promised to get them for him in exchange for money and drugs. We believe Lawson was also funneling drugs into the schools in Florida so he could use that as part of his campaign tactics. Even with him behind bars, his goons are making sure they keep up his handiwork. They're harder to bust and our resources are thin on the case since we have Lawson in custody.

"The list Renato gave Lawson not only included the basic, but included ages and virginity status. Renato's clients didn't want kids off the street, they wanted what they called 'untouched' children. Some of the clients didn't care about virginity because they were just interested in turning those children into sex slaves. Those people paid less. If Lawson delivered a less desirable child, he didn't make as much money. Why he came after Claire, we don't know. There isn't a description on the lists that we have which matches hers."

Cara's words are hard to digest. The father in me wants to round all of these sick bastards up and kill them one by one. The SEAL in me feels the same way, but would torture them first, making sure they felt death knocking on their door. I swallow the lump in my throat and try to push the nausea in my stomach down.

"But she's older now, was there a description of her six years ago?" The words barely tumble out of my mouth. Thinking of my baby, any baby for that matter, being on a list causes rage to build inside.

Cara shakes her head. "Not that we've found."

"Then why come after Claire?"

"Easy target, especially if her dad is out of the picture."

Cara maneuvers back into traffic and heads toward the storage facility. Every time I try to piece this all together, Frannie rears her ugly face in my thoughts. Everything ties to her, but I can't figure out why. I was never meant to be a detective. Shit, even the trained detectives are having a hard time figuring this out.

"You know, if you guys hadn't come back, we'd still be trying to piece this together."

I don't say anything because honestly there's nothing left to say.

We park outside the gate and make our way to the front office, hoping someone is working today. Cara opens the door and walks in, with me right behind her. I recognize the man behind the desk; he's a face I'm familiar with.

"This is the man I rented from," I whisper in her ear as we approach the desk.

"Stay behind me," she says under her breath. I do as she instructs, dropping by head so he can't see who I am. I'm not sure what will happen if he recognizes me, but I'd rather be safe than sorry.

"I'm SA Hughes and this is my partner, Riggs. I'm

following up on a case and believe you may have encountered the suspect. Have you seen this woman?" Cara holds up a picture, but I don't know who its of.

"Yeah, I've seen her around."

"Doing what?" she asks.

"Don't know," he replies and I imagine him shrugging. I also imagine my gun cocked against his head for being an asshole because the image is either of Penny or Frannie.

"Okay. I feel ya," she says, pulling out her phone. "Hey, Allie, I'm going to need that warrant. Yeah, yeah, I want to dump his financials … hold on, Allie."

"Lady, you don't need a warrant, I'll tell you whatever you want to know."

Cara pockets her phone as I stifle a laugh. She didn't call anyone, but she sure as shit made him believe she did.

"Look that chick in the photo, she's nuts, okay."

"We know," Cara says. "What about this woman?"

"Nah, I mean I've seen her, but not for a few years. That crazy chick asks about her, too. What'd she do?"

I can't continue to stand behind Cara, so I move next to her and try not to make any contact with the man behind the counter. I need to hear him clearly. I should've worn a hat or something to cover some of my face. This is why I wouldn't make a good detective.

"Her name is Penelope McCoy and she didn't do anything wrong, we're searching for her."

The man shakes his head. "So's that crazy chick."

"When was the last time you've seen either one of them?"

"The blonde? Probably five years ago or so, but she wasn't blonde. She had jet black hair. The one riding the train to cuckoo land, last month."

"What'd she want when she came in?" Cara asks.

"The same as always. She wants to know who's paying this one's storage bill, but seeing as she's not the police I don't tell her."

"Wait, you're sure the McCoy storage building is being paid for?" I ask as my heart pounds loudly in my chest.

"Uh huh, every month."

"Who's paying it?" I take over asking the questions because while Cara is trying to find Frannie to arrest her, I have other priorities.

"Hold on," he replies as he starts typing away on this computer. "Says here the payee is Amy Jones."

"Does that name ring a bell?" Cara asks, and I shake my head.

"Where does the payment come from?" I'm starting to shake and my palms are sweating. This is the first solid lead we've stumbled upon since I've been back and it all started with a dream, remembering the night Penny and I met.

"Hold on, that's another screen." He uses the mouse to move screens and types with one finger while I wait impatiently. I'm about to push him out of the way when he stands up and comes back to the counter.

"Says the transaction comes from a TF Bank. That's all I got," he says, shrugging.

"She's on the East Coast," Cara mutters as I look at her, both confused and impressed that she just knows this information off the top of her head. "We'll take a look in the storage unit now," she adds, smiling at the man as he walks around the front with a massive set of keys hanging from his belt loop. He's slow, fat, and out of shape, and it takes us far too long to get to my unit. The key I have sits in the box, inside the car, and I realize I should've brought it with me, along with my gun.

He searches for the right key and starts to lift the door. I close my eyes, not wanting to see what's inside.

"Do you have video surveillance here?" I can hear Cara ask him.

"Yeah, but it don't work all the time, and I only save tape for a week before I reuse them."

"Here's my card. If the other woman shows up, I want you to call the police first, then me. Understand?"

"Yup," he says. I hear the faint jingle of his keys as he walks away.

"Are you going to look?" Cara asks, bumping my shoulder. I can tell by the tone of her voice I won't find my wife and daughter's bodies in here, even though that's what I'm suspecting. I shake my head slightly before prying my eyes open.

I start at the end of the unit. The boxes in the back should be our Christmas decorations. Claire's crib is on the side, saved for another child, and boxes of her baby clothes are pushed up against it. In the middle sits my bike with mine and Penny's helmets hanging off the handle bars. I fight the urge to cry as I see the belongings that I never thought I would.

"Is that your bike?"

I nod, biting the inside of my cheek to keep my emotions in check. The last thing I want to do in cry in front of her. I don't care if she's a woman, she's a Federal agent and they're as tough as a SEAL … sometimes.

"Are you going to take it home?" Her question gives me so much hope, but it quickly deflates.

I shake my head. "I'm sure the registration is expired and I can't afford to get pulled over." I can feel her eyes on me, but I'm afraid to look at her. I really need a moment to take all of this in. First, someone named Amy Jones has been paying this rental fee, and for all I know that's my wife. The money is coming from an East Coast bank Cara seems familiar with. The problem now is that I'm on the West Coast with no money to get to where this bank or this Amy person is. Cara makes the first move and steps into the storage unit. She walks around my bike, inspecting it. It's safe to say it won't blow up if I start it since Frannie hasn't had access to. When she gets to the end, she kneels and starts to smile.

"Nope, you're good for another few months," she states, much to my surprise.

"What?" I choke out.

"McCoy, someone has been paying for the upkeep of this bike, and you and I both know it's your wife."

"Or this Amy Jones," I mutter, because that's who we have proof of.

"Semantics. Call your PI and let her know what we've found. I'm going to go talk to Buzz." Cara walks out, our happy moment now over and back to work mode has set in again.

"Buzz?"

"That's what his name tag said," she says, shrugging as she walks away.

When Cara is out of sight, I step in and instead of going to my bike I open one of the boxes holding Claire's clothes. I pick up a pink dress with ruffles on the bottom. I'd like to think I remember her wearing this, but I don't. I bring it to my nose and inhale deeply, imagining the sweet smell of my baby girl. I know it doesn't smell like Claire, or a baby, but I'm telling myself it does because I need to believe I'm going to find her. I need to have faith that this Amy Jones is going to be or know where my wife is. I put the dress down and pick up a pair of socks, putting them in my pocket. If I can't have my daughter with me right now, I'll carry a piece of something she used to wear. It's stupid, I know, but I need it.

My bike looks clean even though there's a layer of dust on it. I find a rag and wipe it down before climbing on. She feels good between my legs—it doesn't feel like I haven't been on her for six years. I think about starting her up, but would rather do it out in the open. Pushing the kickstand back and dropping into neutral, I roll out until I'm in the middle of the alley.

After closing the storage door, I hop back on and make my way to the front office where Cara is. She's standing by her car, talking on her phone, which reminds me to call Marley. I pull out the cell phone Evan gave me and dial her number. It rings and rings until her voicemail comes on.

"Marley, it's McCoy. Call me. I think I found something." I decide not to leave any details because I'm still fearful that she's being watched, although if Frannie is hounding the storage owner, she can't be messing with Marley. I wouldn't put it past Frannie to have a fucking team of assholes working for her though.

The gate opens, allowing me to take my bike through. By the smile on Cara's face, she approves that I'm on it.

"Have you started it up yet?"

"No, I was waiting until I was out here. If I need a tow truck this area is accessible. Plus, I left the key in the car. Did you get what you needed from Buzz?"

Pulling out her notebook, Cara nods. "I just verified what he said earlier and I asked him about the tags on your motorcycle. He says they came from the DMV every year. I asked him how he knew to put them on and he said the last time he saw Penelope, she asked him to take care of the bike and only let you in there."

"So he recognized me?"

"Yeah, he must've. Did you call your PI?"

This time I'm the one nodding. "Left a message to have her call me."

"It's a good lead, McCoy. Come on, let's go get some food. I'm starving."

After I get the key out of the red box I hop back on my motorcycle and turn the key, engage the clutch, and push down on the kick-start. She roars to life underneath me, and for the first time in I don't know how long, I'm smiling. This is a small step, but it's monumental one.

chapter 14
Amy

IT'S BEEN A FEW DAYS since my blackout, and thankfully Ray seems to have forgotten about it and so has Adam. He hasn't said anything the last couple of times he's been in the store and for that I'm thankful. I couldn't quite figure out why Ray was so sour about my blackout until I went to work the next day and everyone was asking if I was okay. If I was being asked here, then that means Ray was being asked at work and he likely didn't want to take attention away from his students. Plus, hearing your wife is blacking out is probably cause for concern. I can't really blame him.

Of course the day after the blackout, which let's be honest was really my mind going elsewhere, I didn't get any work done. The store was full of concerned neighbors and citizens; even the town's resident doctor stopped by to make sure I was okay. It was overwhelming and I'm hoping it's now behind us. I don't want to be treated with kid gloves or have people staring at me, wondering if it's going to happen again. That day with Adam was an isolated incident.

I thought about taking a few days off, but that would

only prove to be troublesome for me. Being alone in my house with my thoughts with nothing to occupy my time would defeat the purpose of forgetting about everything and that's what I need to do, forget.

The bell chimes on the door and once again I find myself lost in thought about nothing in particular. I'm afraid to think about my life before I arrived in Pittsfield. No, I shouldn't say that. My life was great. I was in love, happy, and my man loved me with everything that he was. I never doubted how he felt about me. But that all changed when Frannie— No, I shouldn't think about it. Those thoughts, that life, it needs to stay locked away. Ted Lawson *cannot* hurt my family anymore.

I smile at the couple that just walked in. They're tourists. It's easy to tell the people that haven't been here before because they walk in and cringe when the screen door slams shut. Their steps are timid because they're not sure where they should go. Eyes wander, searching for the bathroom sign, and they rush off as soon as they see it. I chuckle at this particular couple because that's what they just did, only to stop by the glass-covered pastries and point to the large cinnamon rolls and cookies. Even if they only meant to stop and use the restroom, they'll purchase something as they leave. Laura has the store set up perfectly that way.

As soon as customers walk in, the counter is off to the left with the store opening up on the right. Directly in front of them is a table full of Vermont specialties and diagonally from there, you'll find our coffee and pastries stand with the bathrooms in the back corner. Groceries and the deli are straight ahead when you walk in. It's truly the perfect little country store.

Another couple, followed by a family, walks in— meaning I should leave my duty of dusting. I stand at the counter with my hands behind my back, making eye contact with them when they look my way. The goal is to make them feel welcomed. That's what Laura did for me, same with Ray. Claire and I were barely making it, but we had each other and I was determined. I never liked working at the gas station. It's freezing in the winter and stifling in the summer, but it paid my rent and put food on the table for Claire. People used to drop things off for her when we were at work. We'd walk home, a mile down the busy stretch of the road, and find a bag of clothes. She'd be so excited and on the inside I was, too, but as soon as she went to sleep for the night I cried my eyes out in the bathroom. My life wasn't supposed to be like this. When my husband died I should've been able to pack up my home and find a new place for us to live. I have no doubt I would've gone to stay with Ryley, who was pregnant at the time. I've always wondered how she's doing today and whether or not she had the baby.

I've been tempted to hunt for her on the web, see if I can find a picture of her, anything to curb my curiosity, but at the same time, I don't want to know. I don't want to risk someone looking over my shoulder, or somehow knowing I looked her up. That part of my life is dead and buried, and as much as I miss it, I'll never be there again.

The first couple that walked in comes up to the counter. Both of them are carrying cinnamon rolls and cups of coffee.

"Traveling far today?" I ask, as I ring them in.

"We just moved to New York from Oklahoma and we've been exploring as much of New England as we can. We're looking for the perfect place to host our wedding. It's so beautiful up here but it's so cold," the woman says while I make change from the twenty that her fiancé gave me.

"Yes it is. Enjoy your trip and please drive carefully. Oh, and congratulations. Weddings in the fall are simply gorgeous around here."

She waves good-bye as her fiancé pulls her out of the store. I don't have much time to recover, not that I need it, before the family comes up to the counter with their arms full of snacks. As I ring them in, the kids pretend to box behind their parents, the dad reads the newspapers, and the mom fiddles with her phone. They're likely locals from another town, not interested in conversation.

After I give them their total and they pay, I wait for the last two people, who decide they don't need anything after using the rest room. I wave good-bye and glance at the clock; two hours left.

Laura's never been strict on electronics in the store, as long as it's clean, she doesn't care what we do. I pull out my tablet—determined to read—when my finger accidentally hits my email button. I rarely check my email since everyone I know lives in town and my parents had passed away long before … well, for a long time now.

Email after email comes in, most of them junk, but one from late last night catches my attention. **You told me to email!** I look around the store to make sure it's empty before I open it. I know I shouldn't but this can't be a coincidence.

> **Dear Amy,**
> **Earlier today an FBI lady and her partner came in asking questions about you and your storage unit. They said you were missing and were shocked to find that you've been paying. They confiscated the motorcycle for evidence or something. Buzz.**

My heart drops to the floor, followed by my stomach and knees. Pain radiates through my legs when I hit the ground and the breath I need to keep me from hyperventilating isn't anywhere to be found. *She's* found me. *She's* coming for me. *She's* coming to take my baby away from me.

She took the last thing I had of Tucker. And with that knowledge my heart breaks into a million pieces. The day

I found out he died, I ran. I knew Lawson was coming to take Claire and would likely kill me if I didn't hand her over. There was no way in hell that scum was getting my baby. So I left and walked away from everything. I held out hope that one day I'd return and have something left over from my life with Tucker. Now I have nothing except Claire and she doesn't even remember him.

I try to control my breathing before someone comes in. The last thing I want to do is start more gossip about the status of my health. I try to type a response, but my fingers aren't working correctly and everything seems blurry. Resting my hands on the counter, I stare down at the words, memorizing them before I shut my tablet off and put it back in my bag. This is exactly why I never look on the web. It never yields anything good, just torment and pain.

When Laura walks in I try to hide the indifference I'm feeling about myself right now. It's taking everything within me to not run. All I can see is Claire and I in a car, driving until I'm far away from here and there are no traces that I ever existed, except I can't do that to Ray. He's been so good to us, loving Claire as if he's her father. He's been there through all the bumps and bruises, the late night homework sessions and that first crush. Ray is a good man and deserves to know what I'm bringing down on him.

"Are you okay?"

"I'm fine," I say with the wave of my hand. "I stumbled a little getting my tablet out of my bag. I'm just sore." I fumble my way through the muddy waters that I'm creating. Laura looks at me and shrugs, and I can't tell if she's bought my story or not. Either way, I'm leaning against the counter for support because my knees hurt.

"Well I'm here if you want to go home."

"Thank you." Breathing out a sigh of relief, I gather my things quickly, almost forgetting to take off my apron. I'm almost free until I touch the handle on the door and my name is called.

"Amy?"

I swallow the lump in my throat and turn around. I smile softly at my boss and friend, praying my tears stay at bay.

"Are you sure you're okay?"

"I'm fine," I tell her, but know my face doesn't agree.

"You know you can talk to me. I won't tell anyone, if you're having troubles at home. I'll help you."

I shake my head adamantly. "Ray and I are great." I nod my head, hoping I'm conveying my message.

"Is there someone else?"

Yes, but he's dead and my last physical memento of him has been stolen. Furrowing my brows, I shake my head. "No, of course not, Laura. I should go." I point to the door with my thumb over my shoulder. "My knees hurt."

I don't wait for her to saying anything, and I hope she realizes I won't be at work tomorrow. I need time. These past few days have really done a number on me and I have to find a way to get past this.

And I either need to tell Ray everything or I need to run because Frannie is coming after us and I can't let her hurt my family. Ray will be better off if Claire and I aren't here. He'll be safe. I know he won't understand and he'll tell me to stay, and that he'll protect me, but he can't. He's a gentle man, a kind soul who wouldn't hurt a fly.

There's only one way I'm safe and that's if she's dead.

chapter 15
Tucker

THE NAME AMY JONES STARES back at me, almost mocking me because it knows that I'm limited in what I can do to find out who this person is. My cell phone sits next to me, the ringer switched on as I wait for Marley to call back with details on where I'm going to find Amy Jones.

Marley and Cara spoke briefly today when Marley returned my call. Cara informed her that we'd fly to the East Coast once Marley could locate this Amy Jones. I'm not convinced this person is my Penelope, but Cara has hope. I guess that's part of her job, to be optimistic.

"A watched phone will never ring," Carole says as she enters the dining room in her wheelchair. When her and Ryley were in their accident, Carole ended up taking the brunt of the impact. If I remember correctly, she had a broken pelvis to go along with two broken legs, but I can't be for sure. Ryley told me her mom goes through extensive rehab and has to learn to walk again, which Carole says will be accomplished by the summer so she can hold Nate's arm as he walks her down the aisle to her seat for Ryley and Evan's wedding. And because it'll be on the beach, Carole has to be confident in her steps since walking in sand is a bitch for anyone. Unless Carole wants to wear her combat boots.

"I know, but I'm afraid to leave it."

"It's portable, it can go with you." She points out the obvious, except I'm afraid that if I move it from its spot my cell coverage will weaken and I'll still miss the call or won't be able to hear Marley clearly.

"You're going to find them, Tucker. Penelope is out there just waiting for you to come and get her."

I shake my head. "I don't think so. She thinks I'm dead and knows people are looking for her. If I were her, I'd be hiding in plain sight just so I could watch my surroundings. I wouldn't trust anyone, which is why I'm confused about this Amy Jones person. Whoever she is, she knows where to find Penelope."

"And what are you going to do when you find her?"

Cry. Scream. Jump for joy. "I don't know." I shrug. "I'm trying to tell myself that my situation will be different from Archer's or Rask's, but the truth is, it'll likely be the same. I'm going to have to convince her I'm alive and pray that my daughter remembers me, but I doubt she will."

"And what if Penelope has moved on?"

Shaking my head, I drop my head into my hands and sigh. "I can't think about that. I don't know what I'll do if she's remarried. I wouldn't blame her, though, because it's been six years and she should remarry and find happiness, but she's my wife ... at least for a few more months. If I don't find her soon, it's not going to matter what I think."

"How are you liking Marley?"

I crack a brief smile. "Marley is efficient. You were right when you suggested that I try using a female PI."

Carole smiles and rests her hand on my mine. "Cara shared with me what Marley found. Penny is brave, Tucker. She did what any mother would've done in her position. She couldn't turn to you and feared for her daughter's safety. You can't hold that against her."

"I don't. I just pray that wherever she is, she's safe and happy. And that Claire is loved and enjoying life."

A phone rings off in the distance and even though I know it's not mine, I pick it up and say hello. Carole must think I'm a goof because she's laughing.

"I'm freaking out."

"I know," she says, patting my hand. "But Marley will call when she finds something. I've known her for a long time, and she's always been efficient."

EJ comes into the room with his camo pants on and a shirt that says 'Future SEAL'. It makes me wonder how Ryley and her family feel about his desire to go into the Navy. I think, under the circumstances, they'd probably discourage him when he's older. I know I would now.

"Wanna go fishing, Uncle Tucker?"

"Thanks, Buddy, but I'm going to hang out here with your grandma."

"Why?" He puts his hands up in a shrug. I guess to him, hanging out with grandma over going fishing with him and his grandpa doesn't make much sense. Honestly, it doesn't make sense to me, either. For all I know Marley won't call for days.

"EJ, don't be bothering Tucker," Ryley says as she enters the room. EJ huffs and crosses his arms over his chest.

"Fine." He stomps off to the door that leads to the garage.

"Is he mad at me?" I ask Ryley.

Stifling a laugh, she shakes her head. "No, he's looking for someone to bait his hook since my dad makes him do it himself. EJ says the worms are too wiggly."

"Ah, I see. Clever little dude."

Ryley and Carole both nod. The mood is light and somewhat cheery even though I'm on edge. Cara's voice echoes down the hall, and as much as I'm straining to hear her, I can't. She hangs up as she walks into the dining room, pocketing her phone.

We're all silent as she pulls out a chair and sits down. On the inside I'm freaking out because she's sporting her FBI face. She's either hiding something or about to rip my heart out of my chest.

"Marley called," she begins, and my mouth drops open. I bring my phone to life and see that I don't have a missed call, which means Marley didn't call me. What the fuck does that mean?

"I know what you're thinking, McCoy, but it was easier for her to call me. She's located Amy Jones; the only problem is that there are over three hundred registered with the bank. Of those three hundred, she found that one hundred and sixty of them have children who match Claire's age."

"Well shit," I mutter.

"Penny has chosen one of the most common names in the United States to hide under. There are over six hundred thousand Amy's in the US."

Making eye contact with Cara, I shake my head. "We don't know that Amy and Penny are the same person."

Cara sighs. "I get your hesitation, but I'm working under the assumption they're the same person until I find out otherwise. Marley is sending me a map of all the Amy Jones' near the bank locations. We'll leave tonight to fly to New York and start there. Unfortunately, we'll need to split up to cover more ground."

Ryley comes over to me and gives me a hug. I can feel tears on my neck, but don't call attention to it. I can't imagine what she thinking or going through right now. Years ago she lost Evan and her friend, Penny, only to assume that Penny left, unable to handle the heartache. I've never wished so hard that Penny would've confided in her about what happened, but I understand why—fear, it's crippling. And I'm sure the last thing Penny was thinking about was Ryley and her feelings. She was in mom mode, protecting our daughter.

Both Ryley and Carole leave me at the table to collect my thoughts. Visions of Penny running into my arms flood my mind. That's the reunion I want. Realistically, the reunion I'll get is Penny telling me she's in love with someone else. It'd make sense. For all I know she's been with them longer than she was with me and I really have no leg to stand on.

Rising, I turn to stare out of the sliding glass door. Jensen and EJ are visible from where I am. It looks so peaceful on the lake, and now I wish I had gone fishing; at least then my thoughts would have some company.

"Wherever you are, Penny, I'm coming for you."

I've never flown on a commercial airline at night before. It's different looking out of the window and seeing nothing but a dark mass of nothing below you. Before, I'd never be able to look out until the hatch door opened and I'd be ready to jump into the unknown. Somehow, flying now, makes me miss my parachute and jumping at night. At this moment, I'd really like the security of my chute.

This time, I walked through the airport like everyone else except for the fact that I had a badge in my hand. When I asked Cara why the difference, she filled me in on how her friend Riggs is on vacation and he brought his badge over to the Clarke's with the understanding that Cara would return it before he came back from Mexico. And that I wouldn't kill anyone. The latter I can't promise because if I see Frannie, she's dead. If it's by my hands or a gun, it doesn't matter as long as I'm the one doing it.

Torturing her would be ideal. Pulling her fingernails out. Smashing her kneecaps. Breaking each finger one by one. I'd cause so much pain she would beg me to kill her, but I wouldn't. I'd let her sit there for hours with an audiotape in the background playing the sounds of screaming children begging for their moms and dads, crying uncontrollably. She'd hear them pleading, asking their attackers to stop raping them. I'd play it over and over again until she begged me to end her life.

The fact that I have these thoughts sickens me. I can't help it. The mere mention of her sends me into a rage that I've never known before. It's worse now than when we stumbled up on Renato. Frannie, of all people, should've been protecting my daughter. We let her into our home, welcomed her with open arms, only for her to have an agenda that would be the end of my family. She needs to pay.

I startle awake when the plane touches down. I must've fallen asleep, and feel worse now than I did when I boarded. Gazing out the window, the early morning sun casts a bright glow over New York. The stores and businesses are starting to open and people will start their commute to work. The streets are going to be crowded with cars, foot traffic, and the NYPD standing in the center of an intersection telling everyone which way they can go.

Cara and I deplane and immediately head for the car service area. Instead of checking luggage, we only brought duffle bags with a few items. Inside mine, I have a large sum of money, which she was able to procure before we left. I think that when I grow up I want to become an agent like her. I've seen her create magic out of thin air with this trip. She flashes her badge, allowing us to bypass the travelers waiting in the taxi line. We both slide in the cab, and then Cara gives the driver an address and tells him there's double pay if he hurries.

He does.

My eyes are glued to the people we're passing, wondering if Amy is in the mix. She could be here, walking the streets of Manhattan carrying a briefcase. Before Claire was born,

Penny wanted to own her own boutique. Maybe she's here now working at Saks, or Macy's.

The driver stops at a hotel about a block off Times Square. It's shady and not what I'd expect Cara to stay in. I have a feeling she's not, though, and this will be my residence for the time being. She checks us in and I follow her down the hall to the last door. When she draws her gun, my heart rate spikes, and for the first time in a long time it's out of fear. She holds her hand up, fist closed, telling me to wait, and since she has the gun, I listen. Cara enters the room, pointing her gun left then right before disappearing into the bathroom.

"All clear," she says, holstering her gun as I walk in.

"Um … what was that?" I ask, closing the door behind me.

"Precaution. I've had to call in some favors, and one of the people I spoke to yesterday has been an outspoken supporter of Lawson. I don't know how much of my conversation they overheard."

"Well that makes me feel safe."

She nods. "Open your duffle." Cara crosses the small room and closes the curtains.

After setting it down on the bed, I do as she instructs. Inside are the clothes she asked for, my pictures of Penny and Claire—both with age progression—and the cash she put in there earlier. I look at her in confusion, wondering what I'm missing.

"Hidden inside the fold of your pants is a piece. Only fire if you feel you're in imminent danger. If you get arrested, your one phone call is to me and only me, and you don't say anything to anyone. Understand?"

"Yes." The feel of the cool metal as it touches my fingertips brings me an odd sense of calm. Even when I wasn't on duty or deployed, I always had an accessible weapon.

"Here are the lists that Marley sent, along with detailed maps. Each red dot is an Amy Jones. It's either her maiden or married name. The records Marley was able to get a hold of didn't break it down for her. You're going to go door-to-door and introduce yourself as Riggs. If a woman answers, ask if she's Amy Jones, you'll know right off if it's Penny as she'll be able to tell it's you. If it's a man, show him the picture of Penny and ask if he's seen her.

"If you do encounter Penny, don't panic. She's liable to freak out. Give her the address to this place and ask her to meet you and call me straight away."

"Easier said than done, but I understand." I don't know how I'm not going to panic if I see Penny. I'll be in full freak out mode whether I intend to be or not.

"When you're out, never take the same route back home. You need to work under the impression that someone is following you. You have enough money to eat three meals, buy extra clothes if you need to, and for your transportation. The room is covered.

"Now, I'm heading north to cover the New England area. We will check in each night at eight p.m. If I don't hear from you, I'm going to assume you've been compromised. If that's the case, buy a new phone and call me, so that your call cannot be traced in any way. Memorize my number."

"And what if I don't hear from you?"

Cara looks at me for a minute before sighing. "You will, but if you don't head back to Coronado and wait for Riggs to return to the Clarke's. He knows what's going on and will take over for me."

"Okay." Suddenly I'm not so sure I like this. I'd like to go back to sitting on Evan's deck, watching the shipyard across the Sound.

"McCoy, everything is going to be fine. We don't know what Frannie is capable of so we need to move as if she's out there. We also don't know who Lawson has working for him on the outside."

"Hughes, how is it that you're able to work on this case?"

"When you were getting reacquainted with your bike, I filed a kidnapping report with the Bureau and asked to be assigned. The message Penny wrote on the picture, and the fact that her credit hasn't been used since before you died, was enough to get a case open. By next week, all Federal buildings will have Penny's face hanging in them."

"What if she runs?" I ask, choking back a sob.

"We'll be there to catch her."

I want to pull her into a hug, but it's not the right thing to do at this moment. So I nod and offer the best smile I can even though I'm falling apart on the inside. She smiles back before exiting the room, leaving me with my thoughts and a map to every Amy Jones in the surrounding area.

Time to find my wife.

chapter 16
Tucker

HOUSE AFTER HOUSE, I KNOCK and wait. Some answer, some don't, some slam their door in my face when they see I don't have a car, likely thinking I'm sort of creep, and some say they'll keep their eyes out except we both know they won't. How many people actually look out for a missing person they have no ties to, when the Feds—even the fake Feds—are searching for them? Not many I can imagine.

Before I started out this morning I bought a clipboard to keep my maps and notes straight, making sure to go back after dinner to those houses where there was no answer or people were out at work.

When Penny moved to Coronado, she started working in an office on base as a secretary. Some of our best dates were lunch dates. I used to stop by to see her, bringing her something to eat. We'd take a stroll on the beach before both of us had to go back to work. When Claire arrived, Penny talked about daycare, but I didn't want them separated like that and suggested she stay at home. The plan was for her to go back to work once Claire started preschool, but they never made it that far.

I walk up the stairs and knock on the next door. It's a small modest house, something that would've driven Penny nuts. She loved having space and walls to decorate.

"Can I help you?" The woman who answers is definitely not Penny. She's too short and very young.

"Are you Amy Jones?"

"Who's asking?"

"I'm SA Riggs with the FBI," I say, showing her my badge. "Do you know this woman or have you seen her?" I hold up the photo of Penny and she takes it. This is the first house I've stopped at where the resident has actually taken the photo from my hands. She doesn't need to know that they're potentially sharing the same name. I'm here to find an Amy Jones who knows my wife and is paying her storage bill. I'm trying not to get my hopes up at the way she's studying the photo of Penny. This woman is probably just concerned that a woman is missing and that's all.

"Does she look familiar?" I hedge.

"Yes she does, but I can't place her." She shakes her head, maybe clearing her thoughts. My heart falls when she hands the photo back to me. "I'm sorry."

"But you've seen her?"

She bites her lower lip, seeming unsure of herself. "I don't know. Maybe it was her, but I've met a lot of people recently."

"Where do you think you've seen her?" I'm trying to remain calm when in reality I want to reach out and shake her.

"Like I said, I'm not sure. My fiancé and I have been doing a lot of traveling recently, trying to find a wedding venue. We've come across a lot of people. But the woman I'm thinking of isn't blonde."

"What color hair did she have?"

"Dark brown I think. Is she in trouble?"

I shake my head. "No, she's been kidnapped and we're

trying to locate her."

"Oh, that's sad."

"Yes it is. Where have you traveled recently?"

"Oh gosh," she says, inhaling deeply. "All over New York, including upstate and Long Island, and throughout New England, too. I'm sorry, but I don't remember exactly. My fiancé might, but he's not home right now."

"What time will he be home? I can come back."

"Usually about six or seven, depending on if he catches the right train."

"Great, thank you," I say as I turn away and walk down her steps. I can feel her watching me, so I stare down at my clipboard and make notes even though I'm dying to call Cara and Marley. I know Cara only wants to touch base at night, but this is too important. I pull out my cell phone and hover over Cara's name, but at the last second press Marley's number. She'll be able to find out where this Amy Jones has recently visited.

"Marley Johnson," she answers on the third ring, much to my relief.

"This is McCoy." I keep my voice down because Amy Jones is still standing in her doorway watching me.

"How's the East Coast weather?"

"Great. The ninth address on the list knows something. She says Penny looks familiar but can't place her, and also says she has dark hair, maybe brown. She's been traveling recently all over New York and into New England looking for a wedding venue."

"But she can't tell you where?"

"No, she can't place her." I glance over my shoulder at Amy and smile, hoping to relieve any suspicion she's feeling right now. Here I am standing on her sidewalk talking on my cell phone instead of in a car. I need to get moving before she decides to call the cops on me.

"Okay, give me a few hours to pull her financials."

"Thank you, Marley."

"Of course, Tucker. I'll call you in a few. In the meantime, keep knocking on those doors. We're getting close. I can feel it."

"Hey, Marley … I just want to thank you for doing what the others couldn't."

"Tucker, if I didn't try, I wouldn't be doing my job properly. We're going to find them and you'll have your family back."

Marley hangs up, leaving me speechless and torn. I have no doubt we'll find them, but I'm not so confident that I'll have my family back. Even though it's what I want most in the world, I may have to accept the fact that they've moved on without me and I'll be the dad Claire is forced to come see during vacations and the rare holiday.

Hard decisions will have to be made if they've moved on. I don't want to disrupt their lives. I don't want to be the dad that makes their daughter regret them because I interrupted her happiness. My feelings aren't going to matter if she doesn't remember me or wants nothing to do with me.

I wave to the one Amy Jones who may have changed everything for me and continue down the street until I'm about a half mile away and knocking on the next door.

"What the fuck did he do now?" the lady behind the screen door screeches.

"Ma'am, I'm SA Riggs, have you seen this woman?"

"You ain't here for Junior?"

"Not unless he has something to do with this woman's kidnapping."

"Oh I'll kill him." She leaves the door and starts yelling down the hall. I should leave, but I'm interested in knowing who Junior is and why he's in so much trouble with his mother.

When Junior comes to the door, I estimate that he's about fifteen years old and maybe one hundred and ten pounds if he ate a sandwich.

"Wasn't me," he says as if he doesn't have a care in the world.

"Step outside, son."

"Ah, man, I didn't do it. I was home all night." He steps out, swinging the screen door so hard it hits the porch rails.

I grab him by the back of the neck so he's looking at me. "Where's your father?"

He shrugs. "Gone."

"So that makes you the man of the house, and from what I can gather you're stressing your mother out. Get your act together and take care of her because she doesn't need to worry about you. Am I clear? If I have to come back here, I'm taking you in for the disappearance of this woman, got it?"

"Yes, sir."

I let him go back into the house only to see his mother start hitting him with her dishtowel. It can't be fun having an unruly teen, and it's clearly not the first time the authorities have come to the door. When I'm a SEAL again, I'm going to come back and talk to him about enlisting. The service will teach him everything his mom is trying to do, but will demand that he respects himself while doing it.

Sirens, laughter and the odd screaming keep me pacing the floor while I wait for Cara to call. I'm going stir crazy, as the minutes and seconds tick on without any word from her. With her professional training she is more versed on how an investigation should go. Me, I wanted to go back to that one Amy Jones and sit in her living room until she's recounted every place she'd been until she remembers where she saw Penny. One thing's for sure, Penny is alive. She's out there somewhere, and so is Claire. I'm certain of that fact, unless that lady isn't remembering correctly, and then we're back to square one and I'm still going door-to-door like a shitty salesman, but with nothing to offer. Only doors aren't slammed in my face; instead, it's the look of pity I receive as a result of what these people feel for Penny, even though they don't know her.

I hear a scuffle in the hall, but through my peephole I can't see what's going on. Voices are getting louder and coming closer to my room. Pressing myself against my door, I try to decipher what I'm hearing but the words are muffled. You would think for a low-end hotel, the doors would be thinner, but that's not the case.

I freeze when I hear my name, and by my name I mean Tucker McCoy, not the name I'm checked in by.

"I don't have a guest by that name, ma'am." The manager's voice is right outside my door. Through the peephole I can see him and the back of another person. When that person turns to pound on my door, I see her. It's Frannie.

Rage fills me instantly and I'm tempted to open the door, but I'd be hauled away for murder. When I take her out, it'll be in the privacy of a place that I chose, not in a hotel.

"I know he's here," she snaps, pounding on my door. *How the fuck does she know I'm here?* Cara was right, there's a mole inside her division—and it's probably the Lawson follower.

I place my foot against the door and stretch until the gun Cara left me is firm in my hand. As carefully as I can, I check the magazine to confirm it's loaded and flip off the safety.

For a brief moment I think about opening the door and welcoming her with open arms and once the manager walks away, gagging her. Bed sheets are easy to rip. I could tie her to the chair and torment her until the Feds came to pick her up, except I wouldn't be able to explain to them how I'm in the possession of an agent's badge.

Either way I'm fucked. I can't kill her and I can't take her as a hostage. Life is really unfair sometimes.

Of course, life also has a funny way of turning the knife even more at the most inopportune moments. My phone starts ringing, the chimes echoing throughout the room.

"Someone is in there," she says, pounding on the door again and asking for her husband.

I have no choice but to let the phone go to voicemail, which I know will alert Cara that something is not quite right. After seven rings, it goes off again. I realize that I need to get out of this room while Frannie is still in the hallway.

Sliding the door chain on as quietly as I can, I grab the lone chair in the room and position it under the doorknob to keep her out. Picking up my bag and making sure I've left nothing behind, I head to the window.

As my luck would have it, not only is my phone ringing again, but the window hasn't been opened in years.

"Shit," I mutter as I push with all my might to get it to shift. When it finally does I wiggle out, drop to the street, and sling my duffle bag over my shoulders.

First stop is the Army Navy store—no more playing a helpless Fed. I need to have the tools that I'm used to. I just hope they don't ask for ID.

When I'm far enough away from the hotel I pull out my phone and call Cara back.

"Productive day I hear."

"Frannie showed up at the hotel. I had to bail."

"Fuck. I knew that piece of shit in my office was working for Lawson. Where are you?"

"Doesn't matter, Hughes. She's here and I need to get lost. I'm heading to the Army Navy store to get the gear I need to survive. If I see her, I'm going to kill her and I can't do that if I'm carrying your buddy's badge. I need to ditch it someplace safe until you can retrieve it. I'm going hunting."

"No, Tucker, you need to get on the train and head north to Boston. You'll meet Ryley, Rask, and Archer there."

"Why?"

"I found her, McCoy."

chapter 17
Amy

"ARE YOU READY?" I YELL up the stairs to Ray and Chloe; both of them are taking their own sweet time getting ready. "We're going to be late."

Ray appears first, followed by Chloe. They both come thundering down the stairs. Ray pulls up short and kisses me on the lips before brushing past me.

"I'm not kissing you," Chloe remarks with a smart little roll of her eyes. I remember when I was her age; my mother would tell me she's going to slap my eyes straight if they kept rolling like that. I can't say that to Chloe, though. For one Ray wouldn't like it, and secondly, it would make Chloe cry. I've coddled her so much since we left California and I can't bear to see her cry.

"I didn't want you to kiss me anyway," I say, walking past her and sticking my tongue out. It only takes a few seconds for her to start chasing after me to give me a kiss, but it's the hug that follows which means more than she'll ever know.

After my email from Buzz, I decided that telling Ray could wait. When I changed my name I chose something so common that it'd be hard to trace. The money I put into the bank is cash that I mail in. Once a month I travel to the bigger city and mail it. If it's being traced now, after six years, then so be it. But I will not strike fear in my husband's life about someone that may or may not be coming to get me.

If I told Ray now, he'd worry and he'd fuss over me. I can't have that. He'd want me to quit my job and I need to stay busy. My mind has to have something to do so I'm not constantly worrying, although despite my best endeavors, that's exactly what I'm doing.

I feel like everyone who comes into the store is staring at me. The cracks are starting to show, and I'm afraid I won't be able to keep my lies straight. Yesterday, before I went to work I had to remind myself what my name was, where I'm from, and that Chloe doesn't have a biological father. They're all lies that I've told people in town so that when someone does come looking for Penelope McCoy, people won't know who they're talking about.

"Are you going to put a coat on?" Ray asks, shaking me out of my thoughts.

I smile softly at him and grab my coat before following him outside. This afternoon we're heading to the Village Green for the winter flea market, arts festival, and snow-sculpting contest. I'm not a big fan of the cold, but Chloe has fun at it and Ray has a duty to make appearances at the town gatherings.

"Mom, did you know they had to bring trucks of snow in for this?"

"Yes, I saw them yesterday dumping it all. Then the drivers came in for lunch."

"One of these years I'm going to enter," Ray says as I look at him sideways. He's never sculpted anything in his life.

"Well I'm sure we'll get plenty of snow this year for you to practice." I pat his hand with mine as he navigates down the road. We don't live very far from the Green and probably should've walked.

The Green is bustling with people, a lot of them I don't recognize, which is a good thing. Tonight at the store, Laura is working and I told her if she needs me to let me know. I'll happily step out of the cold and into the store for warmth. But she won't call. I know she overheard Ray saying how much he was looking forward to tonight.

Ray parks and we get out linking hands as a family. There's live music coming from the gazebo and a few people are dancing.

"Are there fireworks tonight?" Ray asks. I nod, remembering the flyer that hangs in the store stating as such.

As soon as we hit the Green, Chloe runs off to find her friends. My heart races, knowing she won't be next to me, but I can't let my fear get in the way of her having a healthy and fun relationship with her peers.

Ray pulls me through the crowd and onto the makeshift dance floor, spinning me around before setting us right into a dance. The band playing has a pretty good following and you can tell a lot of their fans are here, singing right along with the lead singer.

Once our dance is over, Ray takes me by the hand, still dancing as we move toward the front of the market area. Each booth we stop at turns into a chat session, and it takes us about twenty minutes before we're moving on to the next.

"Oh taste this." I hold up a cracker with maple honey mustard for Ray to take.

"Hmm, that's good. We should buy some. Hey, I'm going to go check to the snow sculptures." He kisses me quickly before running off to the other end of the Green. I nod, and turn my attention back to the stall.

"I'll take a jar." The lady behind the table isn't local and has obviously traveled to town to sell her products. "You should ask Laura at the General Store if she'd like to sell this. I'm sure you could work something out. We have other

Vermont made products in there."

"Thanks, I'll give her a call." She hands me my bag just as I pay for my purchase. "Thanks, again."

I wave and start toward the next tent.

"Hello, Penelope."

I freeze at the sound of my name, a name I haven't heard roll off anyone's lips since I left California. I close my eyes and fight the impending tears before turning very slowly.

"I'm sorry, I think you have the wrong person." I'm not very convincing with the infliction in my voice, but I do my best to hide anything that might give me away.

"I don't, and you know it." She flashes her badge, but it's so fast I can't tell who she is. As I look at her face, I find that she looks familiar and it dawns on me that I had seen this very same woman the day before.

"You were in the store yesterday. How do you know who I am?" I try to keep my voice low and not draw any attention to myself.

"We've met a few times, a long time ago."

I quickly glance around to see if anyone is paying attention to us. Thankfully they're not.

"I'm sorry I don't remember, but you need to leave."

She shakes her head. "I'm sorry, you know I can't. Let me show you my badge again." She does and this time I look at the name. Cara Hughes. I rack my brain, digging up long buried memories.

"Nate's girlfriend?" She nods as I cover my mouth and feel the first of what's sure to be many tears falling.

"You need to come with me, Penny."

"I can't," I tell her, shaking my head. "I—"

"Ray is with Claire, they're watching the contest. You're going walk with me, side by side, and people will be none the wiser."

I nod and whisper, "Okay." If Ray has Cl ... Chloe— it feels so good to say her name in my head, and to hear someone else say it—if Ray has her, she'll be safe.

I follow Cara across the street to where her car is parked. She waits until I'm in the passenger seat before she climbs in. I guess she's waiting to see if I'm going to run or not. I want to, I want to grab Chloe and run far away from here.

"We aren't going very far," she says, starting the car and maneuvering into the road. The last time I saw her was maybe a month or so after the guys deployed. I don't remember everything correctly, but I think she was still in college and just visiting. It seems like she's doing pretty well for herself.

Thinking about those days brings my mind to Ryley. Oh how I've missed her.

"Ryley, how is she? Do you know if she had her baby boy?"

Cara nods as she turns into the parking lot of a hotel about a half-mile from where the Village Green is.

"His name is EJ."

Evan Junior. Evan has a namesake and he isn't even around to see him grow up. I wipe away tears that have been steadily falling down my face since I started walking to the car.

"How much does Ray know about your life?"

"Nothing. He doesn't know anything. He thinks my name is Amy Jones and Claire's ... I mean Chloe's dad left us. He doesn't know about Tucker or anything else." I trail off, not wanting to bring anything up that happened after Tucker deployed. I realize for the first time in years I've used my daughter's given name and it feels good. It feels like a weight has been lifted off my shoulders and I can breath just a little bit.

"We know about Lawson and the police report you filed. The last sighting of Frannie was in New York City yesterday, so she's getting close."

"How'd you find me?"

"Your storage unit. Buzz was kind enough to give us your

name. You've been classified as a missing person by the Feds. I had the case assigned to me because of my relationship with Nate."

"Are you guys still together?"

"We are, but weren't for a long time. A lot of things have happened to a lot of people. Come on, let's go inside."

I hesitantly get out of the car, still clutching the brown paper bag containing my jar of maple mustard. Cara walks up the stairs and opens the door, allowing me to step in first.

My jar of mustard hits the floor when I see Ryley stand up from the bed. Her lower lip quivers as her arms open for me. I rush to fall into them, letting years of tears out while she holds me.

"I thought I'd never see you again." I'm blubbering, but Ryley doesn't seem to care. She holds me against her, stroking my back and hair.

"You should've told me."

"I couldn't. I had to run to protect Claire. He was going to take her from me."

"Ssh, it's okay, Penny. Everything is going to be okay."

"How can you say that? Frannie is close and I'm going to have to run again. Claire, I mean" I take a deep breath and remind myself to call my daughter Chloe. I can't get in the habit of saying Claire or I might slip. "Chloe is established here and I'm going to have to take her away from her friends."

"That's not going to happen. None of us will let that happen."

"Penny," Cara says my name to get my attention. "I know this is a lot to take in, but I have to tell you that I have a team of agents arriving very shortly. We want to use you to draw Frannie here so we can arrest her."

I shake my head vehemently. "No way. I can't put Chloe in harm's way."

"She won't be, I promise," Cara states. But she can't protect us. No one can. I have to disappear again. I have to run, change our names, and find another place to hide. I can't let Frannie find us because if she does, *he'll* be right behind her. *He'll* win and I'll never let him have my baby. I don't care if he's in jail. He has people on the outside working for him.

I see the look of determination on their faces and realize that they're not going to listen to me.

"Look, I understand that you think I'm missing, but I'm not. You can see me standing here, but my life as Penelope McCoy, it's over. Cla— *Chloe* and I, we have a good life and you being here is disrupting it. I need to get back to my family."

I bypass Cara and avoid Ryley's outstretched hand. By tomorrow my daughter and I will be gone and poor Ray will be come home thinking everything is okay until we don't return from the grocery store. If I could fake my death I would.

"Penny, please don't go, I have something to tell you." Ryley's voice is full of desperation.

I shake my head as I turn the doorknob, and find myself eye-to-eye with a chest. I look up slowly and gasp, trying to catch my breath. My hand covers my mouth and tears cloud my vision. I feel hands on me before everything turns black.

chapter 18
Tucker

WITH TODAY'S LACK OF SECURITY measures in place, it's a shock that there aren't more attacks happening on trains and buses. Buying the train ticket was easy. I was even thanked for my service now that I'm dressed in some Army issued fatigues. There's no way in hell I'll ever be caught dead walking around in the blueberry Navy working uniform. Besides, I think Frannie would expect that, and as much as I'd love to run into her out on the street, I need to get my ass to Boston.

As soon as Cara said the words, "I found her," everything stopped, including myself. Breathing didn't exist. The lights and sounds of New York City came to a halt and it was if they were no longer functioning. The streets were deserted; the people of Times Square were gone. And so was Cara because my phone died as soon as she said those three words.

I frantically looked around for help, but there wasn't anyone I could ask. Every store I stopped at that morning didn't have what I needed and pay phones are non-existent these days. Not that I would've been able to call her since her number was stored in my phone and I didn't have it memorized like she asked me to do. The smart thing would've been for me to write her number down just in case. But I didn't.

All I knew was that Penny had been found, and by the tone of Cara's voice, she sounded happy. Which to me means Penny is alive and well. My next move was to get the train. I had to get to Boston to meet my friends.

I don't know how long I stood on the street corner—with my mouth hanging open and a dead cell phone in my hand—until my brain could tell my legs to move, and once they did it was like I couldn't stop.

The first thing I did was ask directions to the nearest Army Navy store. I still needed some clothes I'd be comfortable in and that was the only place to provide them. When I walked in, I felt at home. A weird sense of calm washed over me. It could've been because this wasn't an ordinary AN store, this was a store run by an arms dealer. The militia runs it. I was with my kind, or at least people who understood my desire to outfit myself. The first thing I found was an Ontario MKIII Navy knife, followed by my boots and the rest of my purchases were gravy: box cutter, Leatherman, zip ties, and a couple of rounds for my gun. I was going to be prepared in the event Frannie is on my train.

Once I arrived at the train station I was able to calm down. I stood in the corner, waiting for my train to flash on the screen and bolted to the door. The last thing I wanted to do was share a seat with someone—I wanted people to be scared to sit with me. It should be easy. I'm a master at looking pissed off. Hell, I've only been doing it continuously for the past six months.

I rest my head against the window with my duffle bag held tight in my arms. I lucked out and was able to nab a four-seater that no one else wanted to sit in with me. I don't blame them because I'm not much of a travel companion.

The scenery flies by and it's only when we arrive in a town and slow down or come to a stop that you're actually able to take some of it in. When the train is traveling at seventy plus miles per hour, everything is a blur, much like my life right now.

I know each stop brings me closer to Penny, but the train is taking forever. I caught the first train to Boston without thinking about the stops it would have to make. The express train is the one I wanted, but instead I'm on the slow one.

The train comes to a full stop and people move down the aisle to get off. I watch their reflections in the window, not needing to see their face. Most often, they'll smile or tell me thank you. Thing is, they have no idea what exactly they're thanking me for. If they had a clue they wouldn't be able to sleep at night knowing what kind of monsters are out there lurking, and I'm talking about the Lawson types.

Unfortunately my luck has run out when an elderly woman sits down across from me. Considering her age I don't think I have to fear her unless she's hiding an AR-15 in her bag. If she is, we're all dead so it wouldn't matter.

"You look lost," she says in a sweet grandma voice. The only thing missing are milk and cookies to soothe my scraped knees.

"I'm not sure if that's a compliment or an insult."

"Just an observation." She waves her hand, as if to end the conversation that probably didn't start off the way she wanted.

"My Richard was in the service." She digs through her bag, pulling out two long needles and a ball of yawn. I've always been fascinated by the knitting skill, but never thought it'd be something to learn. My grandma ... well, the woman that raised me, she used to knit all the time and asked me if I wanted to learn. The answer was always no. Thinking back, I should've taken her up on her offer because that would've been something I could pass on to Claire.

"What branch?" As much as I'd love to sit in silence, if her husband served, she deserves my attention. She's put in her time as his wife, the least I can do is listen to her story for the rest of my ride.

"Navy. We met in New York City on September second, nineteen forty-five."

"Were you a nurse?" I give her a true smile with a slight hint of laughter. She already amuses me.

"You know that day?" she questions.

"Of course I do, ma'am. I know my history, especially when it has to do with the Navy."

"Are you a sailor?"

"Yes, ma'am." I was at one time and that's all she needs to know.

A big smile forms on her face as she clasps her hands. "My Richard loved the Navy. He was a proud member for thirty-five years."

"Well I hope to be in it as long as he was. Serving my country is what I was born to do."

"What do you do in the Navy? Richard was a cook and on R and R when we met that day."

I figure there's no harm in telling her what I do. "I'm a SEAL, ma'am. Have you heard of us?"

"Oh yes, Richard was very impressed with the training you young men have to go through. He wished the SEALs were around when he was younger. He always said he would've been one."

"I have to say, I enjoy it. The training, not so much, but being in the Navy is rewarding."

"I never saw myself as a Navy wife, though. How about you, are you married?"

"Yes, ma'am," I reply without hesitation. "I'm on my way home right now."

"Well, she's a lucky woman."

"No, ma'am, I'm the lucky one."

Our conversation continues as she tells me about her children and grandchildren. I leave out that I have a daughter because she would expect me to tell her stories and I don't want to keep lying. Too many lies and one forgets what the truths were to start with. I'd rather her remember me as the sailor who sat across from her and listened to her stories about Richard.

When the train pulls into my stop, I have a pang of regret that our time has come to an end.

"Well, ma'am, this is my stop."

She looks out the window and sighs. "It was nice meeting you. What's your name?"

"McCoy. Tucker McCoy."

My name must mean something to her because her face falls and she starts looking at me harder. The smart thing is to get up and make haste, but I sit in front of her.

"You were one of those boys that the Navy declared dead, but you weren't."

Why, of all the times I meet someone, does it have to be the one person who actually caught the news the day they aired something? The Navy has done a miraculous job keeping a lid on our whereabouts.

"Yes, ma'am."

"Shame on them."

I couldn't agree more and leave her with her last words hanging over us. I pray for her safety when she gets off the train and that she doesn't tell anyone or she's liable to meet Richard sooner than she intends.

As soon as I step off the train and enter the terminal, Nate is waiting for me.

"Where are Archer and Ryley?" I ask after we shake hands.

"Evan is in the car. There's no parking in this damn city. Ryley is already with Cara."

"How'd you get here so fast?"

"Private jet."

"Lucky bastard," I mutter under my breath.

I think it's funny that Nate, who I know from being in the service, trainings, and hanging out with his brother, was sent in to get me when it should've been Evan.

"We have about a two and half hour drive to where Cara is so we need to get going."

One thing you can always count on when you're with a SEAL is fast moving feet. Archer's strides are long and quick as he dodges the people coming toward us. Outside, Evan is standing next to a car with its hood up.

"You've got to be kidding me," I exclaim, throwing my hands up in the air. I want to get to my wife, and knowing that she's only a couple of hours away and the car is broken down frustrates the hell out of me. *Why? Why me?*

"Ready?" Nate hollers to Evan who nods and slams the hood down.

"What the—"

"He was parked illegally. He had to do something or he would've gotten a ticket."

"Wow, I'm impressed." I climb into the back while Nate gets in the front. I barely have time to buckle my seatbelt before Archer has us weaving in an out of traffic. Again, I find myself staring out the window at the passing cities as they turn into the sprawling land.

"I can't imagine breaking down out here," Evan says while we're in the middle of nowhere.

"Where are we heading?" I'm so excited to see Penny that I hadn't even asked where we're going.

"Vermont. The town's called Pittsfield. Cara says there's nothing there except a gas station, general store, a few restaurants, and some bed and breakfast places."

"And that's where Penny and Claire are?"

"Yes." Nate looks out the window instead of at me, clearly hiding something.

"What else?"

He shakes his head. "When we get to the hotel, Cara is going to get Penny and bring her to meet Ryley. We're going to wait in the next room. Well, you and I are. Evan will go in so she knows you guys are alive."

"Cara said I was supposed to meet Rask at the train station, not you. What changed?" I know Evan would never compromise me, or us for that matter, but I'm not sure of Nate. Did he sell his brother and the rest of our team to the highest bidder?

"Rask went with Ryley and Cara. Nate and I needed to pick up some supplies in Boston and it's easier to get them when I'm with him."

I guess that makes sense, and I'm happy I didn't come right out and accuse Nate of being a traitor.

"I want to see my wife."

"We know you do, but we have to trust Cara. Things are sensitive and with Frannie close by, she doesn't want to take any chances. Cara is already on thin ice for calling in favors."

"How is Penny? Did she say? And Claire?" I'm starting to grow antsy and feel like Evan isn't driving fast enough for my liking. Nate stalls, looking out the window without giving me an answer.

"Is she married?"

The silence that fills the car is enough to shatter my heart into a billion pieces. A lone tear falls before I wipe it away angrily. My wife is fucking married—illegally, but according to my death certificate legally. And even though I had suspected it, having it confirmed in not so many words feels like my life is being shredded all over again.

"Fuck," I yell, slamming my fist into the backseat.

"Her name is Amy Barnes and Claire is now called Chloe. Cara is unsure how long she's been married, but it's close to five years. Penny works at the general store in town and her husband is a middle school history teacher. Cara observed that Claire is a happy child, while Penny seems nervous when she's around her."

I stop listening because it's not going to matter that I'm alive. My wife has moved on, rightfully so, even under an assumed name. Deep in my heart I know she's going to ask me to go away, at least for a few months until our seven years abandonment has expired and she can be with her husband. The shitty thing is, I'll tell her yes because it'll make her happy and she deserves to be happy.

Evan gets off the highway and pulls onto a windy two-lane road.

"This area was decimated by a hurricane that came up the coast. It did millions of dollars of damage and took out this road, effectively cutting the state in half. This is the main traveled road from the southern end to the central part of the state. They used granite to reinforce the bank that washed away with the rain."

Nate fills me on why there's a massive wall of rock one side of the road. Across the river you can clearly see where the water rose and destroyed the lands. Large trees are uprooted and banks have been torn apart by the rushing waters.

"Seems like a pretty state." And probably one that I'm going to have to get to know if my daughter is here.

"It's nice to look at, but frigid in the winter," Nate replies.

"I hate snow," Evan adds, and I happen to agree with him.

He pulls into a hotel and I quickly spot Ryley gazing over the balcony. We get out and traipse up the stairs. She pulls me into a hug, already knowing that I've been told the bad news.

"She'll be here soon," Ryley says, offering me a warm smile. "I'll talk to her. This will work out, I promise."

Nate taps me on the shoulder and I follow him to the room right next to hers.

"We'll listen from here," he says, pointing at the equipment that Rask is playing with.

"When did we become spies?"

Evan laughs behind me. "When Lawson become senator."

143

chapter 19
Tucker

EVEN AS THE SUN SETS *for the night, it's still blistering hot outside. My shirt is drenched with sweat and I'm in dire need of a shower. I should've never gone for that last run along the beach, but when Archer dared me, I couldn't let his cocky attitude beat me at anything.*

Music plays throughout our house and knowing my neighbors, they'll likely call patrol on us because of a disturbance. I've told Penny she has to watch that sometimes, but she never seems to remember. Not that I blame her because as I stand in the doorway to the kitchen, watching her dance in her bikini to the likes of the Eagles, I'm mesmerized and forget why I'd be upset because she's enjoying herself.

It's easy to tell that she's been out in the sun today. Her hair is piled high and I can see the outline of her sunglasses resting on top of her head. The straps of her hot pink bikini shake each time she shimmies her hips to the beat of the song. Every few seconds she sings a word or two even if they're the wrong ones.

That's one of the first things that clued me in that I was in love with her—her singing. It didn't bother me, or get on my nerves. I didn't care that she was out of key and didn't know the song. The best part is that she'd make up her own lyrics and even though they weren't right, they made the song better and I quickly found myself using her lyrics instead of the actual ones in the song.

I don't even know how she's mine. How did I end up so lucky to be graced with a woman like her? Sure she was dared to talk to me, but what transpired after has been nothing short of amazing. Every day I'm thankful for her friends deciding to take a trip to San Diego and venturing across the bridge. They could've walked into any bar, but they chose Magoos instead. They could've dared her to talk to any other frog in the bar, but my lonely ass appealed to them and they sent her my way.

"What's all this?" I step into the kitchen as Penny turns around. The smile that forms as soon as she sees me is the most amazing thing I have ever seen.

"You're home early." Penny walks toward me and rests her forearms on my shoulders while clasping her hands behind my neck. When my wife is half naked and standing in front of me, you can bet your ass that I'm going to touch her. My fingertips press into her back, right where her bikini starts. It takes very little effort to slide my hand inside so that I'm palming her ass.

"I'm late, actually, and very sweaty. Wanna take a shower?" I waggle my eyebrows at her, but don't really need to. She knows what I want because she can feel me growing against her.

"Yes, but I have something to tell you first."

"Tell me," I say, eyeing the sweet valley of her neck. I can easily picture myself placing a hickey there. If she didn't work on base, I'd do it just so everyone knew she belonged to someone. Sometimes a ring isn't enough.

Watching her face for some indication of what kind of news this is going to be since she's taking her sweet time spitting it out, I see indifference. I don't like that. Penny needs to feel like she can tell me anything. I cup her face gently and make sure her eyes meet mine.

"You can tell me anything, you know this."

"I'm afraid you might be upset with me." Her voice falls.

"Are you leaving me?" My instincts tell me to step back and put some distance between us, but I don't. I pull her even closer, if that's possible, so she can feel my heart beating for her.

"I'm pregnant," she says so quietly I barely hear the words, but I hear them nonetheless. The words seep in, followed by the images of Penny with a swollen belly, my hands on her stomach feeling a baby kick—a baby we created together. Me, standing in a blue hospital gown holding my son or daughter—a child I never thought I'd have.

"Say it again," I plead, needing to hear her say the words that will make us parents, the words which are going to change everything for the better.

"I'm pregnant," she says, shrugging with a look of sorrow across her face, obviously expecting that I'd be upset.

"I'm going to be a dad?" I ask, for reassurance. Penny nods hesitantly and that's not good enough for me. I pick her up and twirl her around the kitchen, laughing. "I'm going to be a dad!"

I put her down and drop to my knees. "I'm going to be a dad," I whisper against the skin protecting my unborn child. I kiss her softly, resting my forehead there for a brief moment before standing back up.

"I love you, Penelope."

"Are you sure you're okay with this? Some of the other wives said it's not a good idea to be pregnant so early in our marriage."

"Are any of those women sharing our bed at night?"

She shakes her head.

"Are any of those women our friends?"

She shakes her head again.

"Well then you let them worry about their own marriages and we'll worry about ours. I'm fucking ecstatic. You have no idea how happy I am that we're going to have a baby."

"Yeah?" she asks, sniffling.

"Yeah, now lets go take that shower so I can show you how happy I am."

I take her by her hand and lead her to bathroom, kicking the door to as I go by. As soon as we step into the bathroom, I pull the straps on her bathing suit.

"Wait, I saw this news report where this lady was pregnant by two different men. Can that happen if we have sex right now?"

Penny shakes her head and pushes me toward the shower. "No, Tucker. But I hear that I'm going to get really, really horny."

"Well shit, more sex for me. Bring it on, baby."

I *hate* waiting. I feel like I've been waiting my entire life to see my family again. For me it's been a lifetime. The pictures I received didn't do the longing justice, and each time I think about one of the packages that was sent to me, I wonder if that's what Claire even looks like. That's why Cara had the age progression done—there isn't anyone we can trust. I take out the last photo I have of Claire and study it. When I left her, she looked like me, but does that mean she still does? The picture tells me she does, but how I can be sure?

I can't. I can't know for sure until I see her with my own eyes, until I can feel the contours of her face with my fingertips. Even if I see her today, it'll likely be years before I get to hug her. She doesn't know me. She won't remember me.

And worse, she calls another man dad.

I won't hear that word from her today, probably never, and I don't know if I can cope with that. It would be one thing if I had done something to hurt her, to lose her desire to refer to me as her father, but I didn't. I went to work, expecting to return quickly. And when I finally came home, I expected my family to be waiting for me.

A car door slams and the gravel in the parking lot crunches underneath their heavy footfalls. I remember walking up the steps to this room and imagine whoever is outside doing the same.

I stand to go to the door, but Nate steps in front of me and Evan puts his hand on my shoulder.

"Let Cara and Ryley do their jobs," Evan says lowly. Right now I want to break him; tell him to get out of my way so I can go to Penny. No one stopped him from running to Ryley so why can't I go to my wife?

"I know she's next door. I can feel her, Archer. My heart is racing with anticipation knowing she's just beyond that wall. She doesn't know I'm alive and won't believe Ryley. What if she leaves? What if she runs before I get a chance to show her I'm alive? You got these moments with Ryley, why deny me what you had?"

"It's not that, McCoy. Think about what Rask is going through with his parents. Think about your daughter. She was a toddler when you left, she's not going to remember you. You can almost guarantee that Penny didn't bring any pictures of you with her for fear that Claire would say something. Imagine Penny living in fear for the past six years, always wondering who was behind her. Imagine her looking at Claire and seeing you. Or her daughter calling another man dad. I've been there, McCoy. I've experienced it firsthand. The one I was destined to be with was engaged to another man. I'm there now with my son calling another man dad and waiting for him to say those words to me. Each time EJ looks at me, I think this is going to be the day that he says it, but he doesn't. He either calls me Evan or doesn't say anything at all. Part of me wants to demand that he call me dad, but the other part of me wants him to do it on his own.

"This can't be you, McCoy. Think about Penny and what she's being told. Think about the shock of knowing she's been

148

found and what's going through her head. Her only goal in life is to protect Claire from Lawson and the only way she knows how to do that is hide. We need to treat the situation with kid gloves and trust Cara and Ryley to convince her that they're safe.

"Penny thinks we're all dead and yet here we are, McCoy. She doesn't know if she can trust Ryley and probably doesn't remember Cara. If you go over there, she's going to panic and that will be the last time you see her."

He's right and I hate it. I hate that Penny is over there and three Navy SEALs are here holding me captive. One of them I could take, but not all three. I'd be down on the ground in the matter of seconds with my hands pinned behind my back. And I'm pretty sure Nate is packing.

Why he can have a gun and I can't isn't fair. What if I need to shoot a wild animal or Frannie?

"Evan, Cara is asking for you," Rask says without making eye contact with him.

Evan's hand squeezes my shoulder to get my attention. "We cool?"

I nod, but I'm not. Not really. I want to understand, but I'm not there yet. Penny loved me once, surely that love is strong enough that as soon as she sees me, she'd know it was me and not think I'm an imposter.

"Let me go talk to her, show her I'm alive. We need to ease her into this. She didn't have anyone to help her grieve your death. She did it while she was on the run, protecting Claire."

"Fine," I say, holding my hands up.

Evan nods and moves toward the door Nate has just opened. Even if I want to make a run for it, he'll be there to stop me.

"Tell her …" My voice breaks as I try to compose myself. "Tell her I love her, that I've never stopped."

Evan smiles. "You'll be telling her yourself shortly."

Fucking right I will be.

chapter 20
Penny

WHEN SOMEONE SAYS THEY'VE HAD their lives flash before their eyes they mean it in the literal sense. It's the unprepared slam of brakes because you catch a glimpse of a child running and a ball rolling down a driveway in front of you. Your tires screech, and as you slam on the brakes your body jerks forward. Your heart races so fast that the sound is drowning out the radio and all you think is, *What if this was my child?*

Or it's when you go to pick your child up from school and they're not on the playground like they're supposed to be. So you search and search until tears are running down your face, only to remember you let her go home with a friend for the first time. The images you've *had* to store and recreate in your mind because you have *nothing* left but your memories, don't do you justice because you can't remember the way your baby smelled or how it felt to hold her. Right now you can't recall what it was like to lie in bed with your husband while you both stared at your sleeping daughter between you. The smile and laughter you thought you had memorized has faded.

And even as you remember, it's still not enough to quell

the thoughts running through your head so you drive by, except this isn't a suburban area and you can't see up their almost mile long driveway. You pick your fingers raw on the drive back to your house so you can call the other mother to make sure your only reason for living is there. And the next time your daughter asks you if she can go and stay at her friend's house, you offer the alternative because you can't bear the thought of her being away from you.

I've had a few moments in my life where my life flashed before my eyes. Regardless of how safe I've felt, I've lived with fear for the past six years. Fear of the unknown, fear that Ray would find out my life is a lie, fear that the random knock on the door in the middle of the night would reveal Frannie or Ted Lawson and I'd be powerless to stop them.

But nothing has ever prepared me for what I'm feeling now. My life and the life of my daughter is a continuous movie reel showing me everything that I remember and conjured up in my mind.

As I stand here, my heart beats slowly as the fear I've been trying to avoid seeps into my system. The shock I'm going through will eventually go away when my endorphins kick in and my fight or flight reactors engage.

I've been duped. I should've never listened to Cara and jumped at her vague answer regarding Nate. And Ryley—the one person who in a matter of moments made me believe I could trust someone—has lied. They're not here to flesh out Frannie, they're here to deliver me to her. *They* work for her.

I step back from the man in the doorway and shake my head. I'm trapped. I have nowhere to run and everyone in town is at the Village Green. It's the perfect set up and I've walked right into it. The thought of Claire being taken and Ray being hurt as he tries to save her run rampant through my mind. I let out a cry, only to be comforted by Ryley.

"Don't touch me," I scream. "You people are sick. I just want to be left alone. Why couldn't you leave me alone?"

"Penny," the man in the door says my name, as if he

knows me. He doesn't. He can't.

He's dead.

I look at Ryley, who has tears rolling down her face. I can't understand why she's crying. Has her mission failed?

"Penny, I know you're in shock right now, but please listen to me," Ryley says as she reaches for me. I step back and try to remain upright when the back of my knees touch the bed.

"I don't have to listen. This is sick, Ryley. Having someone pose as your dead fiancé to get me to help you? Why would you do that?"

"I'm not dead, Penny. Give us a chance to explain, please," the imposter pleads. I slowly shake my head, but know I have no choice. He digs into his pocket and pulls out a piece of paper, handing it to me.

"What's this?"

He sighs, running this hand over the top of his hat. "Read it, please. It'll help with what I'm about to tell you."

Unfolding it carefully, I read the words at the top of the page:

NO HAPPY HOMECOMING FOR SEALS DECLARED DEAD BY NAVY

By Art Liberty

In an instant I think back to six or seven months ago when Ray said he saw a news report, something about a conspiracy. His words are clear, "*Anyway, it was about a Navy SEAL who was reported dead, but they found him alive.*" *Him.* He said him, not *them.*

"What about—"

Ryley sets her hand on my shoulder and then I know. Evan was the one they found alive, not my Tucker.

"Finish the article, Penny."

Nodding, I wipe away my tears with the back of my hand so I can see clearly.

That is the joyful scene that we have become used to seeing on the internet, television, social media and newspapers. But that was not the welcome home reportedly experienced by four members of Navy SEAL Team Three, based in Coronado, CA.

They deplaned after a long flight from their theater of operations to be met by – no one. Instructed to take taxis from the airfield, the SEALs made their own way home to families that were anything but overjoyed to see them. The reason? All four were dead, according to the Navy. Funerals had been held with full military honors. "Taps" was played, a rifle salute was performed, and in a meaningful ritual peculiar to the Navy's elite warrior SEALs, fellow SEAL team members removed their Trident insignias and embedded them into the lids of the caskets in a poignant and symbolic goodbye to fallen brothers-in-arms.

"Is this some type of joke?"

"No," he replies, shaking his head. "We're alive and we're home. We've been back for a little over six months. Shit's bad, Penny. We had no idea what was going on back home."

"And we had no idea Frannie was sending the guys care packages," Ryley says. "They came home thinking we knew they were alive, that they were still on their mission."

"This is unbelievable. This is the type of stuff that happens on television, not in real life," I whisper, sitting down to re-read the article again, focusing on the word "four". Ray heard one and that one could be Evan, if it's the same story, but this four.

Four Navy SEALs dead, only to return home six years later.

There were four in Tucker's deployment, Evan being one of them. My hopes soar as I try to form some sort of coherent sentence, but I can't. My breathing picks up, my heart rate increases, and I feel dizzy.

Tucker …

Claire …

… Ray.

It's only in that moment I realize what the article is telling me. "It says four. Are you telling me that Tucker is alive?" My voice breaks as I look at Evan, desperate for confirmation.

"Yes," he, Ryley, and Cara all say at the same time.

"Where?" I stand on shaky legs and brush past Evan, toward the door. "Where is he?" I open the door and step out, only to hear another door open. Nate, Evan's twin brother, steps out first and holds up his hands, stopping me from gaining entry into the other room.

"Move out of my way," I demand, trying to push past him, but he's much bigger than I am and doesn't budge. Rask steps out next and nods toward me before stepping into the room I just left.

"He's been looking for you since the day he got back." I turn my head toward Evan, who's standing in the doorway. "*Every day.* He hasn't given up hope that he'd find you and Claire."

Nate steps aside, no longer blocking me from the room where Tucker should be. I step hesitantly, until I'm in front of the door. I rest my hand against the cold wood as tears drip down my face. There's no use wiping them away because I feel more and more coming. I swallow hard and take in a deep breath before pushing the door open.

My hand covers my mouth, but the gasp is loud enough to draw his attention toward me. He stands, unsure of himself … of us, and lets out a sob that breaks me on the inside. We both step to each other, the door behind me crashing closed, causing us both to jump.

Something is holding me back. Is it Ray? Or am I so unsure of myself right now I don't know what to do?

"Is it you?"

"I should be asking you the same thing, Penelope. I've been waiting for this moment since the day I left." Tucker reaches out and strokes my cheek. My face leans into his hand and it's only a matter of seconds before I'm enveloped in his arms.

"Oh God, Penny, you don't know how long I've been waiting to do this."

"I have a good guess," I say, trying to lighten the mood, but nothing is going to lift the heavy clamor of reality. I grip his shirt in my fingers and breathe him in. My heart is telling me to remind him how much I love him, but I can't.

"I dreamt about this day for so long, only to have my dreams shatter and change when I arrived home. I had this big long speech in my head all set and ready to go, and then you walked into the room. There's an elephant in the room and we should talk about it before I lose my nerve or before I do something you'll hate me for. I won't be able to live knowing that you hate me, Penny," he says, breaking my train of thought.

I nod against this chest, but am unwilling to leave his hold. What if he disappears on me?

"I don't want to let you go." I bring him closer, wrapping my arms around his waist. He's lost weight since I saw him last.

"Believe me, I'm not letting you out of my sight, but we need to talk." He pulls my arms away from his sides and leads me over to the bed, sitting across from me and never letting go of my hands. "I love you and Claire more than my life and I know you're married," he says as I feel my stomach and heart crash to the floor. "I also know you're living a life under a different name and that you've paid for my storage unit this entire time."

"Are you the one who took your bike?" I choke back a sob.

"I am. It's staying with the Clarkes right now. Penny, so much as happened to us over the past six years I don't even know how to start. I know about Lawson and what he did with Claire."

"How do you know?"

Tucker sits up straight, releasing my hands; they fall limp to my side. The only one I told was the police officer because the MPs didn't believe me that something happened in our home. The police officer tried to talk to Lawson, but had nothing to keep him on.

"My private investigator uncovered the police report you filed and the thing is, Penny, we believe it because Lawson was the reason we were over there. He's the reason you were told we were dead. I remember the day before we left. Claire and I were outside and I was taking pictures."

I nod, remembering all too well the photos I hid in the house. Lawson was in one of them and I knew he was bad.

"I confronted him, and the next thing I know we were off and never coming back."

"He kept you there?"

Tucker nods and lets his tears flow. "That man is ten shades of fucking crazy. He's part of a sex ring we uncovered. Archer killed their leader right off, but there were so many waiting to take his place. God, to think of what would've happened to Claire if you hadn't ran."

"I had to, Tucker. He was going to take her from me."

He stands and comes over to me, resting his forehead against mine. His lips graze mine briefly, igniting something that died in me a long time ago.

"Do you love him?"

I nod.

"Is he good to Claire?"

I nod again.

"Okay," he says without moving. I don't know what that means. Hell, I don't know what any of this means. My husband, the one I thought was dead, is holding me now and all I can think is that this is a dream, a really fucked up dream. When I wake, where will I be?

Tucker stands and walks toward the front of the room. "I've had some time to think, and while not all my thoughts are rational, I'm not going to ask you to leave him. You didn't know I was alive and it's selfish of me to expect you to drop your new life to come back with me. But I want to know

Claire."

I listen to his words and can't believe I'm in this situation. Two husbands, a fake name, and a lie are what my life comes down to.

"I need some time, Tucker. This is all too much for me to take in right now. I mean, you're alive. So are Evan, Justin, and River ... I need time to deal."

"River's dead, Penny. He died after we came back. It's a mess that's all I can say."

Tucker walks back to me and pulls me in his arms. "I love you. I hope you never questioned my love for you in all these years."

I shake my head. "I haven't."

He kisses me just below my ear, but I pull away before he can get any closer to my lips. Ray doesn't deserve to be cheated on. I don't care if Tucker's my husband, too.

Or is Ray not my husband?

"I need to get back. I need to tell Ray what's going on. He doesn't know ... anything."

Tucker clears his throat. "The threat is eminent, Penny. She's out there. I saw her in New York so it's just a matter of time. We'll be watching your house, following you around to make sure she doesn't hurt you."

I nod, expecting nothing less.

chapter 21
Penny

GETTING BACK INTO CARA'S CAR was the last thing I wanted
to do. I have never felt as torn in my life as I do now. To
say I've been dealt a shitty hand is an understatement. I've
always prided myself on being a good person: volunteering
at soup shelters, donating when I can, and helping those who
need assistance. So someone tell me why this is happening to
me? My life has been good. I can't say it's been great because
I've had a hole the size of the Grand Canyon in my chest,
but it's been gradually filling. I live a quiet, peaceful, life and
keep to myself. I don't engage in rumors and gossipmongers
and always treat people with respect. And yet my world is
crumbling down around me.

Why? What did I do to deserve this?

In a matter of minutes I'm going to have to paste a smile
on my face and act like everything is okay when it's not even
close. I'm going to have to ask my husband if he's ready to go
home and explain to him where I've been for the past hour.
He's going to want to sit down, watch a television show, and
maybe enjoy a hot cup of cocoa. I'm going to sit with him

because it's what I always do and instead of flipping through my magazine or working on a crossword, I'll sit there with my heart pounding so hard my ears will vibrate. My palms, already clammy, will be so cold my fingertips will start to turn blue and no amount of rubbing them down my pant leg will warm them up.

I'm going to have to tell him, the man who took my daughter and I in when we had nothing, that I've been living a lie. I should've never gotten involved with him, but the thought of providing for Claire was too great to deny.

I love Ray, I do. He may not be the love of my life because that title belongs to Tucker, but he has my heart. He's a good, caring, and attentive husband who dotes on my daughter. I couldn't ask for more, except it was Tucker that I was still with. But fate, or whatever the hell you want to call it, intervened and took him away from us.

Cara drops me off behind the store, making it easy for me to slip back into the crowd. If anyone notices me, they won't think twice about seeing me come from the general direction of the store. Cara even hands me the bag of maple mustard I bought right before she approached me. It's a good thing she remembered because that was the last thing I was thinking about.

I walk across the street and step into the crowd. More people have arrived and I'm hoping I can use it to my advantage. People I know from town greet me as I pass by; I offer a slight smile, but keep moving. I never realized how hard it is to smile when you're falling apart on the inside. Right now, my throat has this lingering pain that I can only describe as a building sob. I have to keep swallowing because if I don't, it's going to explode right here, in front of everyone.

I'm weaving in and out of patrons, shoulders bumping mine, bodies jostling into me. Each touch makes me more and more nervous. My body tenses at the sound of my name. Not Amy, but Penny. It's a name I'm not used to hearing.

Could Frannie be here? Would she call out my name? Surely there has to be another Penny in this crowd, it's not that uncommon.

My name is called again, and I stop to look around. I spin, looking in all directions for the voice that keeps saying my name … only to realize that it's *Claire* coming my way. She's not saying Penny; she's saying Mom and Ray's right behind her. If anything, he yelled Amy to get my attention. So why did I hear Penny? I go to open my mouth to call her name, but shut it quickly when I realize that the name that's about to fall off my lips is her birth name, and until this past week when my life started to unravel, I haven't thought of her as Claire in a long time and now that I've said her name and heard, I can't get it out of my head.

This time I'm not careful about the people I'm bumping into as I make my way to Claire and Ray. I pull her into my arms and bury my nose deep into her hair. She wiggles, trying to break free, but I hold on for a second longer.

"Geez, Mom, you're trying to smother me," she mutters, pulling away. She fixes her hair and pulls her coat down all while giving me a glance that tells me she's annoyed. Usually I'd say something to her, but not tonight.

Ray wraps his arm around me and I fall into him. For so long he's been my security and I can't help but feel safe in his presence. Tucker makes me feel that way, too, though, and those feelings have me conflicted. The fact that he accepts that I'm married should please me, but it scares me. Was he held captive? Is he not the same man that left on deployment? I've read numerous articles about post-traumatic stress and how the tiniest thing can trigger a response. Is Tucker denying himself the chance to be angry that I'm married? Will this come back to haunt me?

The more I think about Tucker, Ray, and everything that's going on, the more anxious I feel. Smiling at Ray, I'm trying to convey the same happiness he's always made me feel, but I can see in his face—and his concerned smile—that I'm not successful. His hand slides down my back and into mine, giving me a firm squeeze.

"I think I'm ready to go home," he says, giving me a slight tug. It wasn't a question as to whether I'm ready because I think he knows. I reach for Claire's hand, holding mine out until she grabs it. She does, realizing I'm not going to give up. I want her close to me, at least until we get home. Once we're there, she can stomp up to her room and listen to her music. She'll get over the embarrassment she's feeling right now by the time school starts on Monday.

The drive home is quick and silent. The radio isn't even on to drown out the loud thumping in my chest. Telling Ray about my life isn't even something I can put off until tomorrow or next week, and Claire needs to know, too. From her I expect anger, resistance. It's bad enough that she's bordering on her teenage years, but to find out the life she's been living since around the age of two is a lie, is enough to send her life into a tailspin. She's going to have an identity crisis.

From Ray, I expect hurt. The lies may be too much for him to get over. The fear that I'll leave him for Tucker and the thought of losing Claire, he may never recover from. He'll have every right to ask me to leave. It'll be me and me only; he'd never do that to Claire. He'd never put her in harm's way.

By the end of the night, my husband and daughter will hate me and there isn't anything I can do about it.

"Chloe, I'd like to talk to you before you disappear into your room," I say, as we walk into the house. Ray mumbles something, but is smiling when he passes me.

"I told you she'd find out, Care Bear."

Chloe huffs as she hangs up her coat.

"Find out what?" I ask both of them and find they are sporting mischievous grins.

"Dad bought me cotton candy."

"Oh, was it maple flavored? That's my favorite." I'm not a fan of her eating cotton candy, but tonight I don't care.

"Yes," she says, excitedly. "I should've saved some for you."

"It's okay. Here let's sit at the table. You too, Ray."

The sound of the chairs scraping against the hardwood sends a chill down my spine. I'm already on edge and this is making me more so. I'm jumpy and dreading the words that are about to fall out of my mouth.

Across from me, my husband and my daughter sit. Their hands are folded as they both watch me expectantly. I wish I were about to tell them something to make them smile, but that's not the case.

And now that I look at Claire, I wish she were upstairs with her headphones in, not hearing a word I'm about to say.

The rain is coming down in sheets and the wipers are barely able to keep the windows clear. Of all the times it has to rain in San Diego, why now? Every few seconds my eyes glance in my mirror. Claire is sound asleep with her bunny rabbit tucked under her arms. The lack of traffic on the highway makes it easy for me to spot if I'm being followed. Right now I feel safe.

My GPS indicates that I'm nearing my exit. I don't like this part of town, but this is where Buzz told me to go to get a fake ID. I don't even know how I came to ask him. He had a feeling something was wrong when I was writing the check for Tucker's storage unit. My hands shook and I broke down in front of him. He said his friend could help.

Right now, I feel like I'm back in high school, except I'm running for my life. I shouldn't be doing this; I should be home waiting for my husband's body to come off the plane and giving him a proper burial. I can only hope that Ryley will. That she'll be there for Tucker.

The building is run down with no lights on out front. "Just knock," Buzz said. What if I don't knock and just drive? 'He'll find you, Penny.' This time I can't ignore the voices in my head. *I know I have to follow my instincts and hide. There's no doubt in my mind Ted Lawson killed Tucker and his friends, but why? Why do four men need to die? And Frannie ... why would she do this to River?*

Unbuckling Claire, I pull her to my chest and attempt to shield her from the rain, but to no avail. She's tired and fussy, and doesn't understand the magnitude of our situation.

I knock, just like Buzz instructed, and only seconds later the door opens.

"What?"

"Buzz sent me."

The man in front of me nods and steps aside, slamming the door behind me.

"Is your husband beating you?"

The question takes me by surprise, causing me to let out a gasp. The man stops in front of me and looks at my face.

"Is he?"

I shake my head. "No," *I squeak out.*

"Follow me," *he says, turning away from me. His stride is long and I have to jog to keep up with him as we walk down a long hallway. When we come to a door, he punches numbers onto a keypad before it opens and we step in.*

"She can sleep on the couch."

I'm reluctant to put Claire down, but do so anyway. Right now I'm fucked if he wants to kill me so what does it matter?

"Buzz called, said you were coming. Said some fucked up shit is going on."

I nod, but am confused as to why he'd ask if Tucker was hitting me.

"Why did you ask about my husband?"

"To make sure I'm getting the same story. Give me your license."

I do as I'm told and peer over my shoulder at Claire, sleeping without a care in the world.

"I'm going to give you cash for your car and drive you the

bus station. I've wiped out the cameras on the interstate so no one can trace you here. Your new name is Amy Jones. What do you want to call her?"

"Um … I don't know," I say, shaking my head.

"What's her name?"

"Claire."

He punches a few keys before saying, "Her name is now Chloe Jones. It sounds the same and shouldn't confuse her. She seems young enough to not have many memories."

No memories of her father.

I wipe away tears and stare at the new license he's printed for me. It says I'm from Austin, Texas. I sob when he hands me a new birth certificate for Claire … Chloe, and I see that I'm the only listed parent.

"Amy Jones, whoever it is that's following you will have a hard time finding you now."

"I have something to tell you both," I say, as the tears start. Ray and Claire seem concerned, but I hold up my hand, assuring them that I'm okay, even when I'm not.

Swallowing hard, I glance at my husband, then my daughter. "I'm not who I say I am."

"What do you mean, Amy?" Ray asks, concern and confusion lacing his voice.

I shake my head, biting my lower lip. Maybe Cara should've told them and I could've taken the easy way out. I could be a coward and sit stoically while she details my life on the run.

"Six years ago I was living in Coronado, California and married to a Navy SEAL. He deployed when our daughter was two. One day a man came into our home, brought by someone I considered a friend, and tried to hurt our daughter."

I risk a glance at Claire to see her reaction, but she's only staring at me.

"I reported him first to the MPs but they didn't do

anything, so I went to the police and filed a report. They brought him in, but didn't have enough to hold him. Therefore, they had to let him go. The next day, my husband and his team were pronounced dead, and the man—" I have to stop to catch my breath. It's hard to think about that day, the menace I heard in his voice. "He came back, asking for my daughter, and I did what any mother would do. I ran."

After clearing my throat, I continue. "A friend told me about a guy who helped people escape. I went and saw him, and he gave Chloe and I new identities, and then drove us to the bus. We got off here when I saw the 'help wanted' sign in the window at the gas station."

"Amy," Ray covers my hand with his, "I don't understand. Why are you telling me this now? Why not earlier? Why keep the secret?"

"I'm sorry I lied," I choke out, covering my mouth to keep some of my cries muffled.

"I'm not worried about the lie. You did what you had to do to protect Chloe."

"Is my name Claire?"

My eyes dart to hers as I seek her face for any sign that she's known this entire time.

"Where did you hear that name?" I demand, more forcefully than I intended.

She shrugs. "Some lady at the Green came up and said it."

Some lady … Frannie. Cara and Ryley were with me, and neither of them would do that. It has to be Frannie. There's no other woman it could be.

"What'd she say exactly?" I ask as my voice quivers.

"She said, 'Wow, Claire you're all grown up.'"

My body temperature is now non-existent as dread courses through my body, making me ice cold.

"She's here."

"Who's here?" Ray asks.

"Frannie ... is the woman who brought the man to hurt Claire." Rising, I start to pace. "I have to call Tucker," I say, reaching for the phone.

"Who's Tucker?" Ray all but screeches.

"My husband."

chapter 22
Tucker

THE LOUD VOICES OUTSIDE THE room have me scrambling from the bed. After Penny left, lying down was the only thing I could do to keep myself from falling into a heap of nothingness on the floor. My team members don't need to see that. It's not in our training to let our emotions get the best of us, regardless of the situation. The last thing I need or want is for Ryley to come and comfort me because that's exactly what she'd do.

The door opens, smacking against the wall and causing me to jump even though I'm alert and can hear the rustling outside. Evan stands there, his arm holding the door open so it doesn't come flying back to hit him.

"We have to go."

"Where?" I ask. If he thinks I'm leaving this small town he's nuts. As long as Penny and Claire are here, this is where I'll be. It'll be pure torture watching Penny with another man, but I'll find a way to survive. I won't leave them. Seeing her every day, happy with someone else, is better than never laying eyes on her again.

I made the decision seconds before she walked into the room that if she told me she was happy, I'd step aside. I refuse to be the cause of any more heartache in her life. My death and now subsequent return has and will continue to cause her more than enough grief. Only having Claire in my life will be enough to tide me over until death comes for me … again.

"Penny called—" is all I hear before I'm moving past him. I step out into the open-air hallway to find Cara at the end of it speaking frantically on her phone. Peering inside the other room, I find an arsenal of weapons being lined up on the bed by Rask. He looks up and winks at me, as if this is his favorite thing to do. In hindsight, our guns are the only things that haven't let us down. They do their job when we need them to and I have a feeling we'll be using them tonight as we chase down this bitch who seems to have a hand in destroying our lives. What I still don't understand is why? What on earth could she possibly gain by doing the things she's done? Or has taken part in? I think that is what we all want to know. For me, it's the fact she brought a fucking pervert into my house after we let her into our lives. How much did River know? I have so many questions that will likely go unanswered. The idea of torturing Frannie to give us the answers we so desperately want weighs heavily on my mind. Cara would have to turn a blind eye in order for that to happen. And then there's Lawson. Even though I know Penny is alive, I still want to talk to him. I need to know why he did this and why our lives were targeted. He could've chosen anyone, but he chose the team I'm a part of and I have to know why.

"Get ready," Nate says, throwing a bag at me. I catch it haphazardly as it thumps against my chest. A quick pull of the zipper and its contents are displayed: brain bucket, night vision goggles, ammo, and camo paint.

It's easy to let my mind wander, to let my adrenaline kick

in and consider this another mission, but I know it's not. I can tell myself that I'm going out to do my job, but my heart is telling me otherwise. My wife and daughter are in danger and I'm going to save them. And in the event that I can't, my team will. They won't let me down, not after everything we've been through.

"Can someone tell me what's going on?" I ask, setting the duffle bag down on the bed next to Rask's gun display. He stands tall, as if he's about to tell me, but it's Cara's voice behind me which has me turning around.

"We think Frannie is in town."

"What? Why?" I try to keep my voice level and not show any signs of worry, but that doesn't exactly happen.

"Ten minutes ago I received a call from Penny. She was frantic and not making much sense. When I finally got her to calm down and tell me what's going on, she said she was telling her husband about her life and that her ... your daughter asked if her name was Claire. Penny went on to say that a woman approached Claire this evening calling her by her given name and commenting that she's grown up. Penny called me immediately," Cara says, as if this is an everyday occurrence for her. I want to shake her for her nonchalance, but I know she's doing her job even if I think she's lacking eagerness or excitement in her voice. We're both trained in different ways on how to handle situations. Thing is, no one ever trains you on how to handle your life being ripped apart or for your family to be in hiding. If this were left to me, I'd go in there with guns blazing and the 'shoot first ask questions later' mentality.

"So now what? What's our direction?" Although those are the words sitting on the tip of my tongue, it's Rask who's speaking. Nate and Evan stand in the doorway, making me wonder where Ryley is. Surely Evan isn't going to let her out of his sight, not with Frannie nearby.

"Right now, I'm going to get in the car with Ryley. We're

going to drive out of town to enjoy a nice dinner and discuss wedding plans."

"And us?" Evan asks.

Cara looks at him over his shoulder. I see the faint movement of her cheek and wonder if she's smiling at him.

"You're SEALs, I'm sure you can figure it out."

"What about your job?" Nate asks, as he reaches for her hand.

Cara shakes her head. "What about it? As far as I'm concerned you're moving into position to protect McCoy's wife and child. I don't have a solid lead telling me that Frannie is here." She winks at Nate before moving toward the door.

"Don't do anything I wouldn't do, boys." It's with those final words that she walks out of the room, shutting the door behind her. Silence falls upon the room as the four of us look at each other. I've never been to battle with Nate, but have a feeling he's no different than Evan. Deep down I know I can trust him.

"Who wants to lead?" I ask because it's not going to be me. Keeping a level head is going to keep Penny and Claire safe. If I see them in danger, I won't act rationally.

"I'll do it."

We all turn and look at Rask, wondering why he'd volunteer for something when he's never led before. When we went on our mission, he was just a young kid barely out of BUD/s. I'm not even sure if he had been on a mission before that day. River was our leader then and I don't miss the irony in the fact that we're now hunting this wife.

"Why?" Evan asks Rask.

"Because," he says, shrugging his shoulders, "I have nothing to lose. I don't have a wife or a kid depending on me. I don't have a family to go home to at night. I have nothing except you guys. No one is going to mourn me if I die again."

"I will," I say, adding my two cents. "You're our friend and brother. We care deeply about what happens to you."

"And we're wasting time trying to decide who is going to be line leader. This isn't kindergarten. This is real life. We have some shit to fuck up, and standing around here isn't getting us any closer to where we need to be."

"Let's get over there." Nate slings a duffle bag over his shoulder. It dawns on me that the guys are already dressed in their sand-colored fatigues with their combat boots laced up. My eyes wander from each of them, watching as they prepare for the unknown and wonder how I'm going to be able to do this.

The sound of a shutting door jars me out of my thoughts and I realize I'm left alone in the room, holding my duffle bag. The guns, which were laid out on the bed, are gone, and the only sound in the room is the television and my thumping heart. The guys' voices carry upward from the parking lot and I count three doors slamming before the horn is honked.

Can I do this? Can I go into this knowing another man will be protecting my wife and daughter when it should be my job?

Will I let my life be continually dictated by this mad woman?

The horn honking once more startles me into action as I reach for the duffel bag. With one last look around the now empty room, I leave, letting the door slam shut behind me. As much as I wish to never see this hotel again, I know we'll be back here later, hopefully with Penny and Claire by my side.

As soon as I'm in the car, Nate is driving out of the parking spot and onto the road. It's only a matter of minutes before we're driving through town and turning off onto a road that quickly turns into dirt. So many questions are plaguing my mind, but I don't ask them. Instead, I stare out the windows, letting my gaze move from side to side so I can take in my surroundings. I catch a quick look at Evan and Rask only to see that they're doing the same thing. We're memorizing all that we can in case we need to escape. But unless Frannie has brought an army with her I doubt we'll be retreating at all.

After what seems like twenty minutes, Nate pulls off onto the side of the road and shuts the car off. "Up this driveway is Penny's house. Fortunately for her it was easy to hide here. Unfortunately for her, it's so far off the beaten path that no one can hear her if they're in trouble."

"How'd you know where to go?" I ask, as I slip a pistol from my duffle bag into my boot and drop a few magazines into my side pocket.

"Cara gave me detailed instructions which I memorized," he replies, as he gets out of the car and walks to the rear, popping the trunk open. Evan and Rask follow him, and through the rearview mirror I can see faint reflections of guns being taken out. I say a silent prayer aimed at Penny, letting her know I'm coming for her, before I get out of the car.

The guys are putting on their helmets and checking their night vision when I come around to the end. Rask hands me a rifle, similar to the one I used in Cuba.

"Where'd we get all of this?"

"I have great contacts," Evan says, answering me with a smile. For some reason I don't want to know about his contacts, but am very thankful they like him enough to outfit him with military grade weaponry. The less I have to learn in the heat of the moment the better. I set my rifle down and put on my brain bucket, securing the chinstrap. The night cam is the same one I'm used to, and it comes on as soon as I drop it over my eyes.

Rask leads us up the hill with me following last. My senses are heightened and every few steps I'm turning around with my gun aimed at the woods. I want to yell at Penny for living like this, but I get it. It makes sense to stay hidden when you're trying to be inconspicuous, but to be so far out and away from civilization is not a good thing, especially considering the threat she was facing.

Rask puts his fist up as the house comes into sight. It's larger than anything I could ever provide for her and probably something she dreamed about long before she met me. The wraparound porch likely offers great views of the sun rising and setting each day, not to mention the calm way the summer nights tend to leave us. I can see her sitting out there with a glass of iced tea in one hand and a book resting in her lap.

Just beyond the porch is a large picture window with two shadows reflecting off the light and I'm assuming one is Penny's while the other is her husband's. I don't want to meet the man who has loved my wife and daughter when I couldn't, but I know I need to thank him. And I need to tell him that I'm not here to take Penny away from him. She loves him. I'll never stand in the way of that.

On the second floor one room is lit and I can faintly make out a shadow.

"Claire," I mumble under my breath. If the guys hear me they don't say anything.

Guns are raised and I'm quickly scanning the perimeter as to why. Rask still has us holding position and I'm desperately trying to see what he does. When I place my hand on Nate's shoulder he points ahead, and I follow his finger until my eyes land on the basement. A flashlight is being turned on and off down there, and as I flip my goggles to infrared and do a quick scan I now know why Rask has us on the ready. There are four bodies when there should only be three.

"They have company," Evan says, confirming what I'm seeing.

"Let's move. Archers, take the front. Knock first. Let them have a chance to answer before you bust down their door. McCoy and I will take the back and see if we can dance with their intruder."

Dance? No, the tango doesn't interest me. Grabbing

Frannie by the neck and squeezing the life out of her does, though, and as demented as it sounds I'm really hoping I have the chance to do that soon.

Rask and I duck under windows and pause when he points down to the ground, where glass and wood splinters are littered. I duck my head into the window and try to squeeze in, but can't fit.

"Definitely a small-framed person," I report to Rask.

"A man doesn't leave a broken window like this lying around."

"The glass is on the ground, making it seem like it was broken from inside," I add, questioning why anyone would break the window from inside the house.

Rask's face deadpans as he glances at me. I don't want to know what he's thinking, but if it's anything like the thoughts running through my head right now, I'll be aiming my gun at Ray Barnes while the rest of the team aim theirs at Frannie. I hate that I instantly think he can't be trusted, but this seems suspicious.

"We need to move," he says and I nod, hoping he understands that we need to consider multiple hostiles and proceed with our senses heightened. We step over the glass and around the corner to face the kitchen. The light above the door is broken with glass shards resting on the steps. Whoever did this is hoping that the occupants flee barefoot and cut themselves.

"God she's sadistic."

"And well trained," Rask adds.

He tries the door, turning the handle easily. It makes me wonder if our intruder did the same thing or if she's beaten us upstairs and unlocked the door for a hasty exit. We get our answer the moment we step into the house. The calm, eerie voice causes the fine hairs on my neck to stand tall. Each step that Rask and I take is calculated and meant to catch her off guard. Nate and Evan should also be in the house by now, but

I don't hear them, and calling out to them would be foolish, costing us the advantage.

"Do not answer the door," the voice says from inside the room.

Rask pauses and glances slightly in my direction, nodding. The voice belongs to Frannie Riveria—just as we suspected—and explains why Nate and Evan aren't in the house. In front of us is an entryway into the living room where I'm suspecting Frannie is since that's the last place I saw the shadows of the two people I assumed to be Penny and Ray.

Rask and I quickly enter the room just as the Archers come in, but we're too late. Frannie stands in the center of the room with Penny sitting in a chair, her hands duct taped to the armrests. A gun is pressed up against her flesh, penetrating Penny's temple. It takes everything in me not to rush forward to knock Frannie down and cover Penny for safety reasons, but I don't. I do what my training has ingrained me to do and steady my rifle onto Frannie. This is the scene we saw outside. The only difference is that when we were looking, we saw someone downstairs.

We're late.

"Well, well, well, if it isn't Hogan's Heroes." She doesn't seem to care that there are four Navy SEALs each with a gun aimed at her. She's come to finish off the last person who can testify against her brother and I have a feeling she's not leaving until Penny is dead.

"We aren't in Germany, Frannie, and none of us are prisoners of war," Evan says, training his pistol on her. Nate moves around the back of Frannie, cornering her.

"Can someone tell me what the hell is going on?" Ray's voice quivers as he speaks out. A quick look tells me his hands are tied behind his back and he would've been forced to watch his wife's assassination and probably Claire's, too. For a brief moment I thought he could be involved and relief washes over me that he's not.

"Tell him, Frannie," Evan says, his voice laced with sarcasm. "Tell this man why you're pointing a gun at his wife's head. Tell him why you've been hunting her down for the past six months. And please for the love of God tell us why you would destroy *all* of our lives. Inquiring minds want to know what goes on in your fucked up mind."

"You'll never understand, Evan."

"Try us," Nate says.

"People do things for the ones they love."

"Your brother is a child molester. He doesn't deserve love," Rask says as he drops a bullet into his chamber.

"I love him and once they're dead, we can be together. He'll be free from the prison you sent him to."

"You're fucking sick," Nate adds.

"Penny," I say, getting her attention only to have Frannie yell for us to stop talking, "look at me." I drop to my knees so we're somewhat eye level. Tears steak down her face and her hands shake. Her eyes move to the stairs, her way of silently telling me that Claire is up there. I look at Evan and motion for the stairs, watching as he backs his way up them, his gun never changing position until he's out of sight.

"I think it's in your best interests if you all leave. This is none of your business. You're not even supposed to be alive."

"I think you're fucking crazy," I spit back at her.

There's a soft whimper coming from Ray; I glance over to see a man scared out of his wits. "It's going to be okay, Ray," I tell him, hoping to reassure him.

Frannie makes a move, stepping behind Penny and placing her arm around her neck. "I'm going to count to three then she dies."

"If she dies, so does your brother. I'll fucking torture him, Frannie, and I'll make you watch. You'll be begging me to end his life, and only when I've had enough will I hand you the gun and help you squeeze the trigger, but we won't aim to kill. No, you see I have twelve rounds in my pistol so each shot will be designed to cause him extreme pain. And the last person he sees will be you as you deliver the final bullet which will end his piece of shit excuse for a life," I say, making eye contact with her.

The collective gasps in the room don't catch me off guard. I know what I said is extreme but I mean every word of it. If Penny or Claire die tonight and I don't go with them, Ted Lawson won't see a single day in a courtroom.

"Penny, look at me."

When she does I all but die on the inside. "Claire is safe and you're going to be just fine."

The telltale sound of a gun cocking into place fills the room. Everyone is yelling for guns to be dropped, but I'm only focusing on Penny. She's biting her lip so hard it's starting to bleed. I want to reach out to her, but can't right now. Not until the threat is gone.

"I'm going to kill her," Frannie says, grabbing Penny's hair and pulling her head back. Before I can stand, the faint sound of glass breaking and Frannie lurching forward catches my attention, but it's the second gunshot, which has me tackling Penny to the ground in her chair, knocking the wind out of her, so I can protect her body with mine.

chapter 23

Tucker

PENNY'S SCREAM PIERCES MY EARS, causing me to move away slightly. I can't tell if she's hurt or freaked out. Probably a bit of both if I had to guess. I'm afraid to move, to leave this position for fear that Penny will be hurt more than she already is because I don't know where the hell the shot came from.

"She's down! She's down!" someone yells from behind me. I can't tell if it's Rask or Nate, but I look over both my shoulders to see what they're talking about and find Frannie on the ground looking lifeless.

"What the fuck?" I hear Evan behind me as he comes thundering down the stairs. I hope that Claire has stayed in her room because she doesn't need to see her mother tied up like this.

"Is she dead?" I ask Rask who is the closest to the body. He crawls over to her, pushes her gun away, and feels for a pulse.

"She's gone," he says. I quickly roll off Penny and pull my knife from my boot to cut the tape from her wrists to free her.

"Where's Claire?" Penny cries, panic lacing her voice, and I look to Evan for the answer.

"She's okay. She's upstairs. I told her to keep her headphones on. I don't know if she'll listen to me, but I'm hoping she will. She seems pretty scared."

"Ah … Amy," a pained voice sounds from behind me and we all turn toward it.

Penny scrambles away from me and goes to Ray. I turn away again, not wanting to see them together.

"Oh God, Ray," she screams, getting my attention.

I rush over to her side to find Ray shot and bleeding profusely.

"Who fucking fired their gun?" I yell out, knowing it wasn't me. I heard the glass break and watched Frannie lurch forward—that's when I dove for Penny to keep Frannie away from her. "She fucking shot him," I say as I cut the tape from his wrists so we can lay him down.

"Who shot Frannie?" Evan asks.

I glance from Nate to Rask and they both shake their heads. Rask immediately moves to the window and says, "We must have a shooter outside."

We all look at each other and back at Ray who is bleeding out on the couch.

"Go," Rask says, kneeling down in front of Ray, "I'll see if I can stop the bleeding."

I reach for Penny, but quickly realize she doesn't need me; she's too focused on her husband. It's the way things should be even though watching her care for him breaks my heart. I want to be selfish and want her to worry about me, but that's not going to happen.

Nate, Evan, and I grab our guns and head outside, this time with Evan in the lead. My infrared shows a body sitting in the woods, unmoving as we approach. We rush to the edge of the grass and enter the woods.

"Put your hands up," Evan yells and the shooter does slowly, causing us to move faster, but stay together. We have to work as a team against this unknown threat. Our weapons are drawn, guiding us to his location.

Nate takes the lead from Evan, moving swiftly over the forest floor. Leaves and twigs snap under our feet, indicating to the shooter how far away we are from him. This isn't the way missions should be done, but there hasn't been any rhyme or reason to this one. Nate reaches him first, pinning his hands easily to his back while I keep my gun on him.

"Holy fuck," Evan blurts as he shines his flashlight on the assailant.

"What?" Both Nate and I say at the same time. I lift my night vision goggles and walk around to the front with my gun steady. My mouth drops when I see our supposed to be dead team leader, River. I don't know if I should shoot him, kick him, or tie him up and hand him over to the authorities. What I do know is that I'm about tell him that his bullet missed.

"You killed your wife, not mine," I tell him.

"That was my intent."

"What the fuck, man, I thought you were dead? Your house blew up. I was there. I saw it!" Evan exclaims, with Nate now by his side. Both of them have dropped their guns, but mine remains steady and aimed at his chest. I don't know why or how he's here, but I don't trust him even though he's killed his wife. I turn on my helmet flashlight so I can get a good look at him. There doesn't seem to be a damn thing wrong with him. If he's been hiding or on the run, he's been doing a fine job staying clean and well fed.

"Start talking, motherfucker, before I pump you full of lead!" The sudden outburst of anger rolls through me as I stare at him. If it weren't for him, we wouldn't be in the position we are in today. I wouldn't be standing here with my gun pointed at my team leader while my wife tends to her other husband. We'd all be on base, living our lives and worrying about the next terrorist threat.

I can feel Evan and Nate's eyes on me, but I don't care. As far as I'm concerned *he's* responsible for everything that has happened because *he* brought that crazy bitch into our lives. Without her sick and twisted lifestyle, I'd be home right now nursing a fucking beer. Instead I'm in the middle of nowhere with my finger adding a bit of pressure to the trigger that's going to release the bullet which will kill the man in front of me.

River slowly turns his head to look me in the eyes. He doesn't try to shield the light from his eyes, or move this hands even though I know Nate hasn't tied him up. Instead he remains on his knees, waiting to see if I'm going to end his life.

"I don't know where to start," he says, earning a scoff from me.

"The beginning works."

"Come on, let's take him inside." Evan grabs River's arm, helping him up. I don't agree, but I have a feeling I'm outnumbered when Nate bends to pick up River's belongings. I follow behind, keeping my gun aimed at River's head. One move and he's dead.

Evan takes River through the front door where chaos has ensued. Penny is sobbing and Rask is covered in blood. I glance quickly around the room and see that Frannie is still on the floor and Claire isn't down here, at least not that I can see. I drop to my knees and set my gun down.

"What can I do?"

Rask shakes his head. "The paramedics are on their way, but he's lost a lot of blood. I can't stop the bleeding."

My hand reaches for Penny, pausing briefly before I place it on her back. She doesn't acknowledge me and part of me dies a little on the inside. I know it shouldn't bother me, but it does. She's supposed to be my wife, not this guy who is dying on their couch. She's supposed to seek comfort in me, but can't because her heart doesn't belong to me anymore.

"Holy shit," Cara curses as she bursts through the door, startling all of us with her stealth-like ninja skills. I swear a SEAL trained her with how quietly she can move around. We make eye contact quickly before another holy shit comes tumbling out of her mouth when she spots River being held by Evan.

"I should've left instructions on how not to kill anyone while I was gone."

"We didn't kill anyone," Nate says. "River shot Frannie through the window and her reaction caused her gun to go off and shot Barnes. When we came in, Penny was duct taped to the chair and Barnes had his hands tied behind his back."

"Shit," she mutters, pulling out her phone.

I try to focus my attention back on Penny, rubbing her back for comfort while she whispers into her husband's ear. I turn away, trying not to eavesdrop, giving them the privacy they need.

"The ambulance is pulling in now. Evan, you take River and get the hell out of here. Of all of you he's classified as dead. Where did the bullet that hit Frannie come from?" Cara questions.

Evan pushes River through the kitchen and out back.

"The window," Nate answers.

"Shit, why did he have to go and shoot her?"

That's what we want to know, but haven't got any answers yet.

"Where's Claire?"

"Upstairs, I think." I shrug, not knowing where my daughter is. Even if I went to her, she wouldn't know who I was, so maybe it's best if Cara goes to find her.

"You guys need to go. I don't want you here when the authorities arrive. Take Claire with you."

Nate nods, while I stay frozen next to Penny. I don't

know how this is all going to play out, but leaving her isn't an option.

"What's the plan, Cara?"

The sound of sirens grows closer and Cara appears panicked. I'm sure this isn't how she expected everything to go down. Honestly, it isn't how I expected things to be either. I thought for sure that Ray was part of Frannie's posse by the way the basement window was busted from the inside.

Cara pulls out her gun and aims it at an already dead Frannie.

"Hughes, don't. Your bullets won't match."

She looks at me and for the first time I see fear. She's the only one to offer me help, aside from Marley. I can't let her lose her career over this.

Rask stands and grabs his gear as if it's no big deal that his hands are covered in blood. "You found them like this, a stray bullet from a hunter," he says, before walking through the kitchen.

"McCoy, you go, and I'll go get Claire. You'll be too emotional when you see her upstairs. I'll meet you back at the hotel," Nate tells me.

I nod reluctantly and take my exit through the same door I came in. I glance back at Penny, hoping for a sign that she knows I'm leaving, and I get nothing. My only solace right now is the knowledge that I'll soon be seeing my daughter for the first time in six years. It doesn't even matter that she won't remember me or know anything about me. Just seeing her in person, listening to her talk will be enough to get me through the night.

chapter 24
Penny

"WHO'S TUCKER?"

"My husband."

The words from earlier replay over and over with each step I take in the white sterile hallway. The look on his face and the fear in his voice is something I'll never forget. Calling Tucker my husband was a mistake and one I regret. As soon as the word slipped off my tongue I wanted to take it back, but I couldn't. He heard me and by the expression on his face, I hurt him. It wasn't my intent, and by all means I shouldn't have thought about Tucker in that moment, but I did.

It's odd to think that referring to Tucker as my husband came so easily considering I've been married to Ray for so much longer. I've even known Ray longer. I love him, but I've never lost the love I felt for Tucker.

People cry, they moan in pain from the rooms I pass. Nurses shuffle from room to room helping their patients all while I wait for news on my husband. Only a few make eye contact with me and rarely does a smile form on their face. Their jobs in the ER are not happy ones, but ones that require quick thinking in life or death situations. They don't have time for idle chitchat and pleasantries, especially for wives who refuse to go to the waiting room. I want the doctors to sense me out in the hall so they work harder on saving my husband's life.

The emergency room doors open and in rushes another gurney with life saving measures being taken. An EMT straddles the patient while doing chest compressions. He's barking out orders, telling others what needs to be done to save this person's life. It's too hard to tell whether it's a male or female, but nonetheless it's a life worth saving.

That's what they were doing on the way here while the ambulance sped down the windy road as fast as it could. The drawback to living in a small town is that the nearest hospital is forty minutes away and since the gun was fired and the bullet hit Ray, it seems like hours have passed, maybe even days. I know it's not possible because he'd be dead, but that's what it feels like.

As for Frannie … I hang my head and push away the onslaught of tears that want to escape. I know once I start crying I won't be able to stop and I shouldn't shed a tear for her. She ruined everything. It's hard to wrap my head around the chain of events leading up to today. My life was peaceful, happy, and six or seven months ago my axis rocked slightly when my husband brought up a news report about a Navy SEAL, only the chances that he heard them incorrectly are high, since the four warriors I once loved as my family had returned. If Ray had just said *four* and not *one* things could've been different.

No, that's a lie.

If Ray had said four SEALs I would've started searching for Tucker; he would've been easy to find. The only problem with that is I don't know what I would've done had I found him. Would I go back to him? Divorce him? Or wait for him to come find me like he did now? I wish I knew the answer because then maybe I'd feel something for him, when right now all I feel is hatred. I can't help but feel like he brought Frannie here.

She found me without him, though, and she found my daughter, my house, and shot my husband. But who shot her? There was so much yelling and I was focused on Tucker because I knew he wasn't going to let anything happen to me, but who was going to protect Ray? Before I knew what was happening, I was being tackled to the ground with my back slamming against the chair. Tucker lay over me, and for a brief moment I thought he had been shot until he started talking. His voice soothed away the fear even though he wasn't speaking to me. I couldn't help but feel safe in his arms. I was relieved, yet that relief was short lived when I heard Ray call for me. I knew he was hurt by the way he spoke, and even with him being a few feet away, I couldn't get there fast enough.

I push off the wall and start pacing the hall again. There are so many noises making my head ache; the beeping from the machines, the constant sound of the intercom going off, and the rush of feet coupled with urgent voices. Everywhere I look there's a subdued panic on the faces of the medical staff. They try not to show fear, but I see it. I know what it looks like. I've lived it. I've spent years glancing over my shoulder wondering if Lawson or Frannie were there, lurking. Its only when I stopped being so cautious that my world started changing.

I stand at the opening of the hallway and the ER when another gurney comes in. There is no rushing this time, no one working on the woman lying under the white sheet. Her dark hair hangs off the back, swaying lightly with the movement from being rolled down the hall. *Is that Frannie?* I can't help but think it is as I feel a weight being lifted off my shoulders. With Lawson in jail and Frannie dead, my life should go back to normal. I shouldn't have to worry about anyone coming after my daughter and me, or someone trying to harm my husband. Life can be what it's meant to be: enjoyable.

What I don't understand is why Frannie wanted to harm all of us. From our last moments today, I know she was sick and mentally unstable. It's clear that Lawson being put in jail was a trigger for her. I suppose I have a lot of questions to ask, but I'm not sure I even want to know the answers. I don't want to find out that this was something, which could've been prevented if I had just kept my mouth shut.

"Mrs. Barnes?"

I'm caught off guard by my name being called. The doctor stands in front of me with fresh scrubs on. One would think he hasn't done anything important today, but the expression on his face tells me otherwise. He's tired, ragged.

I nod, unable to find my voice. My arms instinctively go around my mid-section, the same thing they did when I was informed that Tucker had died. I'm bracing myself.

"Your husband experienced a lot of damage from the bullet and the blood loss is extensive."

I know what he's going to say next and I don't want to hear him. No one should lose their husband like this, and I'm going to do it twice in my young life. All I remember when I came in with Ray is the EMT saying GSW to the abdomen. Everything else is a jumble of words about his blood pressure, oxygen, and heart rate. They were rushing to do what they could, to get him into surgery before it was too late.

And it *is* too late.

"Is he dying?"

The doctor doesn't say anything right away. For all I know, he's searching for the right words to comfort me. He doesn't know that I've been down this path before, only this time I'll get to say good-bye. There isn't a pedophile trying to steal my daughter causing me to run in the middle of the night. No, this time I'll be holding my husband's hand while he takes his last breath.

"We did everything we could, but there was just too much damage." He reaches out and places his hand on my forearm in an attempt to comfort me. "You can see him and be with him until the end. Someone will be out shortly to take you to him." With those final words he disappears down the hall, removing the paper cap that covers his hair.

I can't even put into words what I'm feeling. I have an odd sense of calm, riddled with anxiety, and it hurts to breath. Tears are building up in my sockets, waiting for me to give the okay to let the floodgates open, but I can't. I have to remain strong for Ray and for Chloe.

Chloe. No, Claire. What do I call my child now that the truth about our lives is out there? I had no time to explain before … before everything changed. My phone call to Cara, not Tucker, was cut short when Frannie walked into my house. Locking our doors had never been a precaution we had to take and we were about to pay the price.

Ray protected my daughter, sending her to her room as he calmly spoke to Frannie. Even with fear running through my body, I jumped when I heard Claire's door slam and something be moved across the floor. She was blocking herself in because even she sensed the danger.

To my left and through the double doors is the waiting room where friends from the life I gave up sit and wait. If my luck continues, the police are there as well, waiting to take my statement. Rask's last words remind me of what I'm supposed to say, but I don't know if it's believable. I don't know if I believe it myself, but someone shot her from the outside and I really want to thank them, yet punch them at the same time because their bullet caused her to squeeze the trigger and shoot my husband.

"Ma'am, would you like to go see your husband?"

I nod at the portly nurse who offers a sweet, yet forced smile. "I need my daughter first."

She seems to understand and steps in next to me, urging me to walk through the double doors. Each step seems to take an hour until I'm at the door and they're being opened automatically for me. The nurse presses her hand against my back, guiding me to where everyone is waiting.

Ryley is the first to stand, and I immediately notice that she's holding Claire's hand. Flashbacks of images come to me as I remember how close they once were.

"Mommy," she says as she runs toward with tears streaming down her face. I don't know what she saw in the living room, but I hope to God Nate kept her face covered. "Are you okay?"

"Yes, baby, I am. Are you?" I ask, pushing her hair away from her face, my eyes doing a quick scan of her body to check she's not hurt in any way.

"I was scared and I had to hang onto Nate while we climbed out my window, but he told me to not let go and said he wouldn't drop me."

I look up at Nate who looks a little embarrassed. As soon as my eyes meet Tucker's, he goes and stands by his friend, patting him on the back. I'll never be able to repay him, or any of the others for coming and saving us.

"No, Nate would never drop you. Neither would Tucker or Evan."

Claire looks back and all the guys smile at her, all except for one—River. He's staring straight ahead. I faintly remember him coming into my house, and if my husband hadn't been injured I would've slapped him in the face. Why he's even here, I have no idea. For all I know he faked his death, twice, to help his demented wife try to kill us all.

I pull Claire to me, cupping my hands over her cheeks. "Your dad is very hurt. I'm going to take you to see him now, okay?"

My words aren't lost on her as her eyes well up with tears. Tucker moves toward me, but I shake my head. I don't want him near me right now. I want to go be with my husband in his last moments, telling him how sorry I am and how much I love him.

With Claire's hand in mine, we walk through the double doors while the nurse leads the way. Claire's grip tightens when we pause at a nondescript door.

"Is my dad dying?"

I nod and let out the sob that has been building for hours. The tears no longer hold back and they rush down my face, soaking my skin immediately. Claire's the brave one and pulls me into the room to where the man I love is lying on a bed with a tube coming out of his mouth. The nurse moves around us, bringing chairs over to his bedside.

"His heart is starting to slow down. It won't be long," she says as she looks at the machine. Claire lets go of my hand and moves to one side of the bed and picks up Ray's hand.

"I'm so sorry, Dad," she says to him. "I hope you know how much I love you even when you made me study history."

I let out a strangle laugh and try to compose myself. How can my daughter have so much more composure than me? I'm supposed to be the strong one, yet she's teaching me about grace and dignity.

Reaching for Ray's hand, I sit down next to him. He's cold and lifeless already. I bring his hand to my lips and press against it. "I'm so sorry," I whisper against this skin repeatedly.

"Ray, if you can hear me please fight. Find strength in our love and fight to stay with us. We need you so much."

"Yes, Daddy, please stay with me," Claire says through her tears. I reach for her, our hands resting over the top of Ray, cocooning him with our love.

"I can't do this without you, Ray. Please don't leave me."

Claire and I talk to him, reminding him that he has something to fight for. I don't know if I believe in the afterlife or the shining white light people with near death experiences say they've seen, but I do believe in love and faith. And I'm praying that wherever Ray is right now, he's turning away from the light and coming back to me.

chapter 25
Penny

"WOULD YOU LIKE ME TO brush your hair?"

Claire steps up behind me, dressed in a black dress that touches her knees with her hair up in a bun. I don't know who did her hair, but I'm thankful. I can barely brush mine. Years ago, when I lost Tucker, I didn't have time to mourn and part of me wishes I were in a similar situation because every part of my body hurts. The other part of me feels like I didn't do this right with Tucker or I'm somehow not honoring his memory.

With the 'passing' of Tucker I was living in fear, constantly looking over my shoulder and jumping at the slightest noises. I'd sleep up against the door while Claire slept peacefully in bed or battled her toddler demons. Numerous times, I wondered if her night whimpers were dreams about Tucker, but her little mind was probably dreaming of monsters under her bed, not her father dying, not her father never coming home. I can't even remember if I told her.

I stare back at my daughter who looks so much like the father she doesn't know. How did our lives become this cluster mess of lies and deceit? I never wanted to lie to Ray, but I had no choice. There was never a convenient time to sit down and unload my burden on him. And why would I? We were living a life of bliss and nothing was wrong, except my inability to give him a child. That was selfish of me. I didn't know if I could love another child the same way I love Claire. She was my last link to a life that I never wanted to give up.

Today I'll bury my husband when I couldn't do it before. I was never afforded the opportunity to say good-bye to Tucker. Instead of honoring the man who served his country, sitting there like a proud wife and accepting his flag, I was lying on a bed, silently crying my eyes out and holding my daughter for fear that someone was going to take her out of my arms.

"Who did your hair?"

Claire picks up my brush and moves it through my hair, brushing it softly. "That lady, Ryley. She seems nice."

"She is." I smile softly. "When you were little, we used to go to the park with her all the time. She has a little boy now … I don't know why I just told you that," I say, getting lost in thought.

"It's okay. We can talk about it."

Claire sets my brush down and sits next to me on my bench, taking my hand in hers. She's so strong and resilient.

"My name is Penelope," I tell her with a smile. "And your name is Claire. For days now I've been referring to you as Claire in my head because it was your grandma's name and your dad loved your grandma so much."

"What's his name?"

"Tucker McCoy."

"He's downstairs fixing our door," she states as if I'm supposed to know this. "He made me breakfast, too, but it wasn't very good. I didn't tell him that though."

"Oh yeah?" I try not to let my voice crack, but it does. I can't imagine what Tucker is thinking right now. He's spent the past six years believing we've been waiting for him, that he'd come home to a family who missed him. Well, I missed him, but Claire ... she was too young.

"Has Tucker spoken to you?"

Claire shakes her head and starts pulling at her lower lip. "What's going to happen now?"

I bring her into my arms and hold her, trying not to mess up her hair. "I wish I had an answer for you, but I don't. I have a lot of decisions to make and I can't make them without you, but none of them have to be made today, okay?"

"Would you be mad if I didn't want to change my name?"

I shake my head slowly while looking her in the eyes so she knows I won't be mad at her. I can understand why she would want to keep her name the same, it's all she's really known.

"He'll be hurt, though, right?"

I rub my hand up and down back, searching for the right answer. Tucker is as innocent as Claire is and we've all lost so much.

"I think Tucker would understand why you want to keep your name the same."

Claire doesn't say anything for a long time before she stands and picks my hairbrush up. She starts humming "Hush Little Baby" the song I used to sing to her while brushing my hair. I keep my eyes closed and let her do whatever she wants. No one is going to care how I look today, not when the focus should be on Ray.

The sound of a hair clip locking into place has me looking in the mirror. Claire stands behind me, beaming. "I think you look pretty like this," she says with a toothy smile. I turn my head from side to side, as if I'm striking a pose, and smile.

"I love it."

Claire stands at the front of the church, her father's

body resting behind her. The pews are filled with friends, colleagues, and students, along with their parents. I have been touched, hugged, promised visits, and offered condolences from people I don't know. Behind me sits my friends, the ones who saved us. No one here knows what really happened, and the police bought the stray bullet story. They found tracks in the woods and figured it was a hunting bullet gone astray. Not uncommon here.

Ryley wanted to sit next to me, but I told her people would stare. Never, in the years that I've been here, have I talked about anyone other than Claire. I don't want to explain where my sudden barrage of friends came from. This is still my home.

"Most of you know my dad as Mr. Barnes, but to me he was just Dad, except when I wanted something and I would call him Daddy. When I was little he came into my life and showed me what it's like to be loved by two parents." Claire has to pause to wipe her tears and clear her voice. She cries softly, making me want to go to her, but I know she needs to do this on her own.

"He taught me how to swing, ride a bike, ski, and use a bow. My dad used to say that I could be an Olympian in Sky Archery. We were just waiting for the snow to fall before we went out again.

"I know you guys are going to miss him as your teacher, or maybe not because he gave really hard tests, but I'm going to miss him for his laugh, the jokes he used to tell me on our way to school, and how he looked at my mom. Every time he saw her, it was like he was seeing her for the first time. I know my dad loved all of his students, even the ones who gave him a hard time, and he'd want his classes to know that he's proud of all of you."

I hear sniffling and a few sobs coming from the people surrounding me. When she told me earlier that she was going to speak, I didn't know what to expect. Watching her now, as she turns toward Ray's casket, rips my heart into pieces. She doesn't deserve this.

"Dad, I'm going to miss you so much. Thanks for loving me and helping me grow."

With those final words, Claire steps down and returns to her seat next to me, burying her face into my side, the sobs she was keeping at bay being absorbed by my body. The minister returns to the pulpit and asks if anyone else would like to say a few things. To my surprise, Tucker stands and walks to the front.

He clears his throat and while I'm staring at him, he's looking anywhere but me.

"I know no one knows me, but a long time ago Ray did me a favor. It's a favor I'll never be able to repay him for. I'm just sorry that I was too late in thanking him." Tucker bows his head, shaking it slightly. His fingers come to rest against his mouth before I hear an audible intake of air. "Ray, what you did … there are no words for the gratitude I feel."

I try to fight back the tears, but to no avail. Only the small group of us understand what Tucker means, can fully grasp why he's saying thank you to Ray. I want to think Tucker would've done that anyway, once he met Ray, but I don't know. SEALs are different from other men; they're more protective and love more fiercely because they never know if it's the last time.

People are going to ask who he is and I'm going to lie. It's what I'm best at. I don't know if Tucker is going to be a friend from college or some man he helped on the street one day, but I will not tarnish the memory of Ray because of a life I used to live. As easy as it would be to fall back into my old life, to move away from here and start over, I don't think that's what Claire wants. She doesn't even want to be called Claire, and as much as it's going to hurt Tucker, she's my priority.

A couple of Ray's co-workers speak, reminding everyone

what a nice, kind, and loving man he was. Their words hit home, stabbing me in an already decimated heart, reminding me that I couldn't trust him enough to tell him my secret until it was too late. When I received the email from Buzz, I should've run. Ray didn't deserve this. He didn't deserve my deceit. All he asked from me is love and I gave it to him, but as I sit here now I don't think I gave him enough.

The minister says a few parting words and invites everyone to the graveside where my husband will be laid to rest. The cold, shallow, dark dirt will consume the wooden box he lies in and the only thing I'll be able to do is pray that wherever he is, he's at peace. The pallbearers pass me and I'm instructed to stand and follow behind. There's soft music playing in the background but that doesn't calm the hushed whispers I hear as I pass. Maybe staying here isn't the right thing to do after all. I could start over, go somewhere tropical where there's crystal blue water and white sandy beaches.

Or I could stay and face my demons. I have no doubt that I'll be called to testify against Lawson, and when that happens my cover will be up. Everyone will know my name isn't Amy, but Penelope. Everyone will know that it wasn't only Ray I was married to, but Tucker also, and the moment he made his presence known my marriage to Ray became null and void.

Choosing between Tucker and Ray would've been impossible. It would've been heartbreaking and I don't think I could've done it. As much as I love Tucker, Ray's been there when I've been at my worst. He picked me up and showed me how to live.

"Thanks for staying," I say as I come down the stairs and enter the living room. Over the past few days, the guys worked to remove any trace of Frannie dying on the floor and my husband losing most of his blood on the couch. Rask and Evan put in new flooring, which was needed before Ray's wake. And Cara and Nate went sofa shopping for me. It's not something I would've picked out, but nonetheless it serves its purpose.

"I would do anything for you, you know that." Tucker sits on the sofa with his leg crossed over his knee. He turns off the television and watches me as I cross the room. I can feel his eyes on me, the same way I could when we first started dating. The butterflies and minor tremors of excitement I felt back then are still very present. Tucker hasn't changed much; he's aged, but who hasn't? I can still picture him shirtless, with his phoenix tattoo on his shoulder, mowing our lawn. I'd gawk at him, taking in the fine contours of his body. He'd catch me staring, but never say anything. It was like a game for us. Who could go the longest before one of us caved and pounced?

I often lost, but it was worth it.

When Tucker left, we were trying to have another baby. According to Tucker it was practice until the deed was done. Over the years I've wondered how our family would've turned out if he had come home like he was supposed to. If River hadn't met and married Frannie, where would we be now? Still in Coronado or would Tucker be retired? Or would I be sitting here today, in another place, mourning my husband?

"We need to talk."

"I know," he replies, but without infliction in his voice. He knows what's coming and is bracing himself.

"I thought about asking you what you want, but it's not going to change my mind. I have to think about Chloe—"

"Her name is Claire," he says interrupting me.

I nod, agreeing with him. There's no use fighting about her name.

"I have to think about her and what she wants, and right now that is staying here."

"Then this is where I stay."

Tears build and seep over, but at this point I'm so used to crying that I let them fall. "I don't want you to, Tucker. I need some time to figure things out. I need some space away from all of this. Months ago my life was great. I was happy. Then Ray hears a news report and emotions and memories are stirred up. Ted Lawson's name is in the paper, and then I get an email from Buzz. I should've told Ray what was going on and I didn't until it was too late. Now he's dead by the hands of a psychotic woman who I knew would find me someday and I can't help but think I could've prevented this.

"I should've kept running, but I got lazy. I let love and family break my walls down and now I'm barely able to function. My body aches and my mind is freaking out on me. I love you, Tucker, I do, but I also love Ray and having you here will create a lot of questions that I don't want to answer, not yet."

Tucker makes a sudden move and I half expect him to leave; instead, he stands and pulls me into his arms. He feels like home, like this is where I belong, but I can't be there right now.

"I told you I'd walk away from you if that is what you needed, but I can't walk away from Claire. She's my daughter and I want to get to know her. I want to make her breakfast in the morning and walk her to school. I want to run on the beach and have her show me how to shoot a bow. I have so much to learn and I'm begging you not to take that away from me."

Tucker's words cause me to sob into his shoulder. Instead of yelling, he holds me, rubbing his hand up and down my back while trying to soothe me. Any other guy would leave, throw shit around the house and slam the door, but not Tucker.

Not in this situation.

chapter 26
Tucker

RAINDROPS FALL AGAINST THE WINDOW of the plane as we land in Washington. Of all the days, today is not the one I want to see rain. My already somber mood is only getting worse as I stare at the gray sky with no hint of sun.

I yawn and stretch as the plane taxis and rouse Nate who is sleeping next to me. Ryley and Evan flew back to San Diego to get EJ right after the funeral, while we stayed behind for a few more days. Rask, Cara, and River are across the aisle and he, too, is looking outside. Cara has been glued to him since we found him in the woods; of course she did the same thing to me, especially when we had to fly. Cara is good like that—making sure we're getting justice the fair way. Technically, Rask, River, and myself should be handcuffed, but Cara didn't bother with that shit this time.

I have a feeling she's making River testify against Lawson, which isn't a bad idea. I don't care what he does after he spills his guts about his wife. He needs to give us something. He needs to prove that we can trust him again.

Leaving Penny and Claire was not my idea, but hers and

one I had to accept. I could push for a relationship with Claire, but my gut tells me that I'll only damage the foundation. She lost the only father she remembers and if I come in all guns blazing I'll look like a damn fool. Even though it killed me to leave them behind, I did so knowing there's a security detail in place until after Lawson's trial is over.

While we were in Vermont, Cara got word that his trial date was being moved up. She didn't know why, but had a feeling that it had to do with Frannie's death. Without her to testify against him, even though we know she would've never done that, the defense feels like the Feds' case is weak. The only problem with their theory is that they don't know we have River, which again leads me to believe he knows more than he's telling.

The plane comes to a stop and everyone rushes to stand up and push open the overhead storage, then they proceed to stand there and huff while the people in front of them do the same thing. So many people lack plane etiquette.

Nate finally stands and stretches, his head not far from the top of the plane. He leans down and says something to Cara, causing me to turn away. They're sweet to each other and it sends a pang of longing into my heart. Penny and I were once like that and I can only hope we get back there someday. And if not, I suppose I can try to find it with someone else.

Once we're off the plane, a car is waiting to take us back to Evan's. I don't know how long I plan to stay; this rainy weather isn't for me and I miss the beach. Plus, Lawson is in California and that is where I want to be. I plan to keep my eye on that piece of shit and watch every move he makes. And I want him to know I'm there. Being in Washington doesn't afford me the ability to scare the shit out of him.

As soon as we pull into Evan and Ryley's, EJ comes running out. He stops dead in his tracks when he sees River. An expression of confusion takes over his features as he stands there and stares at a ghost. It's about a full minute before he turns and runs back into the house yelling for Ryley.

"Yeah I'd run, too, buddy," I mumble under my breath. I don't care if River can hear me; right now I'm not his friend.

I'm the last one to walk into the house and in time to see Cara direct River to sit down. If I didn't know better I'd say he's under arrest, but he didn't exactly do anything, unless marrying a psycho bitch is a felony.

"Tucker, before you take your stuff downstairs, can you sit please?" Cara asks as she motions to a chair across from River. I choose the one farthest from him for fear that I might develop a nervous tic and beat the shit out of him.

Cara stays standing after Rask, Ryley, Evan, and Nate take seats around the table. It's like she's the teacher and about to school us on some random subject we're being forced to take.

"I know the last thing you guys want to discuss is Frannie, but River has something to say and I think you guys should hear him out," Cara states, standing behind River. I'm not sure how I feel about her solidarity toward him and maybe that's why she's a good agent—she's impartial where I'm quick to judge. I think my judgment is warranted, though, considering his connection to all of this.

River takes a deep breath and finally lifts his head up so he's looking at each of us. Since the shooting, I believe this is the first time he's made eye contact with any of us aside from Evan. I know they're close, but this entire time I've felt like he's hiding something from us. If he tells us that he knew how sick his wife was I'll make sure he's sharing a cell with Lawson.

"I knew something was wrong when we came home. We all did," he starts. "But for each of us it was different. I didn't write her as much as the rest of you wrote home because I didn't have a lot to say. The shit we saw out there—it's not something you tell your newlywed wife. And honestly, after being gone so long, I wasn't sure I was even in love with her. She didn't know I was coming home because I hadn't told her. In fact, after being gone so long, the last letter I sent her told her to find someone else. Six years is a long time to go without moving on and letters do not serve our families justice.

"I know I said this before, about how I thought it was weird that Frannie had my favorite beer in the refrigerator, and my first thought was she never threw it out, but the expiration dates were dates that hadn't even happened yet, which lead me to my second thought—she had started drinking. So I watched her for a few days at lunch or dinner when I'd have one and she wouldn't touch them. I then thought she had done as I asked and moved on and the guy just happened to like my beer. Not uncommon.

"When I got to our house, I knocked, half expecting someone else to answer. When she did, she said, 'Hey, glad you're home' as if I had only been gone a few days and not six years. There were no tears, no slap in the face for me telling her to move on, just a very nonchalant greeting. She was making dinner and there were fresh flowers and the table was set for two. I immediately asked her who she was expecting and she said, 'You'.

"If she knew we were coming home, why didn't she tell the other wives and why didn't she meet us at the airstrip? Those questions immediately started plaguing my mind. While she finished preparing dinner, I went upstairs and started unpacking, and that's when shit got weirder. Clothes hung in my closet that weren't mine and I was okay with that. I had told her to move on, but my clothes were there as well and my shoes had been recently polished. In the bathroom I found a pregnancy test on the counter in broad daylight, and on the wall I found a calendar. The best I could ascertain is that the days she marked with a star were the days her and her boyfriend were together. The sad face was a failed pregnancy test since according to the calendar she had taken one that day and the x's were when her period had arrived.

"I wasn't mad, but overly confused. She welcomed me home, albeit somewhat coldly, kept all my stuff but was trying to get pregnant. She was also eerily quiet, like she'd pop up and scare the shit out of me. I'm a SEAL, I should be able to sense stealth movement, but I just couldn't detect hers.

"That night, I sat at the table and she talked as if I had been home the whole time. Asking how my day was, wanting to know if we wanted to go to Ryley and Evan's for a bar-be-cue this weekend, and wondering if we should have Tucker and Penny over one night for dinner. It's only the next day that I find out what everyone was going through.

"But that night, after dinner, I felt odd. There wasn't anything I could do about it except lie down. I was in and out of consciousness for most of the night, riddled with dreams about Cuba, the fighting, and sex. In the morning I kept having these flashbacks about watching someone having sex and couldn't place them. This happened the first few nights and I had finally had enough so I didn't eat what she cooked because each night I didn't feel right afterwards. I pretended to act the same nonetheless that night only to find out that my wife was having sex in our bed with me next to her."

The collective gasps aren't lost on me. I think at this point I'm so desensitized about Frannie that nothing shocks me these days.

"Oh, River, I'm sorry," Ryley says, reaching for him.

"I'm not because it opened my eyes, I just couldn't tell anyone. The one mistake I made was letting Evan move in. Everything stopped, and I think it's because she couldn't drug you."

"Lucky me," he mutters.

"Yes, lucky you because you weren't subject to spying on

your wife. I asked her over and over again whom she was seeing and the answer was always the same, 'I'm not seeing anyone.' But I knew differently so I'd follow her and she'd end up at different hotels, in the backs of cars, and even in parks. It wasn't bad enough that she was blatantly cheating and lying about it, but she acted as if we were this perfectly happy couple in front of everyone.

"I finally got a good look at the guy, waiting for him to leave the hotel one day, but didn't have a clue who he was. It was only after some Appropriations Committee thing was on CNN did I recognize him as Ted Lawson and that was when I really grew suspicious. Evan had moved in by now, but I couldn't wait. I planted tiny cameras around the house to watch her, to see what she was doing. I had her on tape, putting the cell phone in the bathroom, but Evan got to it first.

"And while you guys were talking to NCIS, I was duping her computer and hacking into Ted Lawson's personal email. Everything about our mission was in there. Everything about how Frannie came into my life, years earlier, was there as well. Lawson's affair with Christina Charlotte was detailed and Frannie's involvement with her murder.

"Aside from the fact that my wife …"

The way he says the word wife is laced with disdain. I don't know how he stomachs using that word to describe her right now.

River clears his throat and starts again. "She was in an incestuous relationship with her brother. They share the same dad, but different mothers. They also have a child together, who is about twelve. She was one of the girls we rescued in Cuba."

River lets out a heavy sigh and shakes his head. "I had no idea she was this fucked up. There were no signs, not that I was looking for any. Mental illness isn't something to mess with and Frannie, whose real name is Donna Ingram, was so caught up in a delusional world that the only way to stop her was to shoot her."

"Explain your house then," Nate demands.

River leans back in his chair and shakes his head. "She knew I was on to her. I refused to sleep with her, or eat her food, and asked her where she was when Ryley and her mom were at the hospital. I knew where she was because I could see her on my phone fucking her brother all over the house.

"The day my house blew up, I had left her a note saying that I knew about her relationship with her brother and I was going to out them, publicly. I didn't know she was responsible for the care packages at that point, and I definitely didn't know Lawson had done anything to Claire. If I had, I would've killed them both.

"Anyway, she left after I confronted her. I held a gun to her head and had fucking tears in my eyes because even after everything I had found out, at one point in my life, I loved her. I was stupid and let her talk me down only to have her run out the back door. I chased her, but lost her. There was a car waiting for her down the street."

"That's not what you told us," Evan says angrily. "In fact, you told us that she left you because you had been apart for so long."

River nods. "I know. I wasn't sure what you knew, but I had a feeling. I knew you'd want her, but I wanted her dead. I wanted to see the life leave her eyes for what she had done to us. It was my job to protect you." He looks at Rask, Evan, and finally me. "I let you down. I bought the evil into our lives and I needed to be the one to extinguish it. That day you guys came over I was at my lowest. I wanted to end my life after you detailed everything you knew. All I could think about was the pain everyone went through because of me.

"I had rigged my house earlier, hoping to end both our lives. I couldn't live with the idea that I failed my team and I couldn't let her continue to live, but my weaknesses got the best of me and instead of blowing up the house with her and I in it, she had escaped. The day you came over, I had a gun sitting on the table and you didn't even notice. I was going to end my life because I had failed you."

"You failed yourself," I say, harshly.

He shakes his head and wipes away the tears on his face. "I had no idea where Penny was, McCoy, or I would've told you." He looks from me back to Evan and Nate. "After you left, I had no choice. I had to hunt her down and prevent her from hurting anyone else. The moment you walked out, I got up and walked out my backdoor, tripping the line to set off the bomb."

"Where'd you go," Ryley asked.

"Back to the hotels where Frannie had met her brother. Every few days I'd have an idea of where she was, but she knew I was after her so she moved around a lot. I hacked Cara's phone and found out where you were looking."

"How'd you know she was in Penny's house?" Nate asks.

"I followed these four SEALs I know and they led me right to her."

chapter 27
Tucker

"I know you said you needed space, but I can't not talk to you now that I know you're alive," I tell Penny who is silent on the other end of the line. "I hate this. I hate that we're not together. I hate that you've lost Ray. I have never been so confused in my life. Loving you has been the easiest thing I've ever done, but not having you in my life is the hardest."

"I know, I wish things were different for us."

Does she? Can I ask her without her closing up and refusing to talk or do I change the subject? There isn't a book on how to win your wife back after she's been married to someone else for so long because she thought you were dead. I need a fucking instruction booklet of things I'm allowed to say, ask, and think when I'm talking to her because the last thing I want to do is upset her.

"I'm sorry, Penny. I never meant for any of this to happen."

"I know you didn't, Tucker." Her voice is soft and there's a hint of tiredness. Glancing at my watch I see it's almost eleven for her and should probably let her go, but this is the first time she's answered since I left her in Vermont.

"I think you're a brave woman. I should've told you that when I saw you, but my words were jumbled and everything was happening so fast. I can't fathom being in your situation, thinking I'm gone and having to deal with Lawson. I'm going to kill him when I see him, Penelope."

"Please don't."

Her simple statement takes me back. In fact, I'm confused. Why wouldn't she want this piece of shit dead?

"Why not?" I brace myself for her reasoning.

"Because you'll go to jail and I can't have that."

My heart starts to beat faster, giving me hope that someday her and I will be together again; that we'll be a family and living the life we thought we would. So much of me wants to dissect her statement and ask her what she means, but I don't want to force her into anything she's not ready for.

"I'm going back to California tomorrow," I say instead, changing the subject. "As much as I love Evan and Ryley, living here isn't my home. Not that a place in Cali will be either, but it's what I know. I also have a hearing next week in front of a JAG judge to get my life back. Carole, Ryley's mom, has been working her tail off for Rask and I."

"What are you going to do?"

"About what?" I ask in regards to her open-ended question.

"About being a SEAL?"

"I don't know. I think I'm going to take a leave of absence and get my head straight. Maybe take up surfing or something like that. Being in the Navy is all I know."

"Oh the women will love seeing you on a surfboard," she says, laughing. Her comment strikes me as odd, but it's her laughter that keeps me focused.

"There's only one woman I care about, Penny, and that's you."

She shuffles the phone, or drops it. I can't be sure. I hear her move around and finally hear a door shut.

"Tucker, I have so much to say and probably should've done it when you were here, but words, even now, escape me. I'm torn up. I'm confused. I feel like I've cheated on you and that makes me feel so dirty. When Chloe goes to school—"

I close my eyes when she refers to our daughter as Chloe. I know Ray didn't give her that name, but for some reason the jealousy inside of me makes it seem like he did.

"Can we call her Claire, please?"

"She wants to be called Chloe. I'm respecting her wishes and you should, too. I know what her birth names means to you, but this is all she's known."

Penny is right, even though I can't see past the red. My grandmother raised me after my mom overdosed. My mother never told my grandma who my father was so she stepped in. Her name was Claire McCoy and from the minute Penny and I found out we were having a girl, I wanted to call her Claire. If it weren't for my grandmother, I probably would've been into drugs like my mother. I should ask Penny about my grandmother, but I already know the answer. I make a mental note to see if what I was told about my grandma dying is true or not.

"I understand," I tell her reluctantly. "I just ... I don't know her and can only remember her from when she was a baby."

"I know, but she needs time just as I do. To say our lives are upside down and inside out right now would be the colossal understatement of the universe. Anyway, as I was saying, when Chloe goes to school, I sit in my shower and scrub my skin until it's raw. I can't get clean and I don't know how to make those feelings go away."

The image of her ripping her skin apart kills me. Sadly, I don't know how to make those feelings go away either because my thoughts are just as dark. Half the time when I'm alone I set my pistol out and wonder if things would be easier if I ended my life. But Penny and Claire flash before my eyes. It's their smiles that give me hope to look past the shit storm my life as become.

I can hear Penny breathing on the other end and the thought of having her here with me, lying next to me goes right to my groin. It's going to be a long time, if ever, before I'll feel her like that again.

"I miss you," I say, biting the proverbial bullet. I know she could hang up on me or tell me not to call her again. She could change her number tomorrow and I'd be shit out of luck because I wouldn't be able to reach her, but I don't care. She needs to know and remember that she's my wife, regardless if she feels like she's still married to Ray.

"Tucker—" she says breathlessly.

"No, Penny, I get it, but you have to know. I haven't lived the past six years thinking you were dead or knowing that you thought I was. I came home to you and Claire with roses in my hand only to be greeted by a stranger. None of the stories I was told about you added up. Ryley said you were gone before my funeral, Frannie said after. I didn't know what to believe, but I refused to believe that you left me.

"I spent day and night thinking about you and our daughter when I was away, and the pictures I received were the only thing to keep me going ..." My thoughts trail off. If Frannie had to follow us to find Penny, how the fuck did she have pictures of Claire?

"Tucker?"

"Yeah, babe, I'm here. Sorry, I just had a thought."

"About what?"

There is no way in hell I'm telling her this so I make something up. "About you and I, on the back of my motorcycle. You know it was my bike which led me to you."

"I know, Buzz emailed me."

"He helped you?"

By the noise against the phone I'm guessing she's nodding. "He did. I knew I was leaving, but didn't know where to go, and I had to pay for the storage unit because I didn't want to lose what I had left of you. He knew I was distraught and for some reason I spilled everything to him. He gave me a name of a guy in downtown San Diego who gave us a new identity and set us on the bus. I never asked him to do anything, but he knew to alert me that the Feds had shown up."

"I'd like to thank him," I say, before adding, "I hired a private investigator, three in fact, but only the last one proved to be worth the money. Her name is Marley and she helped Cara and I track you down. Do you know how many Amy Jones there are that use that particular bank?"

"I do, that's why I used it."

"Clever girl."

She laughs again, but this time adds a yawn.

"I'm going to let you go, but I'm calling again, unless you don't want to talk to me."

"No, I do. It feels good."

"Yes it does," I agree with her easily. "I love you, Penelope."

I don't give her a chance to reply before hanging up. It's for my own sake and not hers. I don't want her to say it because she feels that I need to hear it, and I don't want to hear the pause because she doesn't mean it. All in due time.

As soon as I set my phone down, my name is being called from upstairs. It's like living with parents here. I'm reminded to eat, make sure my laundry is in the laundry room, take off my shoes, and hang up my towel. I feel sorry for Ryley, having to put up with Evan and EJ, plus myself on top of them. The woman needs a damn medal of honor.

When I reach the bottom of the stairs I hear an unfamiliar voice having a conversation with Evan, which sends chills down my spine. I rush back to my room and grab my gun, sliding it into the waistband of my pants. I walk up the stairs slowly, hoping to surprise whoever is in the house. They already know I'm here, but don't know where.

I follow the voices down the hall and into Ryley and Evan's formal living room. This room is a shrine to Evan, Nate, and Archie with all their medals and a large USN anchor hang right above their fireplace. The same windows that face the ocean from the family room extend into here, giving this room another magnificent view.

"McCoy, just in time," Archer says as he stands from the chair he's sitting in. "I'm sure you remember our ever faithful Brigadier General."

I walk around the backside of the black leather couch to see Chesley sitting there, eyeing Archer and then me. I feel my mouth drop open before shutting it, and turn my gaze into a glare.

"You'll excuse me if I don't salute you."

"Understandable," he says, nodding at me.

"Chesley here would like to tell us a story."

"Is that so?" I sit down in the other chair, facing the couch. Archer follows suit, but doesn't give Chesley a chance to speak. "Where's Rask?"

"Went back to Cali with Nate this morning."

Fucker didn't even say good-bye.

"What the fuck are you doing across the Sound?" Evan asks, leaning forward.

"Watching you," Chesley replies immediately. "And it's not what you think. I've had troops in and around the area since you moved in, protecting you and your family. The day Tucker arrived, it made my job easier, and when Rask showed up things couldn't have gotten better for me."

"Except?" I ask.

"Except you all left and I couldn't do my job."

"Which is what, exactly? I'm having a little trouble understanding the word 'protect'," Evan remarks.

"I understand and maybe I should start from the beginning. When I found out my daughter-in-law was having an affair with Senator Lawson, as you can imagine I was livid, especially for my son. But when he called to tell me that Abigail had been kidnapped I did what any grandfather would do, I called in favors."

"You danced with the devil," I add.

Chesley nods. "I did, but didn't know it at the time. I had no idea Ingram was Lawson's father. None of us knew he had any children."

"Why our unit?" Evans asks the question that has been plaguing us for so long.

"Because I needed the best. I wanted Abigail in the best possible hands and returned quickly. I didn't know what Lawson had done to her until she came home and she told my son everything. As soon as we had her back, I went to thank you, only to hear that you had died."

"You waited four months to thank us?" I know I sound incredulous, but who the fuck waits for four months?

"No, I tried to thank you as soon as Abigail returned home."

"Cut the bullshit, Chesley. We had the girl in three days or some shit like that. This was a snatch and grab mission. We did our jobs and should've been home for Sunday dinner." Evan is pissed off and rightly so. All Chesley is doing is feeding us a line of bullshit.

"You may have saved her, but she didn't come back right away. The day after my son called to tell me she was finally home was the day I paid a visit to Ingram. I expected to find you guys being debriefed, but he informed me you had perished and that he was working on bringing your bodies home.

"I attended each of your funerals and prayed that you guys were at peace."

"We weren't," I tell him.

"And neither was I."

"Do you expect us to feel sorry for you?" Evan questions.

"No, but I'd like for you to hear me out."

We both nod and that seems to relax Chesley a little bit. "My son started divorce proceedings as soon as Abigail came back, but Christina wouldn't cooperate. She lied through her depositions to protect Lawson all because she didn't want the Vice Presidential nomination to be revoked. That was more important than her daughter. Without her testimony, we couldn't tie anything to Lawson, and Abigail's testimony wasn't enough. To make matters worse, the men who saved her were dead.

"Fast forward to your return. The minute I found out, I was in Ingram's office being threatened. It was at that point I knew something was up so I played along, figuring you'd come to me for help, but I couldn't get word out to you. Weeks before you arrived, Christina was in a car accident on her way to see Lawson."

I glance quickly at Evan and wonder if he's thinking the same thing. We know Frannie murdered Christina, and I'm willing to bet it's because she was in the way and not because she was going to testify against Lawson as we've been told.

"Why didn't you come forward?" Evan asks, his voice somber.

"And say what? That I believed Ingram was behind four of the Navy's finest being dead for six years all because his son was running a sex ring operation with minors? The case we tried to bring against him had already been thrown out. The courts do not like a desperate man. There wasn't anything I could do except turn over what I knew to the justice department and wait. I knew in order to stay alive I had to keep my mouth shut and keep Abigail protected. With Christina dead, there wasn't a soul, aside from her, to testify against him."

"Except Frannie," I add.

"And your wife," Chesley says. He sits up straighter and keeps his hands clasped in his lap. "I went to see you and your wife when you came back, but found out that she had left, without a trace, and that's when I started putting everything into place. I love a great novel with a conspiracy theory, but this was too much for me. The pieces weren't adding up until Ingram and Lawson were arrested. I obtained a copy of the affidavit and was shocked to see that I hadn't a clue what was going on. Everything I thought I knew was in there, plus some."

"So back to your bullshit claim that you're protecting us?" Evan jumps to the point of why Chesley says he's here.

"Lawson has hits out on all of you."

"How do you know this?" I ask, more eager to hear what he has to say.

"Because my son is in the same prison as he is right now, posing as an inmate and informant for the Feds. Lawson has a big mouth and likes to talk. He has friends in there because he has money and someone is making sure he's protected. The guards know about my son and they make sure he's within earshot at all times, even sleeping in the next cell over."

Evan and I both scoff. "Doesn't Lawson know who your son is, or what he looks like?"

"When you've been through what my son has, you age quickly. He doesn't look the same; his eyes are sunken in and his hair is gray."

"And you're saying Lawson is trying to kill us?" I ask, needing more information.

"Yes, he is, which is why I transferred to the shipyard."

"I don't buy it," Evan says as he stands and looks out the window.

"Remember that night you were toying with the fishing boat and they scrambled away?"

"Yep, figured you were peddling drugs and I didn't want that shit near my kid."

"They were coming to your home to kill you. You scared them away, but not too far because we caught up with them."

Chesley lets his words sit heavily in the room. I don't know if there's anything to say or do right now. Evan thought something was going on, but definitely not this.

"I don't know if I trust you," Evan states, still staring out the window.

"That's fine." Chesley stands. "I came to say my peace and thank you for saving Abigail. And until Lawson and Ingram are dead, and I'm still breathing, I'll be doing what I can to protect your family."

Chesley leaves and I'm tempted to follow him out, but am frozen in place. I don't know if our lives will ever be fucking normal, and at this point I'm thinking they never will be. Not as long as those two assholes are alive.

"What are we going to do?" Evans asks as he turns to face me.

I shrug. "I don't know about you, but I think a visit to Lawson is in order."

"What kind of visit?"

"The kind that puts a bullet between his eyes. Lucky for us, you have the rifle and scope, and I have the talent needed to get the job done."

chapter 28
Tucker

CARA DRIVES THE BLACK ESCALADE with the six of us in it down the highway to the penitentiary where Lawson is being held. I never expected for Chesley to ask to come along, but he did and is riding shotgun next to Cara. It's probably best that he stays up front. I'd hate to turn around in my seat and find him in a headlock courtesy of Archer.

I've been back in Coronado for two months now, living the single life of being attached to my phone at all times. If weren't for Evan, I would've gone back to Vermont and tortured myself, and likely lose Penny and Claire entirely. He persuaded me, recalling how he had to deal with Nate and Ryley as examples, and said leaving Penny was the best thing for us. He's been right.

Penny and I talk every other night. At first, I was the one doing the calling, but she'd surprise me every now and again. The best shock was when I answered one afternoon and Claire was on the other end. When I heard her voice, I lost it. It took me minutes to gain my composure, but now she calls every day after school and we talk about non-trivial things like the weather, how I'd like to see her use a bow, and what California is like. I know how Evan feels as he eagerly awaits EJ to call him dad. I had it once before and am praying I get it again someday.

One of the hardest parts for me is wondering what Claire thinks of me. She knows I'm her biological father and can't cook, but for all I know she sees me as the man who showed up one day and ruined her life. I liken myself to being a fucking tornado—I came in and destroyed everything, only to leave devastation in my path. I want to ask Penny, but I'm afraid of the answer.

The other monumental challenge in my life is finding out that my grandmother is alive and well, living in Florida, thanks to Marley and her detective ways. Grandma was easy to track down and I knew hours after I asked Marley to find her. Once my grandmother received word that I had died, she sold her home and moved, saying it was too hard to be in California without me. Since then, I know she's gone to visit Penny and Claire, making sure they both know they were never far from her thoughts.

One of the highlights after returning to California was the hearing Rask and I had about our identities. After meeting with a judge, he returned our status to living and all our assets were unfrozen. He also made sure we still had full military status and encouraged us to file a lawsuit against the Navy. The judge even went on record saying that he'd testify upon our behalf. Before he slammed the gavel down, he apologized and promised that not everyone is as corrupt as our admiral. I'm slowly starting to believe that.

Once Cara turned everything over to the Department of Justice, they moved in swiftly to detain Ingram. This time the evidence was too much to let him walk away. Surprisingly, Chesley wasn't lying when he said he'd do what he could to bring him down.

When we pull up to the gate, Cara flashes her credentials

and fills out the necessary paperwork. The guard radios ahead and tells us to follow the road until we meet up with another guard. He doesn't get out and check our vehicle for weapons, which is a shame. I laugh when we pull away.

"No car search? How'd you pull that off?"

"I don't know," Cara answers as she drives forward. "Someone must really like us."

"Or they want him dead, too," Chesley mutters as he gazes out the window.

I don't plan to shoot Lawson, but only scare the shit out of him once we're done with our meeting, although the option is there if I want it. I've never been so callous about someone's life like I am with his. He doesn't deserve to live.

The next guard flags us down and shows us where to park. The six of us climb out of the SUV and wait to be frisked. When that doesn't happen we all look at each other. I know for a fact that beside myself, Archer is carrying. I don't know about Rask, but I'm gathering by the smirk on his face he is. River, however, is stoic and hard to read. I wouldn't put it past him to be the one to take Lawson out.

The guard takes us through a series of doors, away from the general populated areas. Each time the door locks in place behind us, I jump. We're at the mercy of the guard and I hate feeling like I have no control over the situation.

We're taken into a private room and told to sit. The hard metal chairs do nothing to calm my nerves as my stomach rolls and the anger builds.

"I should just shoot the motherfucker," I blurt out. "Or slice his throat open." I feel for the knife that is sheathed in my boot.

"I'll do it," River says coldly. We each have our own hatred for Lawson, but River's runs deeper than the rest of ours does. Not only does River feel like he's failed us, he was deceived by his wife for so long that he feels responsible for her actions.

"No one is killing anyone today," Cara reminds us with a stern look.

The door opens and Lawson walks in with his hands in cuffs and his legs in shackles. I can't help but snicker, causing the rest of the guys to do so as well.

"I'm not saying anything, so don't ask," the pompous little fuck says as he sits down. Before I can blink his head is bouncing off the table and back up again, while blood trickles out of his nose.

I look at the guard who has Lawson by the hair. "You'll answer every fucking question or you will become Bubba's bitch tonight. You know he's been asking about you since he found out you like little girls. Says he wants to show you what it's like to be raped. Bubba wants to hear you beg for your mommy."

I have second thoughts about killing Lawson for fear I'd end up on the wrong side of being Bubba's bitch.

"You gonna play nice, Teddy boy?"

"Yup," he says, looking away from everyone.

"That's what I thought. Ask your questions, boys, Teddy has to go outside in a little bit." It's then that I realize why our car wasn't searched—someone wants him dead and they're hoping one of us do it. The guard shouldn't be telling us his whereabouts, but he did and by the look on his face, he's serious.

"The first thing we're going to say to you is this: next week at your trial—if you make it that long—you're going to plead guilty and save the tax payers a lot of money," Cara says, starting things off for us.

He shakes his head. "I'm going to walk."

"How do you figure?" I ask, leaning forward. There's no judge in his or her right mind that would let this scum walk, not with the evidence stacked against him.

"Donna. She's going to testify for me. She won't corroborate anything you guys say. Plus, there's my father.

Do you think he'll testify against me? Besides, the one person left to pin any charges on me is dead now."

The room grows silent as we take in what he's saying. He doesn't have a clue that Frannie is dead. It's Evan who starts laughing first, followed by the rest of us. I place my hand on Evan, letting him know I need to talk.

"Who's dead now?"

"Your wife. I'm sorry you didn't get to say good-bye." He bats his eyelashes as if he means well. I take deep breath and pretend like I'm torn up on the inside. I'm not because I spoke with Penny yesterday and I know she's alive. "I do plan to have some fun with that delectable daughter of yours though."

Before anyone can stop me, my knife is out and digging into his neck. The guard is being ever so helpful by holding his head still for me. A small path of blood starts to drip as he swallows, increasing his heart rate.

"Do you feel that, Lawson? Your pulse is quickening and you're fucking scared." I drag my knife ever so slowly, watching more blood rise to the surface. I pause at his pulse point and see nothing but fear in his eyes. "One move and you're done. You'll bleed out before anyone can come in here and save you. Say one more thing about my daughter and I'll end your life. Do you understand me?" He's afraid to move so he blinks twice, and it takes me a beat or two before I sit back down, leaving my knife on the table so he can see his blood on the blade.

"If you mean Frannie, she's dead," River says as what little color was left in Lawson's face drains away. "I shot her months ago. So really, you're going to walk into court and plead guilty because if I have to get up on the stand and recount everything I know, I'm going to be pissed. But if Penelope McCoy has to get up on that stand and look at your smug ass sitting in the chair, the only way you're leaving the court house is in a body bag. If you think I'm joking, try me."

The guard uses this opportunity to lean down and say, "Wow, I think you've made some really good friends here. They're willing to put you out of your misery."

Lawson rolls his eyes, but otherwise doesn't say anything.

"Why?" River asks. He doesn't elaborate and there isn't really a need to. The question is self-explanatory.

Lawson shrugs. "Donna and I were alone a lot as kids and I started experimenting on her. At first, she was scared and wouldn't come to our dad's a lot or she'd hang out with my mom, even though my mom hated her. My dad had an affair that resulted in Donna so my mom didn't want her around. Anyway, when she hit puberty I guess she got horny and wanted to know what shit felt like so I showed her."

"But you didn't stop there?" Rask states.

"Nope, couldn't. My dad even tried with therapy and it'd work for a bit, but when I went into the Senate all the young interns we're eager to please me. The best ones were the shy and timid ones who wore those short skirts, but still had their cherries. I remember each one I popped."

His head goes flying into the table again, this time much harder. When he's able to lift up, his eyes are dazed.

"Why the cover-up? Why tell everyone we were dead?" Evan asks.

"Because you couldn't just do the job you were sent to do, you had to go and kill my friend and open the hive. All my hard work, lost." He looks off toward the window, likely remembering his victims, although to him they're not victims, but conquests.

"You're one sick mother fucker, you know that?" I say.

He shrugs. "There's no cure for what I have."

"Yes there is, it's called death. The world would be a better place if you weren't in it."

Lawson laughs. "I don't know why you're all so bitter; you got your lives back."

"Our lives and the lives of our families were destroyed.

And since we've been back we've been battling a barrage of shit that you created because you were afraid of getting caught. Did you really think this was all going to go away and that we'd never work to bring you to justice?" Rask questions, but Lawson doesn't answer. He doesn't even look at Rask when he's speaking.

"No, he seriously thought he'd get away with it," River adds much to my agreement.

"Oh and, McCoy, do you ever lie awake at night, wondering how my lovely Donna had photos of your sweet Claire?"

I do every night and am afraid of the answer. I fear that if Lawson tells me, and I tell Penny, it'll shatter her world. I can't do that. Instead, I smugly shake my head and don't give him the satisfaction of needing to know. Some things are better left untold.

"Times up," the guard says, ending our conversation. I don't know if I feel relieved or not, but I do have some perverse satisfaction in knowing that he's bleeding because of me.

Lawson is forced to stand and takes one last look at us. "Is Donna really dead?"

"Yes," we say in unison.

"Shame, I'm going to miss her."

As soon as the door closes, Cara says, "That man is seriously fucked up. If he doesn't plead guilty, he's going to plead insanity and get off."

"That won't happen," River remarks.

"You can't kill him." Cara directs her statement at all of us.

"Watch me." River slams his hands down on the table and stands, pushing his chair out so hard it falls to the ground. Evan and Rask stand as well, while I stare down at my knife. The blood is almost dry and while I'm tempted to save it and make a voodoo doll out of it, I decide not to and wipe his blood on the bottom of my boot.

"The trial starts next week," Cara says, reminding me that I'll see Penny. That gives me only a few days to get the house I bought in order, in hopes she'll stay.

chapter 29
Penny

I KNEW IT WAS ONLY a matter of time before I'd be back in California after everything that happened. I didn't, however, expect it to be so I could testify. But this is where I feel at home, and not like a stranger trying to fit it. From the very moment the sun touched my face, I was leaning my head back and soaking it all in.

Only Claire doesn't understand. She will, though, once she sees the beach and touches the sand with her bare feet. She'll fall in love with the always-blue sky and warm ocean water. I hope that by week's end she'll be trying to convince us to move. Fortunately for her, she won't have to twist my arm too much.

The only question that remains is where will we live. Living in California isn't cheap and it's not like there's a general store down the road for me to work at. I'd have to get a job, which would be hard considering I'm not qualified for anything.

Or there's Tucker's. I know he bought a house, but he hasn't said much about it, other than it's close to base. He still hasn't decided if he's going to retire or stay enlisted. And even though he's asked my opinion, I haven't given it to him. I know what happened to us will never happen again, but he could die in battle. Not that I'd expect them to actually deploy him. Not that my opinion matters. Part of me wants him to stay in because it's all he knows. It's been his purpose in life long before I came into the picture. I'd hate for him to give that up.

"It's hot here," Claire whines, tugging at her sweater. In my head, I can't call her Chloe no matter how hard I try. It's like when Frannie died, something was lifted off of me and I was given a small taste of freedom. I didn't have to hide anymore. But I still look around every corner and watched every person who crosses in front of my path; it's ingrained in me and I don't think I'll ever stop.

"I think you'll love it," I tell her as I pull her through the parking lot of the car rental place. Tucker wanted to pick us up, but I wanted a car. There are things I need to do while here and I don't want to depend on him. Besides, if I need to escape, I want the ability to do so. Or go to the mall. It's been so long since I've been to a mall. When I decide to start shopping I don't want any sideways glances at the amount of stuff I have. No one knows what it's like to go from having massive malls at your disposal to not having one at all.

It only takes a few minutes before I get my bearings straight. Sitting at the first red light, I close my eyes and listen to the traffic whizzing by. Most people move to get away from this type of stuff, and here I am relishing in being back.

"You're being weird."

"I know. I can't help it," I tell her. "I've missed the sun and noise."

"I like the quiet."

I won't argue with her, not today. I can't force this on her. It has to be something she wants. I made that promise to her.

Before I know it, I'm pulling into the storage unit parking

lot and shutting off my car. The last time I was here, I was running for my life to protect my baby. Now I'm back and refuse to let Lawson keep me scared.

"Come on," I say to Claire as I get out of the car. She's right, it is hot, but it feels so good. As soon her door slams, I'm reaching out for her hand. She rolls her eyes, but slips her hand into mine. I don't know if I'll ever tell her about Lawson, but I have told her that I almost lost her once and that'll never happen again.

The chime above the door rings out and Buzz pops his head up. By the look on his face, I'd say he's surprised to see me.

"Hello, Buzz."

"Mrs. McCoy, I didn't expect to see you come in … ever."

I don't correct him on the usage of my last name and technically he's right. Tucker's return nullified my marriage to Ray, not that it was probably legal to begin with since I was using a fake name.

"It's good to see you, Buzz. I wanted to thank you for making sure the agents were given my name."

"I didn't cause any trouble for you, did I?"

I shake my head and offer him a smile. "None whatsoever." I leave out the part where Ray died and Frannie attacked us. He doesn't need to know any of that. I wouldn't want him to feel guilty for trying to help me.

"I have to say, you're looking much better this time around."

Smiling bashfully, I accept his compliment.

"And I see she's all grown up."

I squeeze Claire's hand, but refrain from introducing her. Some things are left unsaid and this is one of them.

"I just wanted to thank you in person."

"You're welcome," he says as I turn and leave.

Back in the car I pull up the directions Tucker sent me, plug them into my GPS, and head off in the right direction.

While I remember most places, going someplace new could be a challenge. It's only a matter of minutes before I'm crossing the bridge into Coronado.

"We're up so high. Oh, Mom, look at those planes."

I try to look but am afraid I'll swerve off the bridge. The first night I met Tucker he showed me the planes and told me he's the guy who protects me while I'm sleeping. I still believe that about him.

"They're all over the place around here."

"And that boat."

"It's a ship, honey. Tucker can take you on one if you want to go."

Claire presses her face to the glass and sighs. "Do you love him?"

"Yes, I do," I tell her truthfully. I never stopped loving him. "But I also love Ray just as much."

"But he's gone and Tucker's not."

"No, Tucker isn't and he's not going anywhere. I think if you give him a chance, you might like him."

"We'll see," she says, sighing again. I can't force her, but I may push her a little. Tucker and her could have a few daddy and daughter days while we're here.

As soon as I'm off the bridge and into downtown, everything is coming back to me. I loved living here. The town is cute, quaint, and very friendly. Not to mention the eye candy that's always walking around. Even when Tucker and I were together, I'd often comment, especially with Ryley, about the very good looking men. Tucker would act hurt, but he knew I only had eyes for him.

My GPS tells me I've reached my destination when I pull up in front of a cute yellow bungalow. Claire is out of the car as soon as I shut it off and walking through the white picket fence gate before I can even verify the address or get out of the car. For someone who is hell bent on not welcoming Tucker, she sure is eager to see his house.

I quickly follow her up the stone path and onto the pergola covered porch. It only takes seconds for me to see myself out here tomorrow morning sipping on iced tea. Tucker didn't buy this house for himself; he bought it with Claire and I in mind. He knew I'd love the porch.

Claire knocks and stands at the door with her foot tapping. I want to tell her knock it off, but it's sort of cute. I don't know if she's thinking the same thing I am, but I figured he would've been waiting at the door for us as soon as we pulled up.

The door swings open and a freshly showered Tucker is standing there with just his shorts on. His chest is wet from his dripping hair and I find myself swallowing hard as I gawk at him. It's been far too long since I've been able to see his perfect, for me, body in the flesh.

"You're early, you said five."

I pull out my phone and look, noting that he's right. "We can leave."

"Don't be silly. Let me get your bags."

He walks by us and toward my rental car to retrieve our stuff. When he first suggested we stay with him I didn't want to. I thought it'd be awkward and uncomfortable, but he insisted, saying he'd sleep on the couch. And now that I'm standing here, I'm sort of pissed he didn't pull me into his arms and give me a sweet welcome.

He comes back with his arms full, so the thought of a hug still isn't possible. He pauses long enough to give me a smile that makes me weak in my knees and winks at me.

"Come this way, ladies," he says, motioning with his head.

I walk in after Claire and take in the beauty of this home. This is exactly the type of home we talked about owning one day when he was retired. The living room is lit by natural light through multiple skylights and a large ceiling fan circulates the air. The kitchen is off to right as you walk in, and is white with light blue accents, giving it an ocean feel.

"This way to your rooms."

We follow Tucker down the hall, stopping behind him when nods to the right. "This is the bathroom," he says and both of us look inside. It's a soft yellow and very feminine with a window facing the side yard.

"This is your room," he says, glancing at Claire. A while back I told him she wanted to be called Chloe, but he refused and I know why. I was hoping that after his grandmother visited us, she'd change her mind, but she hasn't said anything. I don't blame her really since all her friends know her as Chloe.

The both of us step inside and I hear a slight intake of air. Her room is decorated in pink, her favorite color. There are mounds of pillows piled high on top of her bed, but it's the bear that grabs my attention.

"Where did you find that?" I ask him.

"It was in the storage unit."

"I always wondered where I lost it."

Chloe walks over and picks it up. Her fingers rub over his eyes, ears, nose, and mouth before she sits down on her bed and stares at him. I can't help but wonder if she's remembering him or if she just knows it was her toy.

Tucker sets her suitcase down, but doesn't say anything as he leaves the room. I want to stay and watch Claire with her toy, but know I should follow him.

When I step into the room, it looks like ours, except it's different. I was in the process of updating our bedroom before he deployed and had shown him a comforter I liked. It was white with an array of purple flowers. The one on the bed now is purple with white flowers cascading over half the material. I know he did this for me because no man would want to sleep in this, unless he has a girlfriend. The thought of him being with someone else hurts and makes my stomach turn. I know I have no right to ask, but I have to know.

I catch him taking a picture off the dresser and sliding it into the drawer.

"What's that?" I ask.

"It's nothing, just a photo."

"Of your girlfriend?"

Tucker turns around and I can see that I'm wrong. His face is pinched and his cheeks are red. He reaches blindly for the frame and shows it to me. It's our wedding photo. I'm dressed in a flowery summer dress and he's in his dress whites.

"I'm sorry. I thought—"

He doesn't let me finish my sentence before he's standing before me. My heart is thundering in my chest, the sound clearly audible in the room. The moment his lips touch mine, I'm a heap of nothing as he takes me in his arms to hold me up. This is unlike the kiss we shared a while back; this one is full of passion and heat. My toes curl when his tongue traces the outline of my lower lip and when I sigh he uses it to his advantage by letting me taste him. With his hand on my back and the other pressed against the nape of my neck, Tucker kisses me with abandon. Our lips move together, in sync and with rhythm, making up for all the time lost during the past seven years. That's how long it's been since this man kissed me like he owns me.

And he does, heart and soul.

"Don't be nervous," Tucker says as he hands me a cup of coffee. I can't stop the jitters and my legs bounce up and down. I'm nervous and slightly freaked about seeing Lawson in court today. On the way over here, the guys mentioned something about telling him to plead guilty, but they don't know what he's going to do. River assures me that I will not be getting on the stand if he can help it.

Claire is spending the day with Ryley, EJ, and her parents at their house on the lake. Tucker bought her a bow and arrow and suggested she take it over there. When we arrived to drop her off, her mouth dropped open when she saw targets spread around for her to use.

I wanted her to be comfortable while I was away and Tucker promised that Carole and Jensen would take great care of her. Having Ryley at the house helps, though, because she knows Claire.

This was also the first time I got to meet her son. He just had his birthday and is a spitting image of Evan, except for his hair. That is all Ryley. Claire took an immediate liking to EJ and didn't even care when I left.

A group of reporters come into view and I quickly realize that they are surrounding Lawson. We make eye contact and I freeze. His little finger wave causes my stomach to roll and then he's out of sight because River is standing in front of me.

"I think I'm going to be sick." I stand up and cover my mouth. Tucker is right behind me, guiding me to the ladies room. If I expected him to wait outside, I'd be foolish. He follows me in and holds my hair back as I release the contents of my stomach into the bowl. I stand and start to cry, collapsing into his arms. He kisses my forehead and tries to soothe me, but it's to avail.

"I can't do this," I tell him as I weep into his shoulder. "I can't go in there and look at him, knowing what he did to our baby."

"You won't have to. I promise."

Tucker holds me for a moment longer before he takes me to the basin to rinse my mouth out and fix my make-up. When I feel somewhat presentable, he takes my hand and guides me out of the restroom and back to our friends.

"It's time to go in," Nate says, leading the way. He waves at Cara, who is seated up front. We choose to sit in the back, with River, Evan, Nate, and Rask sitting in front of us, blocking our view. I don't want to see Lawson and I definitely don't want him to see me.

When the judge enters, I refuse to stand up. I'm small enough that the bailiff will never notice anyway.

"Be seated," the judge says and I hear the faint sound of papers being shuffled. "It seems we have something to discuss, Mr. Reyes."

"That's Lawson's attorney," Tucker whispers in my ear.

"Yes, your honor. My client has decided to change his plea."

There's a collective gasp from the galley and my heart soars. The only thing I want to hear is for him to say he's guilty. If he pleads insanity, I still have to testify.

"So be it, please rise and enter your plea."

The chair grinds against the linoleum floor as he moves it back to stand. I can barely see them through the gap of shoulders of Nate and Evan.

"What's your plea for the charges against you?"

"I wish to enter a plea of guilty."

The gasp is much louder this time and Tucker squeezes my hand. I lean into him and sigh. 'Thank you,' I mouth to him, but he points at River.

"Sentencing will be tomorrow at nine a.m. where you will hear from your victims." The gavel slams down and when the bailiff says 'all rise' Tucker pulls me out of the courtroom and into this arms. He swings me around like we're two young kids in love.

It's only a matter of moments before the rest of the guys join us, and once my feet are firmly planted on the ground, I slip out of Tucker's hold and into River's arms.

"Thank you, for whatever you did."

He doesn't really hug me back, but I hear a sniffle and know he's grateful that I'm thanking him. I don't know if the guys are treating him the same, but after what he's done for me, I'll never be able to thank him enough. I know, deep in my heart, that if he knew what was going on, he would've never brought Frannie into our lives.

"We should go celebrate," Cara exclaims as she comes out of the courtroom.

"Jensen will be more than happy to fire up the grill and we have to go there anyway," Evan says as he volunteers his future father-in-law for cooking duty.

Tucker pulls me to him and whispers in my ear, "Is that what you want to do?"

I nod. "It'll feel good to be with friends again. It's been a long time."

"The McCoys are in," he says proudly, and I don't dare correct him.

"I'm out," River states. "I have some business to take care of." He doesn't say good-bye, but walks briskly down the corridor and out of sight.

"What's that about?" Nate asks.

Rask shakes his head. "He still feels like he's let us down."

"He'll come around," Cara adds. "Come on, let's go."

The group of us walks out of the courthouse and down the steps. Tucker stops, pulling me to him.

He places his hands on my cheeks and my hands instantly hang on to his arms. I shouldn't have the feelings that I do—the longing, the desire, and most importantly the butterflies when he touches me—but I do.

"You know the picture of us that's in my room?"

I nod, biting my lip in anticipation.

"We took that here, in this spot."

I look around and see that he's right, or almost right.

"I know you've only been here for a day, Penelope, but having you here feels like home. I'm not going to pressure you, or ask you over and over again, but just know that I don't want you and Claire to leave. This is your home. This is the life we had planned out for us. Give us a chance."

Tucker doesn't give me an opportunity to answer him. He places a kiss on the tip of my nose and takes my hand in his until we reach his car. I quickly glance back at the courthouse and remember the day I said 'I do'.

chapter 30
Tucker

IN THE END, I WON. Shortly after Lawson's trial, Penny informed me that her and Claire were moving back to California. All I heard was that they were moving home, where they belonged. It was the same day Claire made it known that once she moved here, we could call her Claire since no one would know her as Chloe. I wanted to hug her, but kept my distance and hands to myself.

Claire and I have come a long way in our rebuilding process. I know living together helps and she sees how much I love her mother. I will say, though, sleeping on the couch is getting old, but I refuse to pressure Penny. For right now I can live with stolen kisses and sweet moments with her.

It's been six months since they moved in, leaving the day after Claire's school let out for the summer. Nate and Cara went and helped them move. I wanted to as well, but we thought it would be best that I didn't. Penny wanted to make sure Ray's reputation stayed intact. I acted like I understood, but really I didn't. Maybe she was afraid that I would kiss her in front of her friends or something. Knowing me, I probably would've slipped and done so and that wouldn't have been good.

My house ... our house finally feels like a home. Pictures of Claire from her years in school decorate the hallway. We don't have many pictures of her when she was a baby with those being left in the house and who knows where they are now, but I have the one I kept in my wallet all these years and that sits on our mantle. I often find Claire staring at it when she thinks no one is watching.

I've also learned how to use a bow and arrow thanks to my well-educated daughter. That is one thing that I have to give Ray credit for, he raised her well and taught her everything he knew about the outdoors, leaving me enough room to teach her what I know. Right now, Claire can tie fifty different rope knots and is learning how to scale a wall. These days when I ask her if she wants to go to the park, she suggests the SEAL beach so she can play on the apparatuses. She's a girl after my own heart and has told me that she's going to be the first female SEAL. I wished her luck after she witnessed a group of BUD/s sleeping with their feet in the air.

Most importantly, Claire loves it here. She loves the weather, the ocean, and is excited to start at her new school. Having her and Penny home, with me, makes me feel complete and it makes me feel like I can conquer anything, like my new job as a SEAL instructor.

Penny and I discussed retirement and both agreed I wasn't ready, but I'm also not ready to go back to combat or deploy on secret missions. When I was offered the job as an instructor, I jumped at the opportunity. I can still train, with the fun stuff, all while kicking snot-nosed punks in the ass. It's the best of both worlds.

Lawson is currently serving twenty consecutive life sentences and Ingram goes on trial in the fall. We're hoping he pleads out, but have a feeling he won't. He's too proud of a man to do so and we'll be required to testify. It'll be worth it this time.

The team is together except Ryley and Evan are still living up north. They come down often, but refuse to move. I know once Carole retires, we'll never see them again. I'm secretly hoping that Jensen refuses to sell his lake house, giving us a place to still hang out.

River is around, every now and again. Sometimes we don't see him for a month, and other times he's at everything we do. I know he's lost and I've tried to reach out to him, but his walls are up. It's a hard thing, as a SEAL, to get over letting your team down and it doesn't matter how many times we tell him he's forgiven, he still distances himself from us.

"You home?" The sound of Evan's voice echoes down my hall. I come out of my bedroom to find him dressed in a cream-colored linen suit.

"Hi, and what are you doing here?"

He hands me the black bag he's holding nods toward my bedroom. "Go put this on, we gotta go."

"Where?"

He looks down at this suit and back at me, with a shit-eating grin on his face. I understand it now; he's getting married today. I quickly look at the fridge, wondering if I forgot, but I don't see an invite.

I change quickly, racking my brain about the date. I must've been so caught up with Penny that I forgot and that's not like me. When I come out, I notice that we're dressed similarly except my tie is blue, while he's not wearing one.

"Where's your tie?"

"In the car, let's go."

"Is Penny with Ryley?"

"Yep," he says, rushing to his car. I get in and he pulls away before the door is even shut.

"Are we late?"

"Nah, just eager that's all."

That I can understand. His wedding to Ryley has been a long time coming. He should've married her a long time ago, but then we died and plans got off track for about six years. Now that we've been back, they've been waiting for Carole to say she can walk on the sand. She must be ready.

We pull into the beach and I immediately see white chairs and lots of white lacy crap flying in the breeze. River and Rask are already there, dressed similarly. We trudge through the sand, shaking hands with the guys when we reach them.

"You stand here," Evan says, putting me in place. I look at him questioningly because I assumed Nate would be his best man, but he shakes his head and stands to my left.

"Wait—"

"Watch," he says as he points down the sandy aisle. Music starts and Cara walks down first followed by Ryley. My mouth is open and catching sand from the wind, but I'm in too much shock to close it.

EJ appears next, dressed just like us, except he's wearing a tie and Evan still isn't.

"Hi, Uncle Tucker."

"Hey, buddy. Do you know what's going on?"

He shakes his head and starts laughing.

I glance back at Evan who has a smug look on his face. "This should be you and Ryley," I say, nodding toward the white chairs with a few of our family and friends.

"Nah, Ryley wants this for you guys. It's important to her. Besides, Carole isn't quite ready yet, but don't worry, McCoy, I will be marrying my girl on this beach very soon."

"I look forward to it."

Evan taps me on shoulder and points toward the aisle where my daughter appears in the same lavender dress as Cara and Ryley and I can't help the tears that are falling.

When the music changes, the few guests who are here stand, and my wife appears with Nate on her arm. Her dress flows in the wind as she lets Nate guide her down the makeshift aisle.

He hands her to me, patting me on the back.

"What's all this?"

"It's our anniversary," she says, stunning me into silence. "I want this life with you and I know you want it, too. I love you, Tucker, and I think it's time we renew our vows in front of our friends and family."

Hearing her say that she loves me makes me feel like I'm ten feet tall. I lean to the side slightly, to see Claire, who is beaming at me. I think she wants this, too. But I have to know for sure.

"Are you okay with this, Claire?"

"Yeah, Dad, I am."

Forget ten feet, I'm now twenty feet tall because not only does my wife love me, but my daughter just called me dad.

Nate, who has stepped around me, is now front and center with his hands clasped in front of him. He leans into me and whispers loudly, "I got ordained this morning so don't worry, this is legit."

I can't help but laugh at this situation and shrug. "Let's do this."

"I can't believe we're having a reception at Magoos." It makes sense that we'd come here—it's our home away from home. The party is loud behind us with Evan signing karaoke and Ryley feeding into his ego. I'm sitting at the bar, entertaining myself by watching Penelope dance with Cara.

"There are worse places," Slick Rick says from behind me. He's also dressed in a matching suit even though he couldn't make the ceremony.

"Did you know about this?" I ask as I turn around and face him.

"I know everything that goes on with my guys," he says as he hands me another beer. The bar is closed tonight for this private party and I hate to think about him losing business because of us. There are a lot more people at the bar than at the wedding and I'm fine with that. It could've just been Penny and me and I would've been happy.

"Is this seat taken?"

I give Penny a sideways glance and remember the first time we met. A fucking dare from her friends sent her over to me.

"I don't know, I guess that depends on what you're looking for."

"Well, I'm looking for a strong man who has tattoos and a motorcycle. Do you know anyone like that?"

I shake my head. "Sorry, you're out of luck."

Penny slaps me on the shoulder and sits down, nestling into my neck. The moment I feel her lips I freeze. Aside from kissing, we haven't done anything and the only time I've been intimate is in the shower with my hand.

"Not to be forward or anything, but does this mean I'm getting lucky tonight?"

"I'm pretty much a sure thing," she replies, batting her eyelashes.

"You know the only action I've seen in seven years is my hand. The second I have you naked, I'm going to come all over you and I won't be able to stop it. I'll be your worst middle school memory."

Penny breaks out into fits of laughter, causing my ego to deflate quickly. "How many of those have you had?" She points to my beer.

"This is my second."

"Do you want to get out of here? We have the night to ourselves."

She doesn't have to ask me twice. I put my beer down and holler to the guys that we're leaving. The amount of catcalls we get in return is enough to make me blush. I all but drag Penny outside, only to realize that I don't have a car. I stop short of the door, prepared to ask Slick Rick to call us a cab, but she pushes me out and into the parking lot where my motorcycle is decorated with toilet paper and cans hanging off the back.

"Well isn't this cute."

Before I know what's happening, birdseed is being tossed at us and we quickly scramble to get on the bike. I push the start button and she roars to life, and feel of Penny's arms wrap around my waist.

Pulling out of the parking lot, I head toward our house, taking the scenic route. A few planes are coming in, but we don't stay to watch. There will be other days for that. Tonight is about us being husband and wife.

Once the bike is parked, I help her off and make sure she's steady before she dismounts. Scooping her up in my arms, I carry her to the door; she unlocks it, taking the keys out of my jacket pocket. When we're over the threshold, I set her down, but only long enough to lock the front door.

This time when I pick her back up I do it so her legs are straddling me and I walk us down the hall. Her lips are greedy as she kisses me, while her fingers nimbly work the buttons of my shirt. As soon as her cool hands touch my burning skin, I hiss. I set her gently on the bed and step away from her.

She watches me undress before she starts taking off her dress. She slips it over her head, showing me her barely-there panties and her perky braless tits.

"Fuck, Penny, this is going to be so damn fast." I stoke my rigid cock along my palm and feel the pre-come already seeping out. Even he knows he's about to get lucky.

Penny leans back, pulls her thong off, and tosses it on the pile of clothes that have accumulated on our floor. Scooting to the edge of the bed, she beckons me with her finger.

"What?"

"Let me taste you," she mewls, looking at me with lustful eyes.

I shake my head slowly, matching the stroke my hand is making along my dick. "The minute your lips touch me, I'm done for. I want to be inside of you when I come."

Penny understands what I need and scoots back on the bed. I crawl toward her, placing my knees between hers.

"Shit, I forgot the foreplay."

She reaches for me, aligning us together. "I'm ready," she says as she lifts her hips.

The contact is almost too much to bear and takes me back to high school when I got laid for the first time. I close my eyes and push in, grunting as I do. The warmth that surrounds me gives me pause. A year ago I didn't think I'd ever feel this way again, but I prevailed and never gave up.

Penny flexes, reminding me that I need to move.

"I just needed a moment," I tell her as I pull out slowly, leaving just my tip in to tease her. I move slowly into her, watching my dick disappear inch by inch. When I'm fully sheathed I lean down and kiss her, letting our tongues battle for dominance while I slowly move in and out of her. Her nails pinch into my backside, encouraging me to give her all that I have.

With every moan and slap of the skin, I'm reminded of how amazing our days were together. Making love to her was always the highlight of my day, it was never a chore or something I felt I had to do. It was something I needed that only she could give me. Sitting back on my knees, I let my hands grip her hips. I guide her with each thrust as my cock disappears into her glorious pussy.

"Penelope," I groan, as my balls grow tighter. When she touches her clit I just about blow but am able to hold it off. I grip the headboard and slam into her, much to her delight.

"Yes, Tucker. Oh fuck, fuck, fuck, yes I'm coming."

"Holy shit, you're squeezing me so tight." The way her pussy milks my cock sends me into a frenzy. I pound into her harder until I blow my load, jerking through the aftershocks of one of the most powerful orgasms I've ever had.

"Fuck." I'm out of breath and my chest is heaving for air. I roll off of her, feeling the immediate loss when our bodies part. Pulling her into my side, she weaves her legs with mine and snuggles into my side.

"You don't know how long I've been waiting for this."

"I think I have a pretty good idea, Tucker."

I laugh, even though the situation isn't comical. I move to my side so I can look at her—so she can feel the words that I'm about to say.

Her hair is crazy and I try to tame it by pushing it behind her ear. I kiss her gently and show her how the rest of her night is going to go. I don't care if I have to drink three pots of coffee in the morning we're not sleeping tonight. We have a lot of time to make up for and this was just the beginning.

"I love you, Penelope McCoy. There wasn't a day that went by that I didn't think about you and Claire. Even though I now know the letters weren't from you, hearing about your life, pretend or not, gave me a lot of hope when I was out there. When I came back, I scoured the city looking for you, determined to find you. I refused to believe that you left me. I knew in my heart that you were out there. I just had to find you. And now you're here, in my arms where you belong.

"Your love for me saved me, Penny, from the demons that threatened to take us away from each other. When I saw you for the first time, I knew I'd die a lonely man before I loved again because you are it for me. You and Claire are the reason my heart beats, and without either of you, I am nothing but a shell of the man you met at Magoos so many years ago."

Tears fall and dampen her face. I kiss them away until I reach her mouth. Her fingers dig into my hair as her tongue meets mine. She moans, and as I try to pull her leg over my hip—because there's nothing hotter than watching the woman you love bounce on your cock—she stops me.

"It's my turn, Tucker. The day I saw you in that hotel room I felt like I could breathe again. For years I have had this ache in my chest, but you made that go away. I was living, but I was not alive until you walked back into my life. I'm sorry it's taken me so long to get here, but I'm here and here to stay forever.

"I love you, Tucker McCoy. I love that you're a man of your word. I love that you will do anything for Claire and me. I love that you're a SEAL despite what they've done to you; you're able to overcome and look past the transgressions of one person, to continue to serve a country that loves you. Most importantly I love that you're mine."

She closes her eyes and I feel her body go soft. The last thing I want to do is sleep, but maybe she needs a nap. We have the rest of our lives to make up for what we've missed. There doesn't need to be a rush on tonight.

"Sleep, my sweet Penny. I'll always protect you."

chapter 31
Claire

IT'S THE FIRST DAY OF my new school. The school I likely would've started if my mom and I hadn't been forced to move. She still doesn't talk about that day, and I'm okay with it. I don't think I want to know, at least not yet. My mom assures me that the person who ruined our lives will never do so again. Sometimes I have to remind her my life isn't ruined, but when I do that I feel like I'm not honoring my dad, Ray.

It's odd to think I have two dads, but I do. I don't know what I'm going to tell kids when they ask me about my life, it's not something I practiced, but everyone knows now. We've been all over the news, and I hate it. For a while the news people were sitting outside our house and they made my parents angry. My Aunt Ryley says the news never came around until Senator Lawson pleaded guilty and everything was out in the open. She's angry, too, mostly for EJ. She says the news in Washington have been following them everywhere. My escape has been at the Clarke's. I have spent a lot of time there this summer. I feel safe there and Jensen reminds me of Ray.

I miss Ray. He's not a secret in our house. My dad, Tucker, he talks about him. He asks questions and tries to make him a part of my life. My mom says that Tucker is trying to make sure I never forget about the man who raised me. And I like that, even though I know it hurts Tucker's feelings.

As I stand looking in the mirror, I wonder what other kid has gone through so much. I'm sure there are a few, and they probably have memories. The only time I remember something is when my mom is talking to my dad and I overhear. I think they're memories, but maybe they're figments of my imagination being pieced together by my mom's story.

Today is going to be a new day for me, and I'm scared.

"Of what?" I hear behind me, causing me to jump slightly. I hadn't realized I actually said the words out loud, but it makes sense. I'm often talking to myself, catching my dad off guard.

My dad stands in the doorway, leaning against the doorjamb. He's dressed for work, but according to my clock, he should already be gone.

"I'm scared about school."

"Why?" he asks, motioning toward my bed. I nod and he comes in and sits down. I stay where I am, though for only a second, and quickly sit down next to him.

"What if the kids don't like me?"

"Impossible."

"You're biased. You have to say nice things because you're my dad."

He nods and pretends to contemplate something. He does that a lot when he's thinking of the right thing to say, dragging out the thought process. Mom says he does it to make him look like a genius.

"You're right, but I also know you as a person. You have to remember that I didn't get to be here while you were growing up, but these past few months I've gotten to know you and I think you're a pretty cool kid. You have a lot to offer your new classmates."

"Like what?" I huff.

"Like you're really smart and you're fun to hang out with. Your dad is like really awesome."

I can't help but roll my eyes and punch him in the arm. He pretends to fall over, but pulls me into a hug instead.

The day he made me breakfast, after Ray died, I wanted to hate him. I didn't want him to be a part of my life and I definitely didn't want to move here. When we came to visit, everything changed. He made his house a home for me and never pressured me into calling him dad, or tried to make me do bonding things. He invited me everywhere, though, and going to work with him quickly became my favorite thing. It was one of his trainees who opened my eyes to the great dad Tucker already was.

"Can I invite friends over?"

"Of course you can. Are you ready to go to school?"

"Yeah, I think so."

"Well I'm taking you today, so if you're not ready, we'll skip work and school and hit the beach. Or we can take our bows over to the Clarke's and shoot."

I love that Tucker loves to do one of the things Ray taught me, and now I'm teaching him. I think that is when I knew everything was going to be okay here.

"Or we could go shopping?"

My dad shakes his head. "No, no way in hell. If you want to shop, your mom can play hooky. You and I are going to do sporty stuff, like scale walls and repel from buildings."

The thought of hanging out at SEAL beach all day does excite me, but making new friends is important, too.

"Maybe after school we can go to the beach?"

He winks. "Sounds good to me."

"Thanks, Dad."

"Anytime, Claire."

He leans down and kisses me on the forehead, reminding me that it's never too late to be a parent.

the end

acknowledgements

Dan & Amy ~ Thank you so much for the… well everything. From listening to all my panics, helping with research, especially the trip to SEAL beach, taking stealthy candid's at Coronado and to opening your lives to me. I love you guys and truly can't thank you enough.

Yvette ~ this concludes your idea! What's next?

Christine ~ you, my friend, are a workhorse. I'm so thankful we entered into a partnership. You've taken so much off my plate. I'm so very grateful.

BT Urruela ~ I was so nervous to email you & ask if you'd pretend to be a Navy SEAL, but you nailed it. I can't thank you enough of helping me bring my character to life and giving him a badass attitude to go with it.

Eric ~ you're a master behind that lens. Thank you for capturing the right image.

Sarah ~ thank you for always making the best covers for me. Each new one is always my favorite.

Emily & Crew ~ you ladies work around the clock to make sure everything is perfect. Thank you.

Megan ~ my lovely mama to be! Thank you for sitting down and reading this story before anyone else. Your feedback was so helpful. I really can't thank you enough.

Leslie, Adriana, Ann Marie, Rachel, Jay and Kirby ~ thank

you, thank you, thank you for taking time out of your busy schedules to read and blurb SAVE ME. You have no idea how much your words mean to me.

Audrey, Georgette, Kelli, Tammy, Tammy & Veronica: You ladies sure do know how to make everything right in my world. I really can't ask for a better group of girls to spend my time with.

The Beaumont Daily: You guys rock!

A special shout-out to my agent, Marisa ~ you have changed my life for the better.

To my family: I know the hours are long, but I do it for you! And a special shout-out to my girls, Madison & Kassidy ~ you are the definition of hard work. You push yourselves, but allow others to push you to succeed as well and you both have. I am so proud to be your mom.

And finally to the readers: How you keep up with all the amazing novels being published I'll never know, but you do it, and you do it proudly. If you're reading this, take a moment, smile and pat yourself on the back because you, my friend, are a superwoman... or superman!

Keep reading for a sneak peek at Roped In
(An Armed & Dangerous Novel)
by New York Times and USA Today
bestselling author, L.P. Dover.

ROPED IN
(An Armed & Dangerous novel)

NEW YORK TIMES AND USA TODAY BESTSELLING AUTHOR
L.P. DOVER

CHAPTER 1
Hadley

"*HADLEY! HADLEY! HADLEY!*" THE CROWD cheered.

I blew a kiss and waved. "Thank you for joining me tonight. I love the energy here in Los Angeles! I have to say, I've missed this place. Make sure to listen to the radio this week for the debut of my new song, *Whispered Words*."

"Sing it now!" one of the fans shouted. It was a little girl with blonde braids and freckles, sitting on her dad's shoulders. She reminded me of myself many years ago, when I stood in almost the exact same spot, watching my idol, Martina Hill perform. One of these days, I was determined to do a duet with her.

I winked at the little girl and shook her tiny hand. "I wish I could, sweetheart, but it has to be a surprise." Then I lifted my gaze to the thousands of fans in the stands and waved again. "I hope you all like it. Goodnight, everyone." They went wild and I laughed as I ran backstage.

Waiting for me at the edge of the stage with a huge smile on his face was the love of my life, Nick Meyers. No one could resist his tousled, chocolate brown hair and gorgeous green eyes. The ladies loved him, almost as much as they hated me for having him.

"You were on fire tonight," he shouted.

Rushing off stage, I jumped in his arms and squealed. "What are you doing here? I thought you weren't going to be able to make it."

Cameras flashed and he grinned, his eyes twinkling mischievously. "I can leave if you want," he joked, releasing me from his grasp.

I gripped his arm and pulled him back to me. "Definitely

not. What would the press think?"

Chuckling, he bent down to kiss me, knowing the reporters were taking note of our every move. "Was that a good enough kiss, or do I need to make it more convincing?" he asked, whispering in my ear.

Rolling my eyes, I playfully pushed him away. "I think you need a cold shower."

"Care to join me?" he quipped, waggling his brows.

"Right now, we have work to do. Get your head out of the gutter." We faced the reporters and he held me close as questions were thrown at us in rapid fire. A lady with bright red hair and huge glasses, pushed through the crowd and held out a recorder. "Miss Rivers, we've heard rumors you and Mr. Meyers are engaged. Is that true?"

Nick smirked down at me and I held back a snicker. It was crazy how rumors got started out of nowhere. The next thing I knew, we'd be married and having a baby. "If she was engaged," Nick began, "I would definitely be letting the world know."

We answered several more questions before it was time to go. I knew I was going to have a gazillion autographs to sign on the way to the dressing room. Relaxation was something I needed to schedule now, or it would never happen. I had to get home and get rested up before my early flight to Texas.

Nick was always patient with me when dealing with the press, but I did the same for him too; he was just as famous. I was a rising, country starlet with one of the best hockey players in the country as my boyfriend. Unfortunately, our romance was all for show, but we played the parts beautifully.

Once we were behind closed doors, I breathed a sigh of relief. "The questions keep getting more outrageous don't they?"

"Same shit show, different day." He helped me pack up my things and stuffed them into my bag.

"I thought you were busy with the team tonight?"

"I was, but I made sure to get away early. I missed my buttercup."

I rolled my eyes, nudging him with my elbow when he pulled me into his arms. "You have a life too, Nick. I don't want you sacrificing everything to be with me. You should've stayed with the team."

"Trust me, baby, I'm not sacrificing a single thing. I enjoy every minute of it."

"Even if you don't get anything in return?" I asked, lifting my gaze to his.

For the last four months, he was mine, but not really. It was his and his sister's idea for him to be my fill in boyfriend. His sister, Felicity Myers, was also my agent and the one who'd introduced Nick to me. I guess they were right, it was safer for people to see me with someone, instead of single and living alone. And I enjoyed having him with me, but I didn't want to drag him into the danger surrounding my life.

His smile faded, his gaze serious. "I get plenty in return, Hadley. I'm happy where I'm at, even if I have to steal your kisses. It's not *that* bad being with me, is it?"

"Are you kidding? You're gorgeous and could have any woman you want, but yet you choose to be stuck with me. It makes no sense."

"It does to me," he murmured.

"I've asked you this before, but I need you to be honest with me." He sighed and nodded for me to continue. "What did Felicity promise you? Surely you didn't just agree to be with me for nothing in return." I had often thought about what it would be like to take things further, but I didn't want to ruin our friendship. When I met him two years ago, we instantly clicked. I considered him more of a best friend than a lover.

Grazing his finger across my cheek, he answered, "My sister didn't promise me anything. I offered to do this. Believe it or not, I like being with you. At least it's gotten that fucking psycho off your back." And there it was, the sole reason for the mess I was in.

"So we *think*," I corrected. "What happens when we can't keep this ruse up? What if he comes back?" What started out as innocent letters had quickly turned into stalking, then to trespassing. Presents were left on my doorstep, and the ever watchful eyes of that creeper could be felt every time I left the house. It got to the point where I was scared to be alone. I used to be able to run around my neighborhood and go shopping by myself, but I couldn't anymore.

Nick stepped closer. "That bastard isn't going to get near you as long as I'm around. I believe this plan will work. Eventually, this guy will give up and find someone else to fuck with. Now stop thinking about him, there's something I wanted to talk to you about and I'm not going to do it here."

"Oh yeah? What is it?"

"You'll just have to find out. Come on," he said, opening the door.

There were two security guys standing by the door, I nodded at them as we passed. Their steps could be heard on the concrete floor, following closely behind. I never thought having a security team was important, until I heard horror stories from other singers. Luckily, I hadn't had anyone break into my house to steal my underwear like my nemesis, Lydia Turner. The attention she got after that incident, inflated her already enormous head. I would've been scared shitless to know some pervert was in my house. Not her; it was just another way to get free PR.

"Where's Scott? He usually comes inside to get me," I mentioned.

Scott Wilson worked security for my father, until he'd been sent to protect me. I didn't mind having a bodyguard, but I had boundaries. Thankfully, Scott and I had come to a shaky agreement; he wouldn't hover, unless I wanted him to. He loved to test my patience though.

"He's waiting out by the car. When I came in through the back, I told him I'd bring you out."

"Wow. Hopefully, he's taking what I said to heart."

Nick shrugged. "Possibly. You ripped him pretty hard the other night. The guy's just trying to do his job."

I sighed. "I know, and I hate how I took my anger out on him and not my dad. Scott's a good guy. I just wish the whole country didn't think I got my career because of my dad and his money."

"They don't. Did you not hear the thousands of fans cheering for you tonight? You have an amazing voice. Money can't buy what comes naturally. Besides, you know why your father's so protective."

I leaned into his shoulder, as memories of my mother came flooding back. It had only been two years since we'd lost her to cancer. The first song I ever wrote was about my parents' love for each other; it was what skyrocketed my career. It didn't help I looked exactly like her. My father couldn't look at me without the pain showing on his face.

"I know," I whispered, blinking back the tears.

Once we were out the back door, there were more security guards who flanked us as we walked toward the car. Up ahead, Scott straightened his suit jacket and opened the car door. He was in his early forties, with a closely shaved head and an athletic build. In New York, he didn't have to worry about the paparazzi taking his picture. Now, he was all over the tabloids as one of the sexiest bodyguards alive.

"You did well tonight, Hadley," he said.

"Thanks, Scott. I really appreciate that. But what I want to know is, how are you going to chase down the bad guys in a suit?" I winked and it made him smile. The last thing I wanted was tension between us when he was obviously going to be working for me long term.

"You'd be surprised what all I can do. But hopefully, we won't have to find out. Get in."

I slid into the car and Nick scooted in next, putting his arm around me as soon as he settled into the seat. Once Scott got in the front, we headed out for the thirty minute drive back to my home in Santa Monica.

"I take it you're not mad at me anymore?" I asked Scott.

He chuckled. "It's hard to stay mad at you, kid. You just need to understand, I have a job to do."

"I know," I said with a nod. "I'm sorry for being a bitch."

His gaze met mine in the mirror. "You're forgiven." All too soon we arrived at the house and he parked the car. "You two have a good night. If you need me, you know where I'll be."

I nodded. "See you in the morning." Nick opened the car door and helped me out.

Scott got out of the car and headed to his apartment over my garage. "Be ready by seven, Hadley. We don't want to miss our flight."

I saluted him. "Yes, sir."

Grinning, he shook his head and disappeared into the garage.

Nick slid his arm over my shoulders and squeezed. "Babe, you ready?"

"Yeah, let me get my keys." We started for the door while I dug in my purse, my heart thundering out of control. Was I ready to hear what he had to say? "So . . . what did you want to talk about?" I asked, voice shaking.

Chuckling, he stopped mid-step. "Nervous much? Surely you must already know." His expression turned serious, his fingers made their way to my cheek.

I *was* nervous, but not in the way he assumed. "Please don't do this, Nick. It'll only complicate things."

"How? When I'm not at my games, I'm with you. Everyone thinks we're together. Why can't we make this real?" Body tense, he stared at me with those blazing green eyes of his. "Is it really just an act with you?"

My heart ached but my decision was firm. I knew he had feelings for me, and I'd made damn sure I didn't fall for him. "It's not all an act, but you're my friend. Being with me will only tear us apart. The media has already tried, you know that. We don't need feelings clouding our judgment."

He scoffed. "Speak for yourself." I watched his jaw muscles clench; it was something he did when he was angry.

"Hey," I murmured, "I *do* need you. But the last thing I want is to jeopardize what we already have." He lowered his gaze at my words. "Now let's go inside and eat some Ben & Jerry's. It'll help clear our minds."

"You got anything for an aching heart? You're killing me here."

I shook my head. "I'm sure you'll be just fine. Now, come on. There are countless girls who'd kill to be yours. It will be easy to forget about me."

Sliding the key in the door, he mumbled under his breath, "Not going to happen," but I pretended not to hear. My heart already hurt enough for him. Inside, the house was pitch black. That was strange. I always kept lights on. Sliding my hand against the wall, I found the switch and flipped it. Nothing.

"Is the power out? I don't remember seeing the rest of the neighborhood this dark."

Nick followed me into the house. "No, the other houses have their lights on," he said, pointing to the neighbor's house through the window. "Let me get a flashlight." Shuffling through the kitchen, he pulled out our junk drawer and grabbed the flashlight we kept in there. He turned it on and brought it over to me. "Maybe the breaker tripped. Wanna check it out with me?"

"Sure," I laughed. "I'm sure Scott will be busting through our door any second." We started for the laundry room, but then a sound above caught my attention. "What was that?" Frozen in place, I kept my gaze on Nick. My heart pounded so hard, I felt sick.

Nick glanced up at the ceiling, eyes blazing. The footsteps were light, but audible as an intruder moved around. "Get out of here, now," he hissed low. His fingers dug into my arm and he pushed me out the door.

I kept hold of his arms. "I'm not leaving you."

He jerked out of my grasp and clutched my face, his grip firm. "Stop being so fucking stubborn. Go get Scott and call the police, now!"

Turning his back on me, I got one last look at him before he disappeared into the darkness. I ran out of the house, hands shaking as I tried to dig for my phone. It felt like I was running through quicksand, similar to that feeling you get when running away from someone in your dreams. You can never move fast enough.

"Hadley!" Scott shouted, rushing out of the garage. I ran to him and he pulled me to the side, shielding me.

"Someone's in the house. Nick's still in there," I cried, my hands shaking out of control.

"Go next door and call the police. Don't step out until I come for you." Once I nodded, he took off inside the house.

Determined, I ran as fast as I could to my neighbor's house. By the time I reached their door, I'd found my phone and called for help.

"911. What's your emergency?"

"I'm Hadley Rivers and someone's in my house. Please send help." I gave the operator my address and hung up just as my neighbor, Gabriella Emerson, opened the door. She was dressed in her workout clothes with her midnight colored hair pulled high into a ponytail.

Her smile disappeared the second she looked at me. "Oh my God, Hadley, what's going on?" she demanded. She quickly dragged me inside, and her husband, Paxton, hurried over. They were both MMA fighters and had seen their fair share of violence over the years. If anyone could help, it'd be them.

"Someone broke into my house. They're still in there," I shouted.

Gabriella grabbed my hands and squeezed. "Calm down, honey."

"I can't! Nick and Scott might be in trouble."

Paxton started for the door. "I'm going over there."

"Pax, wait!" Gabriella called. He took off and she huffed. "Dammit, why doesn't he ever listen?" She rushed out after him and so did I.

Scott had told me not to leave their house, but I couldn't listen. Again, it felt like everything moved in slow motion. I couldn't get to them fast enough. Before we could reach the edge of my yard, a gunshot fired from within my house and I screamed, ducking down to the ground. Paxton and Gabriella did the same and crouched low. Dread settled into the pit of my stomach as another shot fired, and another.

I had to make sure they were okay. Charging toward my house, I didn't get very far until Gabriella tackled me to the ground.

"Dammit Hadley, you're not going in there."

"Nick! Scott!" I shouted.

I tried to fight her off, but there was nothing I could do against an MMA fighter. Paxton glanced back at Gabriella, a silent plea on his face; Gabriella nodded. "Go."

"Nick doesn't have a gun. What if he's hurt?" I cried. Gabriella loosened her grip, but kept a vigilant watch of the house. I wished I was strong like her. I'd be able to take care of myself instead of having others do it.

"Don't worry, everything's going to be fine," she said, but even I could hear the uncertainty in her voice.

"Gabby!" Paxton yelled from inside the house. "I need help in here."

She jerked me to my feet and we both took off for the house. When I got inside, the smell of blood was overwhelming.

Everything came crashing down the second I saw Scott and Nick on the floor, covered in blood. But it was Scott who was unmoving, lifeless, his unseeing eyes staring up at the ceiling.

"Scott!" I cried. Paxton rushed over and took his pulse. The pained look on his face was answer enough. I stumbled over and fell to my knees beside him. "He has to be alive." But he wasn't; he was gone.

"Hadley," Nick croaked. Gasping, I crawled over to him and placed a hand over his. Blood oozed out of the wound in his gut. He glanced over at Scott's still form and closed his eyes. "He . . . saved me."

"Where did the shooter go?" Paxton demanded.

Nick swallowed hard. "Back door." His eyes rolled into the back of his head and his body shook.

"Nick! Hang on, *please*," I cried. Putting my hands over his wound, I attempted to stem the blood flow.

Sirens blared down the street, but they were going to be too late.

Growling, Paxton dashed toward the back door. "I'm going after the fucker."

Tears streamed down my cheeks as I watched Nick's life slowly slip away. Gabriella rummaged through my house and came back with a towel. I took it from her and placed it over the wound.

"Nick, stay with us," Gabriella commanded, as I applied pressure to the wound. It seemed to help, but what did I know.

He turned to me, his sea green eyes glassy and full of tears. His body stopped convulsing, and was replaced with a sense of calm. "I wanted . . . to protect you."

"Did you see who it was?" Gabriella asked softly.

He closed his eyes, his grip on my arm loosening.

"Nick? *Nick*. Don't you dare die on me," I shouted.

The police and paramedics burst into the room and rushed over. Gabriella put her arm around me and everything moved in slow motion. I subconsciously noted how Nick and Scott's blood had soaked through my jeans, but I didn't care. All I could do was sit there, realization staring me in the face. Scott was dead and Nick laid in a pool of his own blood . . . because of me. It was all my fault.